PENGUIN BOOK

THE NIGHT TRAIN
DEOLI
AND OTHER STORIES

Ruskin Bond was born in Kasauli in 1934. He has written
several novels, short stories and books for children in the
course of a long writing career. *The Room on the Roof* (also
published by Penguin), written when the author was only 17,
won the John Llewellyn Rhys Memorial Prize in 1957.
    Ruskin Bond lives in Mussoorie.

THE NIGHT TRAIN
AT DEOLI
and other Stories

RUSKIN BOND

PENGUIN BOOKS

Penguin Books (India) Limited, 72-B Himalaya House, 23 Kasturba Gandhi Marg, New Delhi-110 001, India
Penguin Books Ltd., Harmondsworth, Middlesex, England
Viking Penguin Inc., 40 West 23rd Street, New York, N.Y.10010. U.S.A.
Penguin Books Australia Ltd., Ringwood, Victoria, Australia
Penguin Books Canada Ltd., 2801 John Street, Markham, Ontario, Canada L3R 1 B4
Penguin Books (N.Z.) Ltd, 182-190 Wairau Road, Auckland 10, New Zealand

First published by Penguin Books India 1988

Some of these stories first appeared in *Short Story International*, *Blackwoods* the *Illustrated Weekly of India* and other magazines. 'Panther's Moon' was first published by Random House Inc. A modified children's version of 'Sita and the River' was first published by Hamish Hamilton Ltd.

Made and printed in India by Ananda Offset Private Ltd. Calcutta
Typeset in ITC Garamond

For D—
thanks for the memory

Contents

Introduction

Gentle Reader,

I use the old-fashioned term to address you, because I like it and because I know that only the more gentle kind of person is likely to care much for my stories.

I have never been any good at the more lurid sort of writing. Psychopathic killers, impotent war-heroes, self-tortured film stars, and seedy espionage agents must exist in this world, but strangely enough, I do not come across them, and I prefer to write about the people and places I have known and the lives of those whose paths I have crossed. This crossing of paths makes for stories rather than novels, and although I have worked in both mediums, I am happier being a short-story writer than a novelist.

Perhaps there is too much of me in my stories, and at times this book may read like an autobiography. It is a weakness, I know. It can't be helped; I am that kind of a writer, that kind of a person.

Looking back over the thirty years that I have been writing, I find to my surprise that I have written a number of love stories; or perhaps they are all love stories, of one kind or another. In fact, I can't really write unless I am in love with my subject. Another weakness, according to those who make up the rules for literature. But I have never gone by the rules.

'Romance brought up the nine-fifteen,' wrote Kipling, and I find that in the stories I wrote in the 1950's (when I was in my teens and in my twenties) there is a good deal of romance, often associated with trains. People are always travelling in them and going all over the place, but just occasionally two people meet, their paths cross, and though they may part again quite soon (as in 'The Woman on Platform 8' and 'The Eyes Have It'), their lives have been changed in some indefinable way.

Sometimes the hero (if I may use such a term) tries to prevent that moment from passing (as in 'The Night Train at Deoli'), but it is only the very strong among us who can alter events, change trains so to speak, and very often cause a derailment. 'The Night Train at Deoli' is a favourite with many of my younger readers; that longing for something, someone, just out of reach, is familiar to them.

This is a representative collection of my stories selected by David Davidar from what I have written over the years. The early ones were written in Dehra Dun, when I was a young man struggling to make a living as a freelance writer. In the 1960's, after a spell of office work in Delhi, I moved to the hill-station of Mussoorie, and many of the stories written in this period were, in fact, character studies of people I had known, although occasionally, as in 'Bus Stop, Pipalnagar,' I went back to the years of struggle and youthful hopes.

As we grow older, despair and disillusion assail many of us. Our early hopes and dreams have been trodden in the dust. But I have always sought to buoy myself up by the sentiments embodied in an old-fashioned verse passed on me by my father*:

> *The pure, the bright, the beautiful,*
> *That stirred our hearts in youth,*
> *The impulse to a wordless prayer,*
> *The dreams of love and truth;*
> *The longings after something lost,*
> *The spirit's yearning cry,*
> *The striving after better hopes . . .*
> *These things can never die.*

The longings after something lost. Perhaps that is the dominant theme in my stories. It is a longing that has been experienced by all of us at various times in our lives unless one has become desensitized by power and money.

The longing, the yearning, is there in the early stories and it is there in the later stories. In the 1970's, when I found myself being

*The words are by a little-known poet, Sarah Doudney.

weighed down by both personal and professional problems, I turned to writing for children, and this helped me to find a way out of my difficulties. 'Sita and the River' became *Angry River* and also ended up in several European languages; so did 'Panther's Moon' and a number of stories that are not included here because this is not a children's collection. In writing for children one has to adopt a less subjective approach; things must happen, for boys and girls have no time for mood pieces. So this kind of writing does help me to get away from myself. At the same time, because I have so strong an empathy with children, I can enter into their minds when I am writing about them. As children we are all individualists; it is only as we grow older that we acquire a certain grey similarity to each other.

But I still return to the old themes from time to time. 'A Love of Long Ago' was written even as this book was being prepared for the press. Some of the old longing had returned. When I had finished the story, I thought, 'Well that's it. I am fifty-four now. No more love stories, and no more falling in love . . .' But then, on my way home in the twilight, walking through the streets I had known as a boy I met this girl with the most beautiful smile in the world. She was trying to find a bus to Yamunanagar. But I'll tell you about it another time.

Mussoorie   Ruskin Bond
24 March 1988

The Woman on Platform 8

It was my second year at boarding-school, and I was sitting on platform no. 8 at Ambala station, waiting for the northern bound train. I think I was about twelve at the time. My parents considered me old enough to travel alone, and I had arrived by bus at Ambala early in the evening: now there was a wait till midnight before my train arrived. Most of the time I had been pacing up and down the platform, browsing at the book-stall, or feeding broken biscuits to stray dogs; trains came and went, and the platform would be quiet for a while and then, when a train arrived, it would be an inferno of heaving, shouting, agitated human bodies. As the carriage doors opened, a tide of people would sweep down upon the nervous little ticket-collector at the gate; and every time this happened I would be caught in the rush and swept outside the station. Now tired of this game and of ambling about the platform, I sat down on my suitcase and gazed dismally across the railway-tracks.

Trolleys rolled past me, and I was conscious of the cries of the various vendors — the men who sold curds and lemon, the sweet-meat-seller, the newspaper boy — but I had lost interest in all that went on along the busy platform, and continued to stare across the railway-tracks, feeling bored and a little lonely.

'Are you all alone, my son?' asked a soft voice close behind me.

I looked up and saw a woman standing near me. She was leaning over, and I saw a pale face, and dark kind eyes. She wore no jewels, and was dressed very simply in a white *sari*.

'Yes, I am going to school,' I said, and stood up respectfully; she seemed poor, but there was a dignity about her that commanded respect.

'I have been watching you for some time,' she said. 'Didn't your parents come to see you off?'

'I don't live here,' I said. 'I had to change trains. Anyway, I can travel alone.'

'I am sure you can,' she said, and I liked her for saying that, and I also liked her for the simplicity of her dress, and for her deep, soft voice and the serenity of her face.

'Tell me, what is your name?' she asked.

'Arun,' I said.

'And how long do you have to wait for your train?'

'About an hour, I think. It comes at twelve o'clock.'

'Then come with me and have something to eat.'

I was going to refuse, out of shyness and suspicion, but she took me by the hand, and then I felt it would be silly to pull my hand away. She told a coolie to look after my suitcase, and then she led me away down the platform. Her hand was gentle, and she held mine neither too firmly nor too lightly. I looked up at her again. She was not young. And she was not old. She must have been over thirty but, had she been fifty, I think she would have looked much the same.

She took me into the station dining-room, ordered tea and *samosas* and *jalebies*, and at once I began to thaw and take a new interest in this kind woman. The strange encounter had little effect on my appetite. I was a hungry school boy, and I ate as much as I could in as polite a manner as possible. She took obvious pleasure in watching me eat, and I think it was the food that strengthened the bond between us and cemented our friendship, for under the influence of the tea and sweets I began to talk quite freely, and told her about my school, my friends, my likes and dislikes. She questioned me quietly from time to time, but preferred listening; she drew me out very well, and I had soon forgotten that we were strangers. But she did not ask me about my family or where I lived, and I did not ask her where she lived. I accepted her for what she had been to me — a quiet, kind and gentle woman who gave sweets to a lonely boy on a railway platform . . .

After about half-an-hour we left the dining-room and began walking back along the platform. An engine was shunting up and down beside platform No. 8, and as it approached, a boy leapt off the platform and ran across the rails, taking a short cut to the next platform. He was at a safe distance from the engine, and there was no danger unless he had fallen; but as he leapt across the rails, the woman clutched my arm. Her fingers dug into my flesh, and I winced with pain. I caught her fingers and looked up at her, and I saw a spasm of pain and fear and sadness pass across her face. She watched the boy as he climbed other platform, and it was not until he had disappeared in the crowd that she relaxed her hold on my arm. She smiled at me reassuringly, and took my hand again: but her fingers trembled against mine.

'He was all right,' I said, feeling that it was she who needed reassurance.

She smiled gratefully at me and pressed my hand. We walked together in silence until we reached the place where I had left my suitcase, one of my schoolfellows, Satish, a boy of about my age, had turned up with his mother.

'Hello, Arun!' he called. 'The train's coming in late, as usual. Did you know we have a new Headmaster this year?'

We shook hands, and then he turned to his mother and said: 'This is Arun, mother. He is one of my friends, and the best bowler in the class.'

'I am glad to know that,' said his mother, a large imposing woman who wore spectacles. She looked at the woman who led my hand and said: 'And I suppose you're Arun's mother?'

I opened my mouth to make some explanation, but before I could say anything the woman replied: 'Yes, I am Arun's mother.'

I was unable to speak a word. I looked quickly up at the woman, but she did not appear to be at all embarrassed, and was smiling at Satish's mother.

Satish's mother said: 'It's such a nuisance having to wait for the train right in the middle of the night. But one can't let the child wait here alone. Anything can happen to a boy at a big station like this, there are so many suspicious characters hanging about. These days one has to be very careful of strangers.'

'Arun can travel alone though,' said the woman beside me, and somehow I felt grateful to her for saying that. I had already forgiven her for lying: and besides, I had taken an instinctive dislike to Satish's mother.

'Well, be very careful Arun,' said Satish's mother looking sternly at me through her spectacles. 'Be very careful when your mother is not with you. And never talk to strangers!'

I looked from Satish's mother to the woman who had given me tea and sweets, and then back at Satish's mother.

'I like strangers,' I said.

Satish's mother definitely staggered a little, as obviously she was not used to being contradicted by small boys. 'There you are, you see! If you don't watch over them all the time, they'll walk straight into trouble. Always listen to what your mother tells you,' she said, wagging a fat little finger at me. 'And never, never talk to strangers.'

I glared resentfully at her, and moved closer to the woman who had befriended me. Satish was standing behind his mother, grinning at me, and delighting in my clash with his mother. Apparently he was on my side.

The station bell clanged, and the people who had till now been squatting resignedly on the platform began bustling about.

'Here it comes,' shouted Satish, as the engine whistle shrieked and the front lights played over the rails.

The train moved slowly into the station, the engine hissing and sending out waves of steam. As it came to a stop, Satish jumped on the footboard of a lighted compartment and shouted, 'Come on, Arun, this one's empty!' and I picked up my suitcase and made a dash for the open door.

We placed ourselves at the open windows, and the two women stood outside on the platform, talking up to us. Satish's mother did most of the talking.

'Now don't jump on and off moving trains, as you did just now,' she said. 'And don't stick your heads out of the windows, and don't eat any rubbish on the way.' She allowed me to share the benefit of her advice, as she probably didn't think my 'mother' a very capable person. She handed Satish a bag of fruit, a cricket bat and a big box of chocolates, and told him to share the food with me. Then she stood back from the window to watch how my 'mother' behaved.

I was smarting under the patronising tone of Satish's mother, who obviously thought mine a very poor family: and I did not intend giving the other woman away. I let her take my hand in hers, but I could think of nothing to say. I was conscious of Satish's mother staring at us with hard, beady eyes, and I found myself hating her with a firm, unreasoning hate. The guard walked up the platform, blowing his whistle for the train to leave. I looked straight into the eyes of the woman who held my hand, and she smiled in a gentle, understanding way. I leaned out of the window then, and put my lips to her cheek, and kissed her.

The carriage jolted forward, and she drew her hand away.

'Good-bye, mother!' said Satish, as the train began to move slowly out of the station. Satish and his mother waved to each other.

'Good-bye,' I said to the other woman, 'good-bye — mother . . .'

I didn't wave or shout, but sat still in front of the window, gazing at the woman on the platform. Satish's mother was talking to her, but she didn't appear to be listening; she was looking at me, as the train took me away. She stood there on the busy platform, a pale sweet woman in white, and I watched her until she was lost in the milling crowd.

The Coral Tree

The night had been hot, the rain frequent, and I slept on the verandah instead of in the house. I was in my twenties and I had begun to
earn a living and felt I had certain responsibilities. In a short while a
tonga would take me to a railway station, and from there a train
would take me to Bombay, and then a ship would take me to
England. There would be work, interviews, a job, a different kind of
life; so many things, that this small bungalow of my grandfather's
would be remembered fitfully, in rare moments of reflection.

When I awoke on the verandah I saw a grey morning, smelt the
rain on the red earth, and remembered that I had to go away. A girl
was standing in the verandah porch, looking at me very seriously.
When I saw her, I sat up in bed with a start.

She was a small, dark girl, her eyes big and black, her pigtails tied
up in a bright red ribbon; and she was fresh and clean like the rain
and the red earth.

She stood looking at me, and she was very serious.

'Hullo,' I said, smiling, trying to put her at ease.

But the girl was business-like. She acknowledged my greeting
with a brief nod.

'Can I do anything for you?' I asked, stretching my limbs. 'Do you
stay near here?'

She nodded again.

'With your parents?'

With great assurance she said, 'Yes. But I can stay on my own.'

'You're like me,' I said, and for a while I forgot about being an old
man of twenty. 'I like to do on my own. I'm going away today.'

'Oh,' she said, a little breathlessly.

'Would you care to go to England?' 'I want to go everywhere,' she said, 'To America and Africa and Japan and Honolulu.'

'Maybe you will' I said. *'I'm* going everywhere, and no one can stop me . . . But what is it you want? What did you come for?'

'I want some flowers but I can't reach them.' She waved her hand towards the garden. 'That tree, see?'

The coral tree stood in front of the house surrounded by pools of water and broken, fallen blossoms. The branches of the tree were thick with the scarlet, pea-shaped flowers.

'All right,' I said. 'Just let me get ready.'

The tree was easy to climb, and I made myself comfortable on one of the lower branches, smiling down at the serious upturned face of the girl.

'I'll throw them down to you,' I said.

I bent a branch but the wood was young and green, and I had to twist it several times before it snapped.

'I'm not sure that I ought to do this,' I said, as I dropped the flowering branch to the girl.

'Don't worry,' she said.

'Well, if you're ready to speak up for me —'

'Don't worry.'

I felt a sudden nostalgic longing for childhood and an urge to remain behind in my grandfather's house with its tangled memories and ghosts of yesteryear. But I was the only one left, and what could I do except climb coral and jack-fruit trees?

'Have you many friends?' I asked.

'Oh, yes.'

'Who is the best?'

'The cook. He lets me stay in the kitchen, which is more interesting than the house. And I like to watch him cooking. And he gives me things to eat, and tells me stories . . .'

'And who is your second best friend?'

She inclined her head to one side, and thought very hard.

'I'll make you the second best,' she said.

I sprinkled coral-blossoms over her head. 'That's very kind of you. I'm happy to be your second best.'

A *tonga*-bell sounded at the gate, and I looked out from the tree and said, 'It's come for me. I have to go now.'

I climbed down.

'Will you help me with my suitcases?' I asked, as we walked together towards the verandah. 'There is no one here to help me. I am the last to go. Not because I want to go, but because I have to.'

I sat down on the cot and packed a few last things in a suitcase. All the doors of the house were locked. On my way to the station I would leave the keys with the caretaker. I had already given instructions to an agent to try and sell the house. There was nothing more to be done.

We walked in silence to the waiting *tonga*, thinking and wondering about each other.

'Take me to the station.' I said to the *tonga*-driver.

The girl stood at the side of the path, on the damp red earth, gazing at me.

'Thank you,' I said. 'I hope I shall see you again.'

'I'll see you in London,' she said. 'Or America or Japan. I want to go everywhere.'

'I'm sure you will,' I said. 'And perhaps I'll come back and we'll meet again in this garden. That would be nice, wouldn't it?'

She nodded and smiled. We knew it was an important moment.

The *tonga*-driver spoke to his pony, and the carriage set off down the gravel-path, rattling a little. The girl and I waved to each other.

In the girl's hand was a sprig of coral blossom. As she waved, the blossoms fell apart and danced lightly in the breeze.

'Goodbye!' I called.

'Goodbye,' called the girl.

The ribbon had come loose from her pigtail and lay on the ground with the coral blossoms.

'I'm going everywhere,' I said to myself, 'and no one can stop me.'

And she was fresh and clean like the rain and the red earth.

The Photograph

I was ten years old. My grandmother sat on the string bed, under the mango tree. It was late summer and there were sunflowers in the garden and a warm wind in the trees. My grandmother was knitting a woolen scarf for the winter months. She was very old, dressed in a plain white sari; her eyes were not very strong now, but her fingers moved quickly with the needles, and the needles kept clicking all afternoon. Grandmother had white hair, but there were very few wrinkles on her skin.

I had come home after playing cricket on the *maidan*. I had taken my meal, and now I was rummaging in a box of old books and family heirlooms that had just that day been brought out of the attic by my mother. Nothing in the box interested me very much, except for a book with colourful pictures of birds and butterflies. I was going through the book, looking at the pictures, when I found a small photograph between the pages. It was a faded picture, a little yellow and foggy; it was a picture of a girl standing against a wall, and behind the wall there was nothing but sky; but from the other side a pair of hands reached up, as though someone was going to climb the wall. There were flowers growing near the girl, but I couldn't tell what they were; there was a creeper too, but it was just a creeper.

I ran out into the garden. 'Granny!' I shouted. 'Look at this picture! I found it in the box of old things. Whose picture is it?'

I jumped on the bed beside my grandmother, and she wallopped me on the bottom and said, 'Now I've lost count of my stitches, and the next time you do that I'll make you finish the scarf yourself.'

Granny was always threatening to teach me how to knit, which I thought was a disgraceful thing for a boy to do; it was a good deterrent for keeping me out of mischief. Once I had torn the drawing-room curtains, and Granny had put a needle and thread in my hand and made me stitch the curtain together, even though I made long, two-inch stitches, which had to be taken out by my mother and done again.

She took the photograph from my hand, and we both stared at it for quite a long time. The girl had long, loose hair, and she wore a long dress that nearly covered her ankles, and sleeves that reached her wrists, and there were a lot of bangles on her hands; but, despite all this drapery, the girl appeared to be full of freedom and movement; she stood with her legs apart and her hands on her hips, and she had a wide, almost devilish smile on her face.

'Whose picture is it?' I asked.

'A little girl's, of course,' said Grandmother. 'Can't you tell?'

'Yes, but did you know the girl?'

'Yes, I knew her,' said Granny, 'but she was a very wicked girl and I shouldn't tell you about her. But I'll tell you about the photograph. It was taken in your grandfather's house, about sixty years ago and that's the garden wall, and over the wall there was a road going to town.'

'Whose hands are they,' I asked, 'coming up from the other side?'

Grandmother squinted and looked closely at the picture, and shook her head. 'It's the first time I noticed,' she said. 'That must have been been the sweeper boy's. Or maybe they were your grandfather's.'

'They don't look like grandfather's hands,' I said. 'His hands are all bony.'

'Yes, but this was sixty years ago.'

'Didn't he climb up the wall, after the photo?'

'No, nobody climbed up. At least, I don't remember.'

'And you remember well, Granny.'

'Yes, I remember . . . I remember what is not in the photograph. It was a spring day, and there was cool breeze blowing, nothing like this. Those flowers at the girl's feet, they were marigolds, and the Bougainvillaea creeper, it was a mass of purple. You cannot see these colours in the photo, and even if you could, as nowadays, you wouldn't be able to smell the flowers of feel the breeze.'

'And what about the girl?' I said. 'Tell me about the girl.'

'Well, she was a wicked girl,' said Granny. 'You don't know the trouble they had getting her into those fine clothes she's wearing.'

'I think they are terrible clothes,' I said.

'So did she. Most of the time, she hardly wore a thing. She used to go swimming in a muddy pool with a lot of ruffianly boys, and ride on the backs of buffaloes. No boy ever teased her, though, because she could kick and scratch and pull his hair out!'

'She looks like it too,' I said. 'You can tell by the way she's smiling. At any moment something's going to happen.'

'Something did happen,' said Granny. 'Her mother wouldn't let her take off the clothes afterwards, so she went swimming in them, and lay for half-an-hour in the mud.'

I laughed heartily and Grandmother laughed too.

'Who was the girl?' I said. 'You must tell me who she was.'

'No, that wouldn't do,' said Grandmother. 'I won't tell you.'

I knew the girl in the photo was really Grandmother, but I pretended I didn't know. I knew, because Grandmother still smiled in the same way, even though she didn't have as many teeth.

'Come on, Granny,' I said, 'tell me, tell me.'

But Grandmother shook her head and carried on with the knitting; and I held the photograph in my hand looking from it to my grandmother and back again, trying to find points in common between the old lady and the little pig-tailed girl. A lemon-coloured butterfly settled on the end of Grandmother's knitting needle, and stayed there while the needles clicked away. I made a grab at the butterfly, and it flew off in a dipping flight and settled on a sunflower.

'I wonder whose hands they were,' whispered Grandmother to herself, with her head bowed, and her needles clicking away in the soft warm silence of that summer afternoon.

The Window

I came in the spring, and took the room on the roof. It was a long low building which housed several families; the roof was flat, except for my room and a chimney. I don't know whose room owned the chimney, but my room owned the roof. And from the window of my room I owned the world.

But only from the window.

The banyan tree, just opposite, was mine, and its inhabitants my subjects. They were two squirrels, a few mynahs, a crow, and at night, a pair of flying-foxes. The squirrels were busy in the afternoon, the birds in the morning and evening, the foxes at night. I wasn't very busy that year; not as busy as the inhabitants of the banyan tree.

There was also a mango tree but that came later, in the summer, when I met Koki and the mangoes were ripe.

At first, I was lonely in my room. But then I discovered the power of my window. It looked out on the banyan tree, on the garden, on the broad path that ran beside the building, and out over the roofs of other houses, over roads and fields, as far as the horizon. The path was not a very busy one, but it held variety: an *ayah*, with a baby in a pram; the postman, an event in himself; the fruit-seller the toy-seller, calling their wares in high-pitched familiar cries; the rent-collector; a posse of cyclists; a long chain of school-girls; a lame beggar . . . all passed my way, the way of my window . . .

In the early summer, a *tonga* came rattling and jingling down the path and stopped in front of the house. A girl and an elderly lady climbed down, and a servant unloaded their baggage. They went into the house and the *tonga* moved off, the horse snorting a little.

The next morning the girl looked up from the garden and saw me at my window.

She had long black hair that fell to her waist, tied with a single red ribbon: her eyes were black like her hair and just as shiny. She must have been about ten or eleven years old.

'Hallo,' I said with a friendly smile.

She looked suspiciously at me, 'Who are you?' she asked.

'I'm a ghost.'

She laughed, and her laugh had a gay, mocking quality: 'You look like one!'

I didn't think her remark particulary flattering, but I had asked for it. I stopped smiling anyway: most children don't like adults smiling at them all the time.

'What have you got up there?' she asked.

'Magic,' I said.

She laughed again but this time without mockery. 'I don't believe you,' she said.

'Why don't you come up and see for yourself?'

She hesitated a little but came round to the steps and began climbing them, slowly, cautiously. And when she entered the room, she brought in a magic of her own.

'Where's your magic?' she asked, looking me in the eye.

'Come here,' I said, and I took her to the window, and showed her the world.

She said nothing but stared out of the window uncomprehendingly at first, and then with increasing interest. And after some time she turned round and smiled at me, and we were friends.

I only knew that her name was Koki, and that she had come with her aunt for the summer months; I didn't need to know any more about her, and she didn't need know anything about me except that I wasn't really a ghost — not the frightening sort any way . . .

She came up my steps nearly every day, and joined me at the window. There was a lot of excitement to be had in our world, especially when the rains broke.

At the first rumblings, women would rush outside to retrieve the washing on the clothes-line and, if there was a breeze to chase a few garments across the compound. When the rain came, it came with a vengeance, making a bog of the garden and a river of the path.

A cyclist would come riding furiously down the path, an elderly gentleman would be having difficulty with an umbrella, naked children would be frisking about in the rain. Sometimes Koki would run out on the roof, and shout and dance in the rain. And the rain would come through the open door and window of the room, flooding the floor and making an island of the bed.

But the window was more fun than anything else. It gave us the power of detachment: we were deeply interested in the life around us, but we were not involved in it.

'It is like a cinema,' said Koki 'The window is the screen, the world is the picture.'

Soon the mangoes were ripe, and Koki was in the branches of the mango tree as often as she was in my room. From the window I had a good view of the tree, and we spoke to each other from the same height. We ate far too many mangoes, at least five a day.

'Let's make a garden on the roof,' suggested Koki. She was full of ideas like this.

'And how do you propose to do that?' I asked.

'It's easy. We bring up mud and bricks and make the flower-beds. Then we plant the seeds. We'll grow all sorts of flowers.'

'The roof will fall in,' I predicted.

But it didn't. We spent two days carrying buckets of mud up the steps to the roof and laying out the flower-beds. It was very hard work, but Koki did most of it. When the beds were ready, we had the opening ceremony. Apart from a few small plants collected from the garden below we had only one species of seeds — pumpkin . . .

We planted the pumpkin-seeds in the mud, and felt proud of ourselves.

But it rained heavily that night, and in the morning I discovered that everything — except the bricks — had been washed away.

So we returned to the window.

A mynah had been in a fight — with the crow perhaps — and the feathers had been knocked off its head. A bougainvillaea that had been climbing the wall had sent a long green shoot in through the window.

Koki said, 'Now we can't shut the window without spoiling the creeper.'

'Then we will never close the window,' I said.

And we let the creeper into the room.

The rains passed, and an autumn wind came whispering through the branches of the banyan tree. There were red leaves on the ground, and the wind picked them up and blew them about, so that they looked like butterflies. I would watch the sun rise in the morning, the sky all red, until its first rays splashed the window-sill and crept up the walls of the room. And in the evening Koki and I watched the sun go down in a sea of fluffy clouds; sometimes the clouds were pink, and sometimes orange; they were always coloured clouds, framed in the window.

'I'm going tomorrow,' said Koki one evening.

I was too surprised to say anything.

'You stay here forever, don't you?' she said.

I remained silent.

'When I come again next year you will still be here, won't you?'

'I don't know,' I said, 'but the window will still be here.'

'Oh, do be here next year,' she said, 'or someone will close the window!'

In the morning the *tonga* was at the door, and the servant, the aunt and Koki were in it. Koki waved up to me at my window. Then the driver flicked the reins, the wheels of the carriage creaked and rattled, the bell jingled. Down the path went the *tonga*, down the path and through the gate, and all the time Koki waved; and from the gate I must have looked like a ghost, standing alone at the high window, amongst the bougainvillaea.

When the *tonga* was out of sight I took the spray of bougainvillaea in my hand and pushed it out of the room. Then I closed the window. It would be opened only when the spring and Koki came again.

Chachi's Funeral

Chachi died at 6 p.m. on Wednesday the 5th of April, and came to life again exactly twenty minutes later. This is how it happened.

Chachi was, as a rule, a fairly tolerant, easy-going person, who waddled about the house without paying much attention to the swarms of small sons, daughters, nephews and nieces who poured in and out of the rooms. But she had taken a particular aversion to her ten-year old nephew, Sunil. She was a simple woman and could not understand Sunil. He was a little brighter than her own sons, more sensitive, and inclined to resent a scolding or a cuff across the head. He was better looking then her own children. All this, in addition to the fact that she resented having to cook for the boy while both his parents went out at office jobs, led her to grumble at him a little more than was really necessary.

Sunil sensed his aunt's jealousy and fanned its flames. He was a mischievous boy, and did little things to annoy her, like bursting paper-bags behind her while she dozed, or commenting on the width of her pyjamas when they were hung out to dry. On the evening of the 5th of April, he had been in particulary high spirits, and feeling hungry, entered the kitchen with the intention of helping himself to some honey. But the honey was on the top shelf, and Sunil wasn't quite tall enough to grasp the bottle. He got his fingers to it but as he tilted it towards him, it fell to the ground with a crash.

Chachi reached the scene of the accident before Sunil could slip away. Removing her slipper, she dealt him three or four furious blows across the head and shoulders. This done, she sat down on the floor and burst into tears.

Had the beating come from someone else, Sunil might have cried; but his pride was hurt, and instead of weeping, he muttered something under his breath and stormed out of the room.

Climbing the steps to the roof, he went to his secret hiding-place, a small hole in the wall of the unused *barsati*, where he kept his marbles, kite-string, tops, and a clasp-knife. Opening the knife, he plunged it thrice into the soft wood of the window-frame.

'I'll kill her!' he whispered fiercely, 'I'll kill her, I'll kill her!'

'Who are you going to kill, Sunil?'

It was his cousin Madhu, a dark slim girl of twelve, who aided and abetted him in most of his exploits. Sunil's Chachi was her *'Mammi.'* It was a very big family.

'Chachi,' said Sunil. 'She hates me, I know. Well, I hate her too. This time I'll kill her.'

'How are you going to do it?'

'I'll stab with this,' He showed her the knife.

'Three times, in the heart.'

'But you'll be caught. The C.I.D. are very clever. Do you want to go to jail?'

'Won't they hang me?'

'They don't hang small boys. They send them to boarding-schools.'

'I don't want to go to a boarding-school.'

'Then better not kill your Chachi. At least not this way. I'll show you how.'

Madhu produced pencil and paper, went down on her hands and knees, and screwing up her face in sharp concentration, made a rough drawing of Chachi. Then, with a red crayon, she sketched in a big heart in the region of Chachi's stomach.

'Now,' she said, 'stab her to death!'

Sunil's eyes shone with excitement. Here was a great new game. You could always depend on Madhu for something original. He held the drawing against the woodwork, and plunged his knife three times into Chachi's pastel breast.

'You have killed her,' said Madhu.

'It that all?'

'Well, if you like, we can cremate her.'

'All right.'

She took the torn paper, crumpled it up, produced a box of matches from Sunil's hiding-place, lit a match, and set fire to the paper. In a few minutes all that remained of Chachi were a few ashes.

'Poor Chachi,' said Madhu.

'Perhaps we shouldn't have done it,' said Sunil beginning to feel sorry.

'I know, we'll put her ashes in the river!'

'What river?'

'Oh, the drain will do.'

Madhu gathered the ashes together, and leant over the balcony of the roof. She threw out her arms, and the ashes drifted downwards. Some of them settled on the pomegranate tree, a few reached the drain and were carried away by a sudden rush of kitchen-water. She turned to face Sunil.

Big tears were rolling down Sunil's cheeks.

'What are you crying for?' asked Madhu.

'Chachi. I didn't hate her so much.'

'Then why did you want to kill her?'

'Oh, that was different.'

'Come on, then, let's go down. I have to do my homework.'

As they came down the steps from the roof, Chachi emerged from the kitchen.

'Oh Chachi!' shouted Sunil. He rushed to her and tried to get his arms around her ample waist.

'Now what's up?' grumbled Chachi. 'What is it this time?'

'Nothing, Chachi. I love you so much. Please don't leave us.'

A look of suspicion crossed Chachi's face. She frowned down the boy. But she was reassured by the look of genuine affection that she saw in his eyes.

'Perhaps he *does* care for me, after all,' she thought: and patting him gently on the head, she took him by the hand and led him back to the kitchen.

The Man Who Was Kipling

I was sitting on a bench in the Indian Section of the Victoria and Albert Museum in London, when a tall, stooping, elderly gentleman sat down beside me. I gave him a quick glance, noting his swarthy features, heavy moustache, and horn-rimmed spectacles. There was something familiar and disturbing about his face, and I couldn't resist looking at him again.

I noticed that he was smiling at me.

'Do you recognise me?' he asked, in a soft pleasant voice.

'Well, you do seem familiar,' I said. 'Haven't we met somewhere?'

'Perhaps. But if I seem familiar to you, that is at least something. The trouble these days is that people don't *know* me anymore — I'm a familiar, that's all. Just a name standing for a lot of outmoded ideas.'

A little perplexed, I asked, 'What is it you do?'

'I wrote books once. Poems and tales . . . Tell me, whose books do you read?'

'Oh, Maugham, Priestley, Thurber. And among the older lot, Bennett and Wells —.' I hesitated, groping for an important name, and I noticed a shadow, a sad shadow, pass across my companion's face.

'Oh, yes, and Kipling,' I said 'I read a lot of Kipling.'

His face brightened up at once, and the eyes behind the thick-lensed spectacles suddenly came to life.

'I'm Kipling,' he said.

I stared at him in astonishment, and then, realising that he might perhaps be dangerous, I smiled feebly and said, 'Oh, yes?'

'You probably don't believe me. I'm dead, of course.'

'So I thought.'

'And you don't believe in ghosts?'

'Not as a rule.'

'But you'd have no objection to talking to one, if he came along?'

'I'd have no objection. But how do I know you're Kipling? How do I know you're not an imposter?'

'Listen, then:

When my heavens were turned to blood,
When the dark had filled my day,
Furthest, but most faithful, stood
That lone star I cast away.
I had loved myself, and I
Have not lived and dare not die.'

'Once,' he said, gripping me by the arm and looking me straight in the eye. 'Once in life I watched a star; but I whistled, her to go.'

'Your star hasn't fallen yet, I said, suddenly moved, suddenly quite certain that I sat beside Kipling. 'One day, when there is a new spirit of adventure abroad, we will discover you again.'

'Why have they heaped scorn on me for so long?'

'You were too militant, I suppose — too much of an Empire man. You were too patriotic for your own good.'

He looked a little hurt. 'I was never very political,' he said. 'I wrote over six hundred poems, and you could only call a dozen of them political, I have been abused for harping on the theme of the White Man's Burden but my only aim was to show off the Empire to my audience — and I believed the Empire was a fine and noble thing. Is it wrong to believe in something? I never went deeply into political issues, that's true. You must remember, my seven years in India were very youthful years. I was in my twenties, a little immature if you like, and my interest in India was a boy's interest. Action appealed to me more than anything else. You must understand that.'

'No one has described action more vividly, or India so well. I feel at one with Kim wherever he goes along the Grand Trunk Road, in the temples at Banaras, amongst the Saharanpur fruit gardens, on the snow-covered Himalayas. *Kim* has colour and movement and poetry.'

He sighed, and a wistful look came into his eyes.

'I'm prejudiced, of course,' I continued. 'I've spent most of my life in India — not *your* India, but an India that does still have much of the colour and atmosphere that you captured. You know, Mr.

Kipling, you can still sit in a third class railway carriage and meet the most wonderful assortment of people. In any village you will still find the same courtesy, dignity and courage that the Lama and Kim found on their travels.'

'And the Grand Trunk Road? Is it still a long winding procession of humanity?'

'Well, not exactly,' I said, a little ruefully. 'It's just a procession of motor vehicles now. The poor Lama would be run down by a truck if he became too dreamy on the Grand Trunk Road. Times *have* changed. There are no more Mrs. Hawksbees in Simla, for instance.'

There was a far-away look in Kipling's eyes. Perhaps he was imagining himself a boy again; perhaps he could see the hills or the red dust or Rajputana; perhaps he was having a private conversation with Privates Mulvaney and Ortheris, or perhaps he was out hunting with the Seonce wolf-pack. The sound of London's traffic came to us through the glass doors, but we heard only the creaking of bullock-cart wheels and the distant music of a flute.

He was talking to himself, repeating a passage from one of his stories. 'And the last puff of the daywind brought from the unseen villages the scent of damp wood-smoke, hot cakes, dripping under-growth, amd rotting pine-cones. That is the true smell of the Hima-layas, and if once it creeps into the blood of a man, that man will at the last, forgetting all else, return to the hills to die.'

A mist seemed to have risen between us — or had it come in from the streets? — and when it cleared, Kipling had gone away.

I asked the gatekeeper if he had seen a tall man with a slight stoop, wearing spectacles.

'Nope,' said the gatekeeper. 'Nobody been by for the last ten minutes.'

'Did someone like that come into the gallery a little while ago?'

'No one that I recall. What did you say the bloke's name was?'

'Kipling,' I said.

'Don't know him.'

'Didn't you ever read *The Jungle Books*?'

'Sounds familiar. Tarzan stuff, wasn't it?'

I left the museum, and wandered about the streets for a long time, but I couldn't find Kipling anywhere. Was it the boom of London's traffic that I heard, or the boom of the Sutlej river racing through the valleys?

The Eyes Have It

I had the train compartment to myself up to Rohana, then a girl got in. The couple who saw her off were probably her parents; they seemed very anxious about her comfort, and the woman gave the girl detailed instructions as to where to keep her things, when not to lean out of windows, and how to avoid speaking to strangers.

They called their goodbyes and the train pulled out of the station. As I was totally blind at the time, my eyes sensitive only to light and darkness, I was unable to tell what the girl looked like; but I knew she wore slippers from the way they slapped against her heels.

It would take me some time to discover something about her looks, and perhaps I never would. But I liked the sound of her voice, and even the sound of her slippers.

'Are you going all the way to Dehra?' I asked.

I must have been sitting in a dark corner, because my voice startled her. She gave a little exclamation and said, 'I didn't know anyone else was here.'

Well, it often happens that people with good eyesight fail to see what is right in front of them. They have too much to take in, I suppose. Whereas people who cannot see (or see very little) have to take in only the essentials, whatever registers most tellingly on their remaining senses.

'I didn't see you either,' I said. 'But I heard you come in.'

I wondered if I would be able to prevent her from discovering that I was blind. Provided I keep to my seat, I thought, it shouldn't be too difficult.

The girl said, 'I'm getting off at Saharanpur. My aunt is meeting me there.'

'Then I had better not get too familiar,' I replied. 'Aunts are usually formidable creatures.'

'Where are you going?' she asked.

'To Dehra, and then to Mussoorie.'

'Oh, how lucky you are. I wish I were going to Mussoorie. I love the hills. Especially in October.'

'Yes, this is the best time,' I said, calling on my memories. 'The hills are covered with wild dahlias, the sun is delicious, and at night you can sit in front of a logfire and drink a little brandy. Most of the tourists have gone, and the roads are quiet and almost deserted. Yes, October is the best time.'

She was silent. I wondered if my words had touched her, or whether she thought me a romantic fool. Then I made a mistake.

'What is it like outside?' I asked.

She seemed to find nothing strange in the question. Had she noticed already the I could not see? But her next question removed my doubts.

'Why don't you look out of the window?' she asked.

I moved easily along the berth and felt for the window ledge. The window was open, and I faced it, making a pretence of studying the landscape. I heard the panting of the engine, the rumble of the wheels, and, in my mind's eye, I could see telegraph posts flashing by.

'Have you noticed,' I ventured, 'that the trees seem to be moving while we seem to be standing still?'

'That always happens,' she said. 'Do you see any animals?'

'No,' I answered quite confidently. I knew that there were hardly any animals left in the forests near Dehra.

I turned from the window and faced the girl, and for a while we sat in silence.

'You have an interesting face,' I remarked. I was becoming quite daring, but it was a safe remark. Few girls can resist flattery. She laughed pleasantly — a clear, ringing laugh.

'It's nice to be told I have an interesting face. I'm tired of people telling me I have a pretty face.'

Oh, so you do have a pretty face, thought I: and aloud I said: 'Well, an interesting face can also be pretty.'

'You are a very gallant young man,' she said 'but why are you so serious?'

I thought, then, I would try to laugh for her, but the thought of laughter only made me feel troubled and lonely.

'We'll soon be at your station,' I said.

'Thank goodness it's a short journey. I can't bear to sit in a train for more than two-or-three hours.'

Yet I was prepared to sit there for almost any length of time, just to listen to her talking. Her voice had the sparkle of a mountain stream. As soon as she left the train, she would forget our brief encounter; but it would stay with me for the rest of the journey, and for some time after.

The engine's whistle shrieked, the carriage wheels changed their sound and rhythm, the girl got up and began to collect her things. I wondered if she wore her hair in a bun, or if it was plaited; perhaps it was hanging loose over her shoulders, or was it cut very short?

The train drew slowly into the station. Outside, there was the shouting of porters and vendors and a high-pitched female voice near the carriage door; that voice must have belonged to the girls' aunt.

'Goodbye,' the girl said.

She was standing very close to me, so close that the perfume from her hair was tantalizing. I wanted to raise my hand and touch her hair, but she moved away. Only the scent of perfume still lingered where she had stood.

There was some confusion in the doorway. A man, getting into the compartment, stammered an apology. Then the door banged, and the world was shut out again. I returned to my berth. The guard blew his whistle and we moved off. Once again, I had a game to play and a new fellow-traveller.

The train gathered speed, the wheels took up their song, the carriage groaned and shook. I found the window and sat in front of it, staring into the daylight that was darkness for me.

So many things were happening outside the window: it could be a fascinating game, guessing what went on out there.

The man who had entered the compartment broke into my reverie.

'You must be disappointed,' he said. 'I'm not nearly as attractive a travelling companion as the one who just left.'

'She was an interesting girl,' I said. 'Can you tell me — did she keep her hair long or short?'

'I don't remember,' he said, sounding puzzled. 'It was her eyes I noticed, not her hair. She had beautiful eyes — but they were of no use to her. She was completely blind. Didn't you notice?'

The Thief

I was still a thief when I met Arun, and though I was only fifteen, I was an experienced and fairly successful hand.

Arun was watching the wrestlers when I approached him. He was about twenty, a tall, lean fellow, and he looked kind and simple enough for my purpose. I hadn't had much luck of late, and thought I might be able to get into this young person's confidence. He seemed quite fascinated by the wrestling. Two well-oiled men slid about in the soft mud, grunting and slapping their thighs. When I got Arun into conversation he didn't seem to realise I was a stranger.

'You look like a wrestler yourself,' I said.

'So do you,' he replied, which put me out of my stride for a moment, because at the time I was rather thin and bony and not very impressive physically.

'Yes,' I said. 'I wrestle sometimes.'

'What's your name?'

'Deepak,' I lied.

Deepak was about my fifth name. I had earlier called myself Ranbir, Sudhir, Trilok, and Surinder.

After this preliminary exchange, Arun confined himslf to comments on the match, and I didn't have much to say. After a while he walked away from the crowd of spectators. I followed him.

'Hallo,' he said. 'Enjoying yourself?'

I gave him my most appealing smile. 'I want to work for you,' I said.

He didn't stop walking. 'And what makes you think I want someone to work for me?'

'Well,' I said, 'I've been wandering about all day, looking for the best person to work for. When I saw you, I knew that no one else had a chance.'

'You flatter me,' he said.

'That's all right.'

'But you can't work for me.'

'Why not?'

'Because I can't pay you.'

I thought that over for a minute. Perhaps I had misjudged my man.

'Can you feed me?' I asked.

'Can you cook?' he countered.

'I can cook,' I lied.

'If you can cook,' he said, 'I'll feed you.'

He took me to his room and told me I could sleep in the verandah. But I was nearly back on the street that night. The meal I cooked must have been pretty awful, because Arun gave it to the neighbour's cat and told me to be off. But I just hung around smiling in my most appealing way; and then he couldn't help laughing. He sat down on the bed and laughed for a full five minutes, and later patted me on the head and said, never mind, he'd teach me to cook in the morning.

Not only did he teach me to cook, but he taught me to write my name and his, and said he would soon teach me to write whole sentences, and add money on paper when you didn't have any in your pocket!

It was quite pleasant working for Arun. I made the tea in the morning and later went out shopping. I would take my time buying the day's supplies and made a profit of about 25 paise a day. I would tell Arun that rice was 56 paise a pound (it generally was), but I would get it at 50 paise a pound. I think he knew I made a little this way, but he didn't mind, he wasn't giving me a regular wage.

I was really grateful to Arun for teaching me to write. I knew that once I could write like an educated man there would be no limit to what I could achieve. It might even be an incentive to be honest.

Arun made money by fits and starts. He would be borrowing one week, lending the next. He would keep worrying about his next cheque but, as soon as it arrived, he would go out and celebrate lavishly.

One evening he came home with a wad of notes, and at night I saw him tuck the bundles under his mattress, at the head of the bed.

I had been working for Arun for nearly a fortnight and, apart from the shopping, hadn't done much to exploit him. I had every opportunity for doing so. I had a key to the front door, which meant I had access to the room whenever Arun was out. He was the most trusting person I had ever met. And that was why I couldn't make up my mind to rob him.

It's easy to rob a greedy man, because he deserves to be robbed; it's easy to rob a rich man, because he can afford to be robbed; but it's diffcult to rob a poor man, even one who really doesn't care if he's robbed. A rich man or a greedy man or a careful man wouldn't keep his money under a pillow or mattress, he'd lock it up in a safe place. Arun had put his money where it would be child's play for me to remove it without his knowledge.

It's time I did some real work, I told myself ; I'm getting out of practice . . . If I don't take the money, he'll only waste it on his friends . . . He doesn't even pay me . . .

Arun was asleep. Moonlight came in from the varandah and fell across the bed. I sat up on the floor, my blanket wrapped round me, considering the situation. There was quite a lot of money in that wad, and if I took it I would have to leave town — I might make the 10.30 express to Amritsar . . .

Slipping out of the blanket, I crept on all fours through the door and up to the bed, and peeped at Arun. He was sleeping peacefully with a soft and easy breathing. His face was clear and unlined; even I had more markings on my face, though mine were mostly scars.

My hand took on an identity of its own as it slid around under the mattress, the fingers searching for the notes. They found them, and I drew them out without a crackle.

Arun sighed in his sleep and turned on his side, towards me. My free hand was resting on the bed, and his hair touched my fingers.

I was frightened when his hair touched my fingers, and crawled quickly and quietly out of the room.

When I was in the street, I began to run. I ran down the bazaar road to the station. The shops were all closed, but a few lights came from upper windows. I had the note at my waist, held there by the string of my pyjamas. I felt I had to stop and count the notes though

I knew it might make me late for the train. It was already 10.20 by the clock tower. I slowed down to a walk, and my fingers flicked through the notes. There were about a hundred rupees in fives. A good haul. I could live like a prince for a month or two.

When I reached the station I did not stop at the ticket-office (I had never bought a ticket in my life) but dashed straight on to the platform. The Amritsar Express was just moving out. It was moving slowly enough for me to be able to jump on the foot-board of one of the carriages, but I hesitated for some urgent, unexplainable reason.

I hesitated long enough for the train to leave without me.

When it had gone, and the noise and busy confusion of the platform had subsided, I found myself standing alone on the deserted platform. The knowledge that I had a hundred stolen rupees in my pyjamas only increased my feeling of isolation and loneliness. I had no idea where to spend the night; I had never kept any friends,because sometimes friends can be one's undoing; I didn't want to make myself conspicuous by staying at a hotel. And the only person I knew really well in town was the person I had robbed!

Leaving the station, I walked slowly through the bazaar keeping to dark, deserted alleys. I kept thinking of Arun. He would still be asleep, blissfully unaware of his loss.

I have made a study of men's faces when they have lost something of material value. The greedy man shows panic, the rich man shows anger, the poor man shows fear; but I knew that neither panic nor anger nor fear would show on Arun's face, when he discovered the theft; only a terrible sadness not for the loss of the money but for my having betrayed his trust.

I found myself on the *maidan* and sat down on a bench with my feet tucked up under my haunches.The night was a little cold, and I regretted not having brought Arun's blanket along. A light drizzle added to my discomfort. Soon it was raining heavily. My shirt and pyjamas stuck to my skin and a cold wind brought the rain whipping across my face. I told myself that sleeping on a bench was something, I should have been used to by now, but the verandah had softened me.

I walked back to the bazaar and sat down on the step of a closed shop. A few vagrants lay beside me , rolled up tight in thin blankets. The clock showed midnight, I felt for the notes; they were still

41

with me, but had lost their crispness and were damp with rainwater.

Arun's money. In the morning he would probably have given me a rupee to go to the pictures but now I had it all. No more cooking his meals, running to the bazaar, or learning to write whole sentences. Whole sentences . . .

They were something I had forgotten in the excitement of a hundred rupees. Whole sentences, I knew, could one day bring me more than a hundred rupees. It was a simple matter to steal (and sometimes just as simple to be caught) but to be a really big man, a wise and successful man, that was something. I should go back to Arun, I told myself, if only to learn how to write.

Perhaps it was also concern for Arun that drew me back; a sense of sympathy is one of my weaknesses, and through hesitation over a theft I had often been caught. A successful thief must be pitiless. I was fond of Arun. My affection for him, my sense of sympathy, but most of all my desire to write whole sentences, drew me back to the room.

I hurried back to the room extremely nervous, for it is easier to steal something than to return it undetected. If I was caught beside the bed now, with the money in my hand, or with my hand under the mattress there could be only one explanation: that I was actually stealing. If Arun woke up, I would be lost.

I opened the door clumsily, then stood in the doorway in clouded moonlight. Gradually my eyes became accustomed to the darkness of the room. Arun was still asleep. I went on all fours again and crept noiselessly to the head of the bed. My hand came up with the notes. I felt his breath on my fingers. I was fascinated by his tranquil features and easy breathing and remained motionless for a minute. Then my hand explored the mattress, found the edge, slipped under it with the notes.

I awoke late next morning to find that Arun had already made the tea. I found it difficult to face him in the harsh light of day. His hand was stretched out towards me. There was a five-rupee note between his fingers. My heart sank.

'I made some money yesterday,' he said. 'Now you'll get paid regularly.' My spirit rose as rapidly as they had fallen. I congratulated myself on having returned the money.

But when I took the note, I realised that he knew everything. The note was still wet from last night's rain.

'Today I'll teach you to write a little more than your name,' he said.

He knew; but neither his lips nor his eyes said anything about their knowing.

I smiled at Arun in my most appealing way; and the smile came by itself, without my knowing it.

The Boy who Broke The Bank

Nathu grumbled to himself as he swept the steps of the Pipalnagar Bank, owned by Seth Govind Ram. He used the small broom hurriedly and carelessly, and the dust, after rising in a cloud above his head settled down again on the steps. As Nathu was banging his pan against a dustbin, Sitaram, the washerman's son, passed by.

Sitaram was on his delivery round. He had a bundle of freshly pressed clothes balanced on his head.

'Don't raise such dust!' he called out to Nathu. 'Are you annoyed because they are still refusing to pay you an extra two rupees a month?'

'I don't wish to talk about it,' complained the sweeper-boy. 'I haven't even received my regular pay. And this is the twentieth of the month. Who would think a bank would hold up a poor man's salary? As soon as I get my money, I'm off! Not another week I work in this place.' And Nathu banged the pan against the dustbin several times, just to emphasize his point and giving himself confidence.

'Well, I wish you luck,' said Sitaram. 'I'll keep a lookout for any jobs that might suit you.' And he plodded barefoot along the road, the big bundle of clothes hiding most of his head and shoulders.

At the fourth home he visited, Sitaram heard the lady of the house mention that she was in need of a sweeper. Tying his bundle together, he said; 'I know of a sweeper boy who's looking for work. He can start from next month. He's with the bank just now but they aren't giving him his pay, and he wants to leave.'

'Is that so?' said Mrs. Srivastava. 'Well, tell him to come and see me tomorrow.'

And Sitaram, glad that he had been of service to both a customer and his friend, hoisted his bag on his shoulders and went his way.

Mrs. Srivastava had to do some shopping. She gave instructions to the *ayah* about looking after the baby, and told the cook not to be late with the mid-day meal. Then she set out for the Pipalnagar market place, to make her customary tour of the cloth shops.

A large shady tamarind tree grew at one end of the bazaar, and it was here that Mrs. Srivastava found her friend Mrs. Bhushan sheltering from the heat. Mrs.Bhushan was fanning herself with a large handkerchief. She complained of the summer, which she affirmed, was definitely the hottest in the history of Pipalnagar. She then showed Mrs. Srivastava a sample of the cloth she was going to buy, and for five minutes they discussed its shade, texture and design. Having exhausted this topic, Mrs. Srivastava said,'Do you know, my dear, that Seth Govind Ram's bank can't even pay its employees. Only this morning I heard a complaint from their sweeper, who hasn't received his wages for over a month!'

'Shocking!' remarked Mrs. Bhushan. 'If they can't pay the sweeper they must be in a bad way. None of the others could be getting paid either.'

She left Mrs. Srivastava at the tamarind tree and went in search of her husband, who was sitting in front of Kamal Kishore's photographic shop, talking with the owner.

'So there you are!' cried Mrs. Bhushan. 'I've been looking for you for almost an hour. Where did you disappear?'

'Nowhere,' replied Mr. Bhushan. 'Had you remained stationary in one shop, I might have found you. But you go from one shop to another,like a bee in a flower garden.'

'Don't start grumbling. The heat is trying enough. I don't know what's happening to Pipalnagar. Even the bank's about to go bankrupt.'

'What's that?' said Kamal Kishore, sitting up suddenly. 'Which bank?'

'Why the Pipalnagar bank of course. I hear they have stopped paying employees. Don't tell me you have an account there, Mr. Kishore?'

'No, but my neighbour has!' he exclaimed; and he called out over the low partition to the keeper of the barber shop next door.'Deep Chand, have you heard the latest? The Pipalnagar Bank is about to collapse. You'd better get your money out as soon a you can!'

Deep Chand who was cutting the hair of an elderly gentlemen, was so startled that his hand shook and he nicked his customer's right ear. The customer yelped with pain and distress: pain, because of the cut and distress because of the awful news he had just heard. With one side of his neck still unshaven, he sped across the road to the general merchant's store where there was a telephone. He dialed Seth Govind Ram's number. The Seth was not at home. Where was he, then? The Seth was holidaying in Kashmir. Oh, was that so? The elderly gentleman did not believe it. He hurried back to the barber's shop and told Deep Chand: 'The bird has flown! Seth Govind Ram has left town. Definitely, it means a collapse.' And then he dashed out of the shop, making a beeline for his office and chequebook.

The news spread through the bazaar with the rapidity of forest fire. From the general merchant's it travelled to the shop, circulated amongst the customers, and then spread with them in various directions, to the betel-seller, the tailor, the free vendor, the jeweller,the beggar sitting on the pavement.

Old Ganpat the beggar, had a crooked leg. He had been squatting on the pavement for years, calling for alms. In the evening someone would come with a barrow and take him away. He had never been known to walk. But now, on learning that the bank was about to collapse, Ganpat astonished everyone leaping to his feet and actually running at top speed in the direction of the bank. It soon became known that he had a thousand rupees in savings!

Men stood in groups at street corners discussing the situation. Pipalnagar seldom had a crisis, seldom or never had floods, earthquakes or drought; and the imminent crash of the Pipalnagar Bank set everyone talking and speculating and rushing about in a frenzy. Some boasted of their farsightedness, congratulating themselves on having already taken out their money, or on never having put any in; others speculated on the reasons for the crash, putting it all down to excesses indulged in by Seth Govind Ram. The Seth had fled the State, said one. He had fled the country, said another, He was hiding in Pipalnagar, said a third. He had hanged himself from the tamarind tree, said a fourth, and had been found that morning by the sweeper-boy.

By noon the small bank had gone through all ;its ready cash, and the harassed manager was in a dilemma. Emergency funds could only be obtained from another bank some thirty miles distant, and he wasn't sure he could persuade the crowd to wait until then. And there was no way of contacting Seth Govind Ram on his houseboat in Kashmir.

People were turned back from the counters and told to return the following day. They did not like the sound of that. And so they gathered outside, on the steps of the bank shouting 'Give us our money or we'll break in !' and 'Fetch the Seth, we know he's hiding in a safe deposit locker!'Mischief makers who didn't have a paisa in the bank, joined the crowd and aggravated their mood. The manager stood at the door and tried to placate them. He declared that the bank had plenty of money but no immediate means of collecting it; he urged them to go home and come back the next day.

'We want it now!' chanted some of the crowd. 'Now, now, now!'

And a brick hurtled through the air and crashed through the plate glass window of the Pipalnagar Bank.

Nathu arrived next morning to sweep the steps of the bank. He saw the refuse and the broken glass and the stones cluttering the steps. Raising his hands in a gesture of horror and disgust he cried: 'Hooligans! Sons of donkeys! As though it isn't bad enough to be paid late, it seems my work has also to be increased!' He smote the steps with his broom scattering the refuse.

'Good morning, Nathu,' said the washerman's boy, getting down from his bicycle. 'Are you ready to take up a new job from the first of next month? You'll have to I suppose, now that the bank is going out of business.'

'How's that?' said Nathu.

'Haven't you heard? Well you'd better wait here until half the population of Pipalnagar arrives to claim their money.' And he waved cheerfully — he did not have a bank account — and sped away on his cycle.

Nathu went back to sweeping the steps, muttering to himself. When he had finished his work, he sat down on the highest step, to await the arrival of the manager. He was determined to get his pay.

'Who would have thought the bank would collapse!' he said to himself, and looked thoughtfully into the distance. 'I wonder how it could have happened . . .'

His Neighbour's Wife

No (said Arun, as we waited for dinner to be prepared), I did not fall in love with my neighbour's wife. It is not that kind of story.

Mind you, Leela was a most attractive woman. She was not beautiful or pretty; but she was handsome. Hers was the firm, athletic body of a sixteen-year-old boy, free of any surplus flesh. She bathed morning and evening, oiling herself well, so that her skin glowed a golden-brown in the winter sunshine. Her lips were often coloured with *paan*-juice, but her teeth were perfect.

I was her junior by about five years, and she called me her 'younger brother'. Her husband, who was forty to her thirty-two, was an official in the Customs and Excise Department: an extrovert, a hard-drinking, backslapping man, who spent a great deal of time on tour. Leela knew that he was not always faithful to her during these frequent absences; but she found solace in her own loyalty and in the well-being of her one child, a boy called Chandu.

I did not care for the boy. He had been well-spoilt, and took great delight in disturbing me whenever I was at work. He entered my rooms uninvited, knocked my books about, and, if guests were present, made insulting remarks about them to their faces.

Leela, during her lonely evenings, would often ask me to sit on her verandah and talk to her. The day's work done, she would relax with a *hookah*. Smoking a *hookah* was a habit she had brought with her from her village near Agra, and it was a habit she refused to give up. She liked to talk; and, as I was a good listener, she soon grew fond of me. The fact that I was twenty-six years old, and still a bachelor, never failed to astonish her.

It was not long before she took upon herself the responsibility for getting me married. I found it useless to protest. She did not believe me when I told her that I could not afford to marry, that I preferred a bachelor's life. A wife, she insisted, was an asset to any man. A wife reduced expenses. Where did I eat? At a hotel, of course. That must cost me at least sixty rupees a month, even on a vegetarian diet. But if I had a simple, homely wife to do the cooking, we could both eat well for less than that.

Leela fingered my shirt, observing that a button was missing and that the collar was frayed. She remarked on my pale face and general look of debility; and told me that I would fall victim to all kinds of diseases if I did not find someone to look after me. What I needed, she declared betweeen puffs at the *hookah*, was a woman — a young, healthy, buxom woman, preferably from a village near Agra.

'If I could find someone like you,' I said slyly, 'I would not mind getting married.'

She appeared neither flattered nor offended by my remark.

'Don't marry an older woman,' she advised. 'Never take a wife who is more experienced in the ways of the world than you are. You just leave it to me, I'll find a suitable bride for you.'

To please Leela, I agreed to this arrangement, thinking she would not take it seriously. But, two days later, when she suggested that I accompany her to a certain distinguished home for orphan girls, I became alarmed. I refused to have anything to do with her project.

'Don't you have confidence in me?' she asked. 'You said you would like a girl who resembled me. I know one who looks just as I did ten years ago.'

'I like you as you are now,' I said. 'Not as you were ten years ago.'

'Of course. We shall arrange for you to see the girl first.'

'You don't understand,' I protested. 'It's not that I feel I have to be in love with someone before marrying her — I know you would choose a fine girl, and I would really prefer someone who is homely and simple to an M.A. with Honours in Psychology — it's just that I'm not ready for it. I want another year or two of freedom. I don't want to be chained down. To be frank, I don't want the responsibility.'

'A little responsibility will make a man of you,' said Leela; but she did not insist on my accompanying her to the orphanage, and the matter was allowed to rest for a few days.

I was beginning to hope that Leela had reconciled herself to allowing one man to remain single in a world full of husbands when, one morning, she accosted me on the verandah with an open newspaper, which she thrust in front of my nose.

'There!' she said triumphantly. 'What do you think of that? I did it to surprise you.'

She had certainly succeeded in surprising me. Her henna-stained forefinger rested on an advertisement in the matrimonial columns.

Bachelor journalist, age 25, seeks attractive young wife well-versed in household duties. Caste, religion no bar. Dowry optional.

I must admit that Leela had made a good job, of it. In a few days the replies began to come in, usually from the parents of the girls concerned. Each applicant wanted to know how much money I was earning. At the same time, they took the trouble to list their own connections and the high positions occupied by relatives. Some parents enclosed their daughters' photographs. They were very good photographs, though there had been a certain amount of touching-up.

I studied the pictures with interest. Perhaps marriage wasn't such a bad propostion, after all. I selected the photographs of the three girls I most fancied and showed them to Leela.

To my surprise, she disapproved of all three. One of the girls she said, had a face like a hermaphrodite; another obviously suffered from tuberculosis; and the third was undoubtedly an adventuress. Leela decided that the whole idea of the advertisement had been a mistake. She was sorry she had inserted it; the only replies we were likely to get would be from fortune-hunters. And I had no fortune.

So we destroyed the letters. I tried to keep some of the photographs, but Leela tore them up too.

And so, for some time, there were no more attempts at getting me married.

Leela and I met nearly every day, but we spoke of other things. Sometimes, in the evenings, she would make me sit on the *charpoy* opposite her, and then she would draw up her *hookah* and tell me stories about her village and her family. I was getting used to the boy, too, and even growing rather fond of him.

All this came to an end when Leela's husband went and got himself killed. He was shot by a bootlegger who had decided to get rid of the Excise man rather than pay him an exorbitant sum of money. It meant that Leela had to give up her quarters and return to her village near Agra. She waited until the boy's school-term had finished, and then she packed their things and bought two tickets, third-class to Agra.

Something, I could see, had been troubling her, and when I saw her off at the station I realised what it was. She was having fit of conscience about my continued bachelorhood.

'In my village,' she said confidently, leaning out from the carriage window, 'there is a very comely young girl, a distant relative of mine, I shall speak to the parents.'

And then I said something which I had not considered before: which had never, until that moment, entered my head. And I was no less surprised than Leela when the words came tumbling out of my mouth: 'Why don't *you* marry me now?'

Arun didn't have time to finish his story because, just as this interesting stage, the dinner arrived.

But the dinner brought with it the end of his story.

It was served by his wife, a magnificent woman, strong and handsome, who could only have been Leela. And a few minutes later, Chandu, Arun's stepson, charged into the house, complaining that he was famished.

Arun introduced me to his wife, and we exchanged the usual formalities.

'But why hasn't your friend brought his family with him?'she asked.

'Family? Because he's still a bachelor!'

And then as he watched his wife's expression change from a look of mild indifference to one of deep concern, he hurriedly changed the subject.

The Night Train at Deoli

When I was at college I used to spend my summer vacations in Dehra, at my grandmother's place. I would leave the plains early in May and return late in July. Deoli was a small station about thirty miles from Dehra; it marked the beginning of the heavy jungles of the Indian Terai.

The train would reach Deoli at about five in the morning, when the station would be dimly lit with electric bulbs and oil-lamps, and the jungle across the railway tracks would just be visible in the faint light of dawn. Deoli had only lone platform, an office for the station-master and a waiting room. The platform boasted a tea stall, a fruit vendor, and a few stray dogs; not much else, because the train stopped there for only ten minutes before rushing on into the forests.

Why it stopped at Deoli. I don't know. Nothing ever happened there. Nobody got off the train and nobody got in. There were never any coolies on the platform. But the train would halt there a full ten minutes, and then a bell would sound, the guard would blow his whistle, and presently Deoli would be left behind and forgotten.

I used to wonder what happened in Deoli, behind the station walls. I always felt sorry for that lonely little platform, and for the place that nobody wanted to visit. I decided that one day I would get off the train at Deoli, and spend the day there, just to please the town.

I was eighteen, visiting my grandmother, and the night train stopped at Deoli. A girl came down the platform, selling baskets.

It was a cold morning and the girl had a shawl thrown across her shoulders. Her feet were bare and her clothes were old, but she was a young girl, walking gracefully and with dignity.

When she came to my window, she stopped. She saw that I was looking at her intently, but at first she pretended not to notice. She had a pale skin, set off by shiny black hair, and dark, troubled eyes. And then those eyes, searching and eloquent, met mine.

She stood by my window for some time and neither of us said anything. But when she moved on, I found myself leaving my seat and going to the carriage door, and stood waiting on the platform, looking the other way. I walked across to the tea stall. A kettle was boiling over on a small fire, but the owner of the stall was busy serving tea somewhere on the train. The girl followed me behind the stall.

'Do you want to buy a basket?' she asked. 'They are very strong, made of the finest cane . . .'

'No,' I said, 'I don't want a basket.'

We stood looking at each other for what seemed a very long time, and she said, 'Are you sure you don't want a basket?'

'All right, give me one,' I said, and I took the one on top and gave her a rupee, hardly daring to touch her fingers.

As she was about to speak, the guard blew his whistle; she said something, but it was lost in the clanging of the bell and the hissing of the engine. I had to run back to my compartment. The carriage shuddered and jolted forward.

I watched her as the platform slipped away. She was alone on the platform and she did not move, but she was looking at me and smiling. I watched her until the signal-box came in the way, and then the jungle hid the station, but I could still see her standing there alone . . .

I sat up awake for the rest of the journey. I could not rid my mind of the picture of the girl's face and her dark, smouldering eyes.

But when I reached Dehra the incident became blurred and distant, for there were other things to occupy my mind. It was only when I was making the return journey, two months later, that I remembered the girl.

I was looking out for her as the train drew into the station, and I felt an unexpected thrill when I saw her walking up the platform. I sprang off the foot-board and waved to her.

When she saw me, she smiled. She was pleased that I remembered her. I was pleased the she remembered me. We were both pleased, and it was almost like a meeting of old friends.

She did not go down the length of the train selling baskets, but came straight to the tea stall; her dark eyes were suddenly filled with light. We said nothing for some time but we couldn't have been more eloquent.

I felt the impulse to put her on the train there and then, and take her away with me; I could not bear the thought of having to watch her recede into the distance of Deoli station. I took the baskets from her hand and put them down on the ground. She put out her hand for one of them, but I caught her hand and held it.

'I have to go to Delhi,' I said.

She nodded. 'I do not have to go anywhere.'

The guard blew his whistle for the train to leave and how I hated the guard for doing that.

'I will come again, I said. 'Will you be here?'

She nodded again, and, as she nodded, the bell clanged and the train slid forward. I had to wrench my hand away from the girl and run for the moving train.

This time I did not forget her. She was with me for the remainder of the journey, and for long after. All that year she was a bright, living thing. And when the college term finished I packed in haste and left for Dehra earlier than usual. My grandmother would be pleased at my eagerness to see her.

I was nervous and anxious as the train drew into Deoli, because I was wondering what I should say to the girl and what I should do. I was determined that I wouldn't stand helplessly before her, hardly able to speak or do anything about my feelings.

The train came to Deoli, and I looked up and down the platform, but I could not see the girl anywhere.

I opened the door and stepped off the footboard. I was deeply disappointed, and overcome by a sense of foreboding. I felt I had to do something, and so I ran up to the station-master and said, 'Do you know the girl who used to sell baskets here?'

'No, I don't,' said the station-master. 'And you'd better get on the train if you don't want to be left behind.'

But I paced up and down the platform, and stared over the railings at the station yard; all I saw was a mango tree and a dusty road leading into the jungle. Where did the road go? The train was moving out of the station, and I had to run up the platform and jump for the door of my compartrment. Then, as the train gathered speed and rushed through the forests. I sat brooding in front of the window.

What could I do about finding a girl I had seen only twice, who had hardly spoken to me, and about whom I knew nothing — absolutely nothing — but for whom I felt a tenderness and responsibility that I had never felt before?

My grandmother was not pleased with my visit after all, because I didn't stay at her place more than a couple of weeks. I felt restless and ill-at-ease. So I took the train back to the plains, meaning to ask further questions of the station-master at Deoli.

But at Deoli there was a new station-master. The previous man had been transferred to another post within the past week. The new man didn't know anything about the girl who sold baskets. I found the owner of the tea stall, a small, shrivelled-up man, wearing greasy clothes, and asked him if he knew anything about the girl with the baskets.

'Yes, there was such a girl here, I remember quite well,' he said. 'But she has stopped coming now.'

'Why?' I asked. 'What happened to her?'

'How should I know?' said the man. 'She was nothing to me.'

And once again I had to run for the train.

As Deoli platform receded, I decided that one day I would have to break journey there, spend a day in the town, make enquiries, and find the girl who had stolen my heart with nothing but a look from her dark, impatient eyes.

With this thought I consoled myself throughout my last term in college. I went to Dehra again in the summer and when, in the early hours of the morning, the night train drew into Deoli station, I looked up and down the platform for signs of the girl, knowing, I wouldn't find her but hoping just the same.

Somehow, I couldn't bring myself to break journey at Deoli and spend a day there. (If it was all fiction or a film, I reflected, I would have got down and cleaned up the mystery and reached a suitable ending for the whole thing). I think I was afraid to do this. I was afraid of discovering what really happened to the girl. Perhaps she was no longer in Deoli, perhaps she was married, perhaps she had fallen ill . . .

In the last few years I have passed through Deoli many times, and I always look out of the carriage window, half expecting to see the same unchanged face smiling up at me. I wonder what happens in Deoli, behind the station walls. But I will never break my journey there. It may spoil my game. I prefer to keep hoping and dreaming, and looking out of the window up and down that lonely platform, waiting for the girl with the baskets.

I never break my journey at Deoli, but I pass through as often as I can.

Bus Stop, Pipalnagar

I

My balcony was my window on the world.

The room itself had only one window, a square hole in the wall crossed by two iron bars. The view from it was rather restricted. If I craned my neck sideways, and put my nose to the bars, I could see the end of the building. Below was a narrow courtyard where children played. Across the courtyard, on a level with my room, were three separate windows, belonging to three separate rooms, each window barred in the same way, with iron bars. During the day it was difficult to see into these rooms. The harsh, cruel sunlight filled the courtyard, making the windows patches of darkness.

My room was very small. I had paced about in it so often that I knew its exact measurements. My foot, from heel to toe, was eleven inches long. That made the room just over fifteen feet in length; for, when I measured the last foot, my toes turned up against the wall. It wasn't more than eight feet broad which meant that two people were the most it could comfortably accommodate. I was the only tenant but at times I had put up at least three friends — two on the floor, two on the bed. The plaster had been peeling off the walls and in addition the greasy stains and patches were difficult to hide, though I covered the worst ones with pictures cut out from magazines — Waheeda, the Indian actress, successfully blotted out one big patch and a recent Mr. Universe displayed his muscles from the opposite wall. The biggest stain was all but concealed by a calendar which showed Ganesh, the elephant-headed god, whose blessings were vital to all good beginnings.

My belongings were few. A shelf on the wall supported an untidy

57

pile of paperbacks, and a small table in one corner of the room supported the solid weight of my rejected manuscripts and an ancient typewriter which I had obtained on hire.

I was eighteen years old and a writer.

Such a combination would be disastrous enough anywhere but in India it was doubly so; for there were not many papers to write for and payments were small. In addition, I was very inexperienced and thought what I wrote came from the heart, only a fraction touched the hearts of editors. Nevertheless, I persevered and was able to earn about a hundred rupees a month, barely enough to keep body, soul and typewriter together. There wasn't much else I could do. Without that passport to a job — a University degree — I had no alternative but to accept the classification of 'self-employed' — which was impressive as it included doctors, lawyers, property dealers, and grain merchants, most of whom earned well over a thousand a month.

'Haven't you realized that India is bursting with young people trying to pass exams?' asked a journalist friend. 'It's a desperate matter, this race for academic qualifications. Everyone wants to pass his exam the easy way, without reading too many books or attending more than half-a-dozen lectures. That's where a smart fellow like you comes in! Why should students wade through five volumes of political history when they can buy a few model-answer papers at any bookstall? They are helpful, these guess-papers. You can write them quickly and flood the market. They'll sell like hot cakes!'

'Who eats hot cakes here?'

'Well, then, hot *chappaties.*'

'I'll think about it,' I said; but the idea repelled me. If I was going to misguide students, I would rather do it by writing second rate detective stories than by providing them with ready-made answer papers. Besides, I thought it would bore me.

II

The string of my cot needed tightening. The dip in the middle of the bed was so bad that I woke up in the mornings with a stiff back. But I was hopeless at tightening bed-strings and would have to wait until one of the boys from the tea shop paid me a visit. I was too long for the cot, anyway, and if my feet didn't stick out at one end, my head lolled over the other.

Under the cot was my tin trunk. Apart from my clothes, it contained notebooks, diaries, photographs, scrapbooks, and other odds and ends that form a part of a writer's existence.

I did not live entirely alone. During cold or rainy weather, the boys from the tea-shop, who normally slept on the pavement, crowded into the room. Apart from them, there were lizards on the walls and ceilings — friends these — and a large rat — definitely an enemy — who got in and out of the window and who sometimes carried away manuscripts and clothing.

June nights were the most uncomfortable. Mosquitoes emerged form all the ditches, gullies and ponds, to swarm over Pipalnagar. Bugs, finding it umcomfortable inside the wood work of the cot, scrambled out at night and found their way under the sheet. The lizards wandered listlessly over the walls, impatient for the monsoon rains, when they would be able to feast off thousands of insects.

Everyone in Pipalnagar was waiting for the cool, quenching relief of the monsoon.

III

I woke every morning at five as soon as the first bus moved out of the shed, situated only twenty or thirty yards down the road. I dressed, went down to the tea-shop for a glass of hot tea and some buttered toast, and then visited Deep Chand the barber, in his shop.

At 18, I shaved about three times a week. Sometimes I shaved myself. But often, when I felt lazy, Deep Chand shaved me, at the special concessional rate of two *annas*.

'Give my head a good massage, Deep Chand,' I said. 'My brain is not functioning these days. In my latest story there are three murders, but it is boring just the same.'

'You must write a good book,' and Deep Chand beginning the ritual of the head massage, his fingers squeezing my temples and tugging at my hair-roots. 'Then you can make some money and clear out of Pipalnagar. Delhi is the place to go! Why, I know a man who arrived in Delhi in 1947 with nothing but the clothes he wore and a few rupees. He began by selling thirsty travellers glasses of cold-water at the railway-station then he opened a small tea-shop; now he has two big restaurants and lives in a house as large as the Prime Minister's!'

Nobody intended living in Pipalnagar for ever. Delhi was the city most aspired to but as it was two-hundred miles away, few could afford to travel there.

Deep Chand would have shifted his trade to another town if he had had the capital. In Pipalnagar his main customers were small shopkeepers, factory workers and labourers from the railway station. 'Here I can charge only six *annas* for a hair cut,' he lamented. 'In Delhi I could charge a rupee.'

IV

I was walking in the wheat fields beyond the railway tracks when I noticed a boy lying across the footpath, his head and shoulders hidden by the wheat. I walked faster, and when I came near I saw that the boy's legs were twitching. He seemed to be having some kind of fit. The boy's face was white his legs kept moving and his hands fluttered restlessly amongst the wheat-stalks.

'What's the matter?' I said, kneeling down beside him; but he was still unconscious.

I ran down the path to a Persian well, and dipping the end of my shirt in a shallow trough of water, soaked it well before returning to the boy. As I sponged his face the twitching ceased, and though he still breathed heavily, his face was calm and his hands still. He opened his eyes and stared at me, but he didn't really see me.

'You have bitten your tongue,' I said wiping a little blood from the corner of his mouth. 'Don't worry. I'll stay here with you until you are all right.'

The boy raised himself and, resting his chin on his knees he passed his arms around his drawn-up legs.

'I'm all right now,' he said.

'What happened?' I asked sitting down beside him.

'Oh, it is nothing, it often happens. I don't know why. I cannot control it.'

'Have you been to a doctor?'

'Yes, when the fits first started, I went to the hospital. They gave me some pills which I had to take every day. But the pills made me so tired and sleepy that I couldn't work properly. So I stopped taking them. Now this happens once or twice a week. What does it matter? I'm all right when it's over and I do not feel anything when it happens.'

He got to his feet dusting his clothes and smiling at me. He was a slim boy, long-limbed and bony. There was a little fluff on his cheeks and the promise of a moustache. He told me his name was Suraj, that he went to a night school in the city, and that he hoped to finish his High School Exams in a few months time. He was studying hard, he said, and if he passed he hoped to get a scholarship to a good college. If he failed, there was only the prospect of continuing in Pipalnagar.

I noticed a small tray of merchandise lying on the ground. It contained combs and buttons and little bottles of perfume. The tray was made to hang at Suraj's waist, supported by straps that went around his shoulders. All day he walked about Pipalnagar some-times covering ten or fifteen miles a day, selling odds and ends to people at their houses. He averaged about two rupees a day, which was enough for his food and other necessities; he managed to save about ten rupees a month for his school fees. He ate irregularly at little tea-shops, at the stall near the bus stop, under the shady *jamun* and mango trees. When the *jamun* fruit was ripe, he would sit in a tree, sucking the sour fruit until his lips were stained purple. There was a small, nagging fear that he might get a fit while sitting on the tree and fall off; but the temptation to eat *jamuns* was greater than his fear.

All this he told me while we walked through the fields towards the bazaar.

'Where do you live?' I asked. 'I'll walk home with you.'

'I don't live anywhere,' said Suraj. 'My home is not in Pipalnagar. Sometimes I sleep at the temple or at the railway station. In the summer month I sleep in the grass of the Municipal park.'

'Well, wherever it is you stay, let me come with you.'

We walked together into the town, and parted near the bus stop I returned to my room, and tried to do some writing while Suraj went into the bazaar to try selling his wares. We had agreed to meet each other again. I realised that Suraj was an epileptic, but there was nothing unusual about his being an orphan and a refugee. I liked his positive attitude to life, most people in Pipalnagar were resigned to their circumstances, but he was ambitious. I also liked his gentleness, his quite voice, and the smile that flickered across his face regardless of whether he was sad or happy.

V

The temperature had touched 110 Fahrenheit, and the small streets of Pipalnagar were empty. To walk barefoot on the scorching pavements was possible only for the labourers whose feet had developed several hard layers of protective skin; and now even these hardy men lay stretched out in the shade provided by trees and buildings.

I hadn't written anything in two weeks, and though one or two small payments were due from a Delhi newspaper, I could think of no substantial amount that was likely to come my way in the near future. I decided that I would dash off a couple of articles that same night, and post them the following morning.

Having made this comforting decision, I lay down on the floor in preference to the cot. I liked the touch of things, the touch of a cool floor on a hot day; the touch of earth — soft, grassy, grass was good, especially dew-drenched grass. Wet earth, too was soft, sensuous and smelt nice; splashing through puddles and streams.

I slept, and dreamt of a cool clear stream in a forest glade, where I bathed in gay abandon. A little further downstream was another bather, I hailed him, expecting to see Suraj but when the bather turned I found that it was my landlord's pot-bellied rent-collector, holding an accounts ledger in his hands. This woke me up, and for the remainder of the day I worked feverishly at my articles.

Next morning, when I opened the door, I found Suraj asleep at the top of the steps. His tray lay at the bottom of the steps. He woke up as soon as I touched his shoulder.

'Have you been sleeping here all night?' I asked. 'Why didn't you come in?'

'It was very late' said Suraj. 'I didn't want to disturb you.'

'Someone could have stolen your things while you were asleep.'

"Oh, I sleep quite lightly. Besides I have nothing of great value. But I came here to ask you a favour.'

'You need money?'

He laughed. 'Do all your friends mean money when they ask for favours. No, I want you to take your meal with me tonight.'

'But where?' 'You have no place of your own and it would be too expensive in a restaurant.'

'In your room.' said Suraj 'I shall bring the meat and vegetable and cook them here. Do you have a cooker?'

'I think so,' I said scratching my head in some perplexity. 'I will have to look for it.'

Suraj brought a chicken for dinner — a luxury, one to be indulged in only two or three times a year. He had bought the bird for seven rupees, which was cheap. We spiced it and roasted it on a spittle.

'I wish we could do this more often,' I said as I dug my teeth into the soft flesh of a second leg.

'We could do it at least once a month if we worked hard,' said Suraj.

'You know how to work. You work from morning to evening and then you work again.'

'But you are a writer. That is different. You have to wait for the right moment.'

I laughed. 'Moods and moments are for geniuses. No it's really a matter of working hard, and I'm just plain lazy, to tell you the truth.'

'Perhaps you are writing the wrong things.'

'Perhaps, I wish I could do something else. Even if I repaired bicycle tyres, I'd make more money!'

'Then why don't you repair bicycle tyres?'

'Oh, I would rather be a bad writer than a good repairer of cycle-tyres,' I brightened up. 'I could go into business, though. Do you know I once owned a vegetable stall.'

'Wonderful! When was that?'

'A couple of months ago. But it failed after two days.'

'Then you are not good at business. Let us think of something else.'

'I can tell fortunes with cards.'

'There are already too many fortune-tellers in Pipalnagar.'

'Then we won't talk of fortunes. And you must sleep here tonight. It is better than sleeping on the roadside.'

VI

At noon, when the shadows shifted and crossed the road, a band of children rushed down the empty street, shouting and waving their satchels. They had been at their desks from early morning, and now, despite the hot sun, they would have their fling while their elders slept on string *charpoys* beneath leafy *neem* trees.

On the soft sand near the river-bed, boys wrestled or played leap-frog. At alley-corners, where tall building shaded narrow passages, the favourite game was *gulli-danda.* The *gulli* — a small piece of wood, about four inches long sharpened to a point at each end — is struck with the *danda* a short, stout stick. A player is allowed three hits, and his score is the distance, in *danda* lengths, he hits the *gulli.* Boys who were experts at the game sent the *gulli* flying far down the road — sometimes into a shop or through a window-pane, which resulted in confusion, loud invective, and a dash for cover.

A game for both children and young men was *Kabbadi.* This is a game that calls for good breath control and much agility. It is also known in different parts of India, as *hootoo-too, kho-kho* and *atyapa-tya.* Ramu, Deep Chand's younger brother, excelled at this game. He was the Pipalnagar *Kabbadi* champion.

The game is played by two teams, consisting of eight or nine members each, who face each other across a dividing line. Each side in turn sends out one of its players into the opponent's area. This person has to keep on saying *'Kabbadi, kabbadi'* very fast and without taking a second breath. If he ruturns to his side after touching an opponent, that opponent is 'dead' and out of the game. If however, he is caught and cannot struggle back to his side while still holding his breath, he is 'dead'.

Ramu who was also a good wrestler, knew all the *Kabbadi* holds, and was particularly good at capturing opponents. He had vitality and confidence, rare things in Pipalnagar. He wanted to go into the Army after finishing school, a happy choice I thought.

VII

Suraj did not know if his parents were dead or alive. He had literally lost them when he was six. His father had been a farmer, a dark unfathomable man who spoke little, thought perhaps even less and was vaguely aware he had a son — a weak boy given to introspection and dawdling at the river-bank when he should have been helping in the fields.

Suraj's mother had been a subdued, silent woman, frail, and consumptive. Her husband seemed to expect that she would not live long; but Suraj did not know if she was living or dead. He had lost his parents at Amritsar railway-station in the days of the partition, when trains coming across the border from Pakistan disgorged themselves of thousands of refugees or pulled into the station half-empty, drenched with blood and littered with corpses.

Suraj and his parents were lucky to escape one of these massacres. Had they travelled on an earlier train (which they had tried desperately to catch), they might have been killed. Suraj was clinging to his mother's *sari* while she tried to keep up with her husband who was elbowing his way through the frightened bewildered throng of refugees. Suraj collided with a burly Sikh and lost his grip on the *sari*. The Sikh had a long curved sword at his waist, and Suraj stared up at him in awe and fascination, at the man's long hair, which had fallen loose, at his wild black beard, and at the bloodstains on his white shirt. The Sikh pushed him aside and when Suraj looked round for his mother she was not to be seen. She was hidden from him by a mass of restless bodies,all pushing in different directions. He could hear her calling his name and he tried to force his way through the crowd, in the direction of her voice, but he was carried the other way.

At night, when the platform was empty he was still searching for his mother. Eventually the police came and took him away. They looked for his parents but without success, and finally they sent him to a home for orphans. Many children lost their parents at about the same time.

Suraj stayed at the orphanage for two years and when he was eight and felt himself a man, he ran away. He worked for some time as a helper in a tea-shop; but when he started having epileptic fits the shopkeepers asked him to leave, and the boy found himself on the streets, begging for a living. He begged for a year, moving from one town to the next and ending up finally at Pipalnagar. By then he was twelve and really too old to beg; but he had saved some money, and with it he bought a small stock of combs, buttons, cheap perfumes and bangles, and converting himself into a mobile shop, went from door to door selling his wares.

Pipalnagar is a small town, and there was no house which Suraj hadn't visited. Everyone knew him; some had offered him food and drink; and the children liked him because he often played on a small flute when he went on his rounds.

VIII

Suraj came to see me quite often and, when he stayed late he slept in my room, curling up on the floor and sleeping fitfully. He would

65

always leave early in the morning before I could get him anything to eat.

'Should I go to Delhi, Suraj?' I asked him one evening.

'Why not? In Delhi, there are many ways of making money.'

'And spending it too. Why don't you come with me?'

'After my exams, perhaps. Not now.'

'Well, I can wait. I don't want to live alone in a big city.'

'In the meantime, write your book.'

'All right, I will try.'

We decided we could try to save a little money from Suraj's earnings and my own occasional payments from newspapers and magazines. Even if we were to give Delhi only a few days trail, we would need money to live on. We managed to put away twenty rupees one week, but withdrew it the next when a friend, Pitamber, asked for a loan to repair his cycle-*rickshaw*. He returned the money in three instalments but we could not save any of it. Pitamber and Deep Chand also had plans for going to Delhi. Pitamber wanted to own his own scooter-*rickshaw*; Deep Chand dreamt of a swank barbershop in the capital.

One day Suraj and I hired bicycles and rode out of Pipalnagar. It was a hot, sunny morning, and we were perspiring after we had gone two miles; but a fresh wind sprang up suddenly, and we could smell the rain in the air though there were no clouds to be seen.

'Let us go where there are no people at all,' said Suraj. 'I am a little tired of people. I see too many of them all day.'

We got down from our cycles, and pushing them off the road, took a path through a paddy field and then a path through a field of young maize, and in the distance we saw a tree, a crooked tree, growing beside a well. I do not even today know the name of that tree. I had never seen its kind before. It had a crooked trunk, crooked branches, and it was clothed in thick, broad crooked leaves, like the leaves on which food is served in bazaars.

In the trunk of the tree was a large hole, and when I set my cycle down with a crash, two green parrots flew out of the hole, and went dipping and swerving across the fields.

There was grass around the well, cropped short by grazing cattle, so we sat in the shade of the crooked tree and Suraj untied the red cloth in which he had brought our food . We ate our bread and vegetable curry, and meanwhile the parrots returned to the tree.

'Let us come here every week,' said Suraj stretching himself out on the grass. It was a drowsy day, the air humid and he soon fell asleep. I was aware of different sensations. I heard a cricket singing in the tree; the cooing of pigeons which lived in the walls of the old well; the soft breathing of Suraj; a rustling in the leaves of the tree; the distant drone of the bees. I smelt the grass and the old bricks around the well, and the promise of rain.

When I opened my eyes, I saw dark clouds on the horizon. Suraj was still sleeping his arms thrown across his face to keep the glare out of his eyes. As I was thirsty, I went to the well, and putting my shoulders to it, turned the wheel very slowly, walking around the well four times, while cool clean water gushed out over the stones and along the channel to the fields. I drank from one of the trays, and the water tasted sweet: the deeper the wells the sweeter the water. Suraj was sitting up now, looking at the sky.

'It's going to rain,' he said.

We pushed our cycles back to the main road and began riding homewards. We were a mile out of Pipalnagar when it began to rain. A lashing wind swept the rain across our faces, but we exulted in it and sang at the top of our voices until we reached the bus stop. Leaving the cycles at the hire-shop, we ran up the ricketty, swaying steps to my room.

In the evening, as the bazaar was lighting up, the rain stopped. We went to sleep quite early; but at midnight I was woken by the moon shinning full in my face — a full moon, shedding its light all over Pipalnagar, peeping and prying into every home, washing the empty streets, silvering the corrugated tin roofs.

IX

The lizards hung listlessly on the walls and ceilings, waiting for the monsoon rains, which bring out all the insects from their cracks and crannies.

One day clouds loomed up on the horizon, growing rapidly into enormous towers. A faint breeze sprang up, bringing with it the first of the monsoon rain-drops. This was the moment everyone was waiting for. People ran out of their houses to take in the fresh breeze and the scent of those first few raindrops on the parched, dusty earth. Underground, in their cracks, the insects were moving. Termites and white ants, which had been sleeping through the hot season, emerged from their lairs.

And then, on the second or third night of the monsoon, came the great yearly flight of insects into the cool brief freedom of the night. Out of every crack, from under the roots of trees, huge winged ants emerged, at first fluttering about heavily, on this the first and last flight of their lives. At night there was only one direction in which they could fly — towards the light; towards the electric bulbs and smoky kerosene lamps throughout Pipalnagar. The street lamp opposite the bus stop, beneath my room, attracted a massive quivering swarm of clumsy termites, which gave the impression of one thick slowly revolving body.

This was the hour of the lizards. Now they had their reward for those days of patient waiting. Plying their sticky pink tongues, they devoured the insects as fast as they came. For hours they crammed their stomachs, knowing that such a feast would not be theirs again for another year. How wasteful nature is, I thought. Through the whole hot season the insect world prepares for this flight out of darkness into light, and not one of them survives its freedom.

Suraj and I walked barefooted over the cool wet pavements, across the railway lines and the river bed, until we were not far from the crooked tree. Dotting the landscape were old abandoned brick kilns. When it rained heavily, the hollows made by the kilns filled up with water. Suraj and I found a small tank where we could bathe and swim. On a mound in the middle of the tank stood a ruined hut, formerly inhabited by a watchman at the kiln. We swam and then wrestled on the young green grass. Though I was heavier than Suraj and my chest as sound as a new drum, he had a lot of power in his long wiry arms and legs, and he pinioned me about the waist with his bony knees. And then suddenly, as I strained to press his back to the ground, I felt his body go tense. He stiffened, his thigh jerked against me and his legs began to twitch. I knew that a fit was coming on, but I was unable to get out of his grip. He held me more tightly as the fit took possession of him.

When I noticed his mouth working, I thrust the palm of my hand in, sideways to prevent him from biting his tongue. But so violent was the convulsion that his teeth bit into my flesh. I shouted with pain and tried to pull my hand away, but he was unconscious and his jaw was set. I closed my eyes and counted slowly up to seven and then I felt his muscles relax, and I was able to take my hand away. It was bleeding a little but I bound it in a handkerchief before Suraj fully regained consciousness.

He didn't say much as we walked back to town. He looked depressed and weak, but I knew it wouldn't take long for him to recover his usual good spirits. He did not notice that I kept my hand out of sight and only after he had returned from classes that night did he notice the bandage and asked what happened.

X

Do you want to make some money?' asked Pitamber, bursting into the room like a festive cracker.

'I do,' I said.

'What do we have to do for it?' asked Suraj, striking a cautious note.

'Oh nothing — carry a banner and walk in front of a procession.'

'Why?'

'Don't ask me. Some political stunt.'

'Which party?'

'I don't know. Who cares? All I know is that they are paying two rupees a day to anyone who'll carry a flag or banner.'

'We don't need two rupees that badly,' I said. 'And you can make more than that in a day with your *rickshaw*.'

'True, but they're paying me *five*. They're fixing a loudspeaker to my *rickshaw*, and one of the party's men will sit in it and make speeches as we go along. Come on — it will be fun.'

'No banners for us,' I said. 'But we may come along and watch.'

And we did watch, when, later that morning, the procession passed along our street. It was a ragged procession of about a hundred people, shouting slogans. Some of them were children, and some of them were men who did not know what it was all about, but all joined in the slogan-shouting.

We didn't know much about it, either. Because though the man in Pitamber's *rickshaw* was loud and eloquent, his loudspeaker was defective, with the result that his words were punctuated with squeaks and an eerie whining sound. Pitamber looked up and saw us standing on the balcony and gave us a wave and a wide grin. We decided to follow the procession at a discreet distance. It was a protest march against something or other; we never did manage to find out the details. The destination was the Municipal office, and by the time we got there the crowd had increased to two or three hundred persons. Some rowdies had now joined in, and things bègan to get out of hand. The man in the *rickshaw* continued his speech; another man standing on a wall was making a speech; and someone from the Municipal office was confronting the crowd and making a speech of his own.

A stone was thrown, then another. From a sprinkling of stones it soon become a shower of stones; and then some police constables, who had been standing by watching the fun, were ordered into action. They ran at the crowd where it was thinnest, brandishing stout sticks.

We were caught up in the stampede that followed. A stone — flung no doubt at a policeman — was badly aimed and struck me on the shoulder. Suraj pulled me down a side-street. Looking back, we saw Pitamber's cycle-*rickshaw* lying on its side in the middle of the road; but there was no sign of Pitamber.

Later, he turned up in my room, with a cut over his left eyebrow which was bleeding freely. Suraj washed the cut, and I poured iodine over it — Pitamber did not flinch — and covered it with sticking-plaster. The cut was quite deep and should have had stitches; but Pitamber was superstitious about hospitals, saying he knew very few people to come out of them alive. He was of course thinking of the Pipalnagar hospital.

So he acquired a scar on his forehead. It went rather well with his demonic good looks.

XI

'Thank god for the monsoon,' said Suraj. 'We won't have any more demonstrations on the roads until the weather improves!'

And, until the rain stopped, Pipalnagar was fresh and clean and alive. The children ran naked out of their houses and romped through the streets. The gutters overflowed, and the road became a mountain stream, coursing merrily towards the bus stop.

At the bus stop there was confusion. Newly arrived passengers, surrounded on all sides by a sea of mud and rain water, were met by scores of *tongas* and cycle-*rickshaws*, each jostling the other trying to cater to the passengers. As a result, only half found conveyances, while the other half found themselves knee-deep in Pipalnagar mud.

Pipalnagar mud has a quality all its own; and it is not easily removed or forgotten. Only buffaloes love it because it it soft and squelchy. Two parts of it is thick sticky clay which seems to come alive at the slightest touch, clinging tenaciously to human flesh. Feet sink into it and have to be wrenched out. Fingers become webbed. Get it into your hair, and there is nothing you can do except go to Deep Chand and have your head shaved.

London has its fog, Paris its sewers, Pipalnagar its mud. Pitamber, of course succeeded in getting as his passenger the most attractive girl to step off the bus, and showed her his skill and daring by taking her to her destination by the longest and roughest road.

The rain swirled over the trees and roofs of the town, and the parched earth soaked it up, giving out a fresh smell that came only once a year, the fragrance of quenched earth, that loveliest of all smells.

In my room I was battling against the elements, for the door would not close, and the rain swept into the room and soaked my cot. When finally I succeeded in closing the door, I discovered that the roof was leaking, and the water was trickling down the walls, running through the dusty designs I had made with my feet. I placed tins and mugs in strategic positions and, satisfied that every-thing was now under control, sat on the cot to watch the roof-tops through the windows.

There was a loud banging on the door. It flew open, and there was Suraj, standing on the threshold, drenched. Coming in, he began to dry himself while I made desperate efforts to close the door again.

'Let's make some tea,' he said.

Glasses of hot sweet milky tea on a rainy day . . . It was enough to make me feel fresh and full of optimism. We sat on the cot, enjoying the brew.

'One day I'll write a book,' I said. 'Not just a thriller, but a real book, about real people. Perhaps about you and me and Pipalnagar. And then we'll be famous and our troubles will be over and new troubles will begin. I don't mind problems as long as they are new. While you're studying, I'll write my book. I'll start tonight. It is an auspicious time, the first night of the monsoon.'

A tree must have fallen across the wires somewhere, because the lights would not come on. So I lit a small oil-lamp, and while it spluttered in the steamy darkness, Suraj opened his books and, with one hand on the book, the other playing with his toes — this helped him to concentrate!— he began to study. I took the ink down from the shelf, and, finding it empty, added a little rain-water to it from one of the mugs. I sat down beside Suraj and began to write; but the pen was no good and made blotches all over the paper. And, although I was full of writing just then, I didn't really know what I wanted to say.

So I went out and began pacing up and down the road. There I found Pitamber, a little drunk very merry, and prancing about in the middle of the road.

'What are you dancing for?' I asked.

'I'm happy, so I'm dancing,' said Pitamber.

'And why are you happy?' I asked.

'Because I'm dancing,' he said .

The rain stopped and the *neem* trees gave out a strong sweet smell.

XII

Flowers in Pipalnagar — did they exist? As a child I knew a garden in Lucknow where there were beds of phlox and petunias; and another garden where only roses grew. In the fields around Pipalnagar thorn-apple — a yellow buttercup nestling among thorn leaves. But in the Pipalnagar bazaar, there were no flowers except one — a marigold growing out of a crack on my balcony. I had removed the plaster from the base of the plant, and filled in a little earth which I watered every morning. The plant was healthy, and sometimes it produced a little orange marigold.

Sometimes Suraj plucked a flower and kept it in his tray, among the combs, buttons, and scent-bottles. Sometimes he gave the flower to a passing child, once to a small boy who immediately tore it to shreds. Suraj was back on his rounds, as his exams were over.

Whenever he was tired of going from house to house, Suraj would sit beneath a shady banyan or *peepul* tree, put his tray aside, and take out his flute. The haunting notes travelled down the road in the afternoon stillness, drawing children to him. They would sit besides him and be very quiet when he played, because there was some-thing melancholic and appealing about the tunes.Suraj sometimes made flutes out of pieces of bamboo; but he never sold them. He would give them to the children he liked. He would sell almost anything, but not flutes.

Suraj sometimes played the flute at night, when he lay awake, unable to sleep; but even though I slept, I could hear the music in my dreams. Sometimes he took his flute with him to the crooked tree, and played for the benefit of the birds. The parrots made harsh noise in response and flew away. Once, when Suraj was playing his flute to a small group of children, he had a fit. The flute fell from his hands. And he began to roll about in the dust on the roadside. The children became frightened and ran away, but they did not stay away for long. The next time they heard the flute, they came to listen as usual.

XIII

It was Lord Krishna's birthday, and the rain came down as heavily as it is said to have done on the day Krishna was born. Krishna is the best beloved of all the Gods. Young mothers laugh or weep as they read or hear the pranks of his boyhood; young men pray to be as tall and as strong as Krishna was when he killed King Kamsa's elephant and Kamsa's wrestlers; young girls dream of a lover as daring as Krishna to carry them off in a war-chariot; grown-up men envy the wisdom and statesmanship with which he managed the affairs of his kingdom.

The rain came so unexpectedly that it took everyone by surprise. In seconds, people were drenched, and within minutes, the street was flooded. The temple tank overflowed, the railways lines disappeared, and the old wall near the bus stop shivered and silently fell, the sound of its collapse drowned in the downpour. A naked young man with a dancing bear cavorted in the middle of the vegetable market. Pitamber's *rickshaw* churned through the flood-water while he sang lustily as he worked.

Wading knee-deep down the road, I saw the roadside vendors salvaging whatever they could. Plastic toys, cabbages and utensils floated away and were seized by urchins. The water had risen to the level of the shop-fronts and floors were awash. Deep Chand and Ramu, with the help of a customer, were using buckets to bail the water out of their shop. The rain stopped as suddenly as it had begun and the sun came out. The water began to find an outlet, flooding other low-lying areas, and a paper-boat came sailing between my legs.

Next morning, the morning on which the result of Suraj's examinatons were due, I rose early — the first time I ever got up before

Suraj — and went down to the news agency. A small crowd of students had gathered at the bus stop, joking with each other and hiding their nervousness with a show of indifference. There were not many passengers on the first bus, and there was a mad grab for newspapers as the bundle landed with a thud on the pavement. Within half-an-hour, the newsboy had sold all his copies. It was the best day of the year for him.

I went through the columns relating to Pipalnagar, but I couldn't find Suraj's roll number on the list of successful candidates. I had the number on a slip of paper, and I looked at it again to make sure I had compared it correctly with the others; then I went through the newspaper once more. When I returned to the room, Suraj was sitting on the doorstep. I didn't have to tell him he had failed — he knew by the look on my face. I sat down beside him, and we said nothing for sometime.

'Never mind,' Suraj said eventually. 'I will pass next year.'

I realized I was more depressed than he was and that he was trying to console me.

'If only you'd had more time,' I said.

'I have plenty of time now. Another year. And you will have time to finish your book, and then we can go away together. Another year of Pipalnagar won't be so bad. As long as I have your friendship, almost everything can be tolerated.' He stood up, the tray hanging from his shoulders. 'What would you like to buy?'

XIV

Another year of Pipalnagar! But it was not to be. A short time later, I received a letter from the editor of a newspaper, calling me to Delhi for an interview. My friends insisted that I should go. Such an opportunity would not come again.

But I needed a shirt. The few I possessed were either frayed at the collars or torn at the shoulders. I hadn't been able to afford a new shirt for over a year, and I couldn't afford one now. Struggling writers weren't expected to dress very well, but I felt in order to get the job, I would need both a haircut and a clean shirt.

Where was I go to get a shirt? Suraj generally wore an old red-striped T-shirt; he washed it every second evening, and by morning it was dry and ready to wear again; but it was tight even on him. He did not have another. Besides, I needed something white, something respectable!

I went to Deep Chand who had a collection of shirts. He was only too glad to lend me one. But they were all brightly coloured — pinks, purples and magentas . . . No editor was going to be impressed by a young writer in a pink shirt. They looked fine on Deep Chand, but he had no need to look respectable.

Finally Pitamber came to my rescue. He didn't bother with shirts himself, except in winter, but he was able to borrow a clean white shirt from a guard at the jail, who'd got it from the relative of a convict in exchange for certain favours.

'This shirt will make you look respectable,' said Pitamber. 'To be respectable — what an adventure!'

XV

Freedom. The moment the bus was out of Pipalnagar, and the fields opened out on all sides, I knew that I was free, that I always had been free. Only my own weakness, hesitation, and the habits that had grown around me had held me back. All I had to do was to sit in a bus and go somewhere.

I sat near the open window of the bus and let the cool breeze from the fields play against my face. Herons and snipe waded among the lotus roots in flat green ponds. Bluejays swooped around telegraph poles. Children jumped naked into the canals that wound through the fields. Because I was happy, it seemed to me that everyone else was happy — the driver, the conductor, the passengers, the farmers in the fields and those driving bullock-carts. When two women behind me started quarrelling over their seats, I helped to placate them. Then I took a small girl on my knee and pointed out camels, buffaloes, vultures, and parriah-dog.

Six hours later the bus crossed the bridge over the swollen Jamuna river, passed under the walls of the great Red Fort built by a Moghul Emperor, and entered the old city of Delhi. I found it strange to be in a city again, after several years in Pipalnagar. It was a little frightening, too. I felt like a stranger. No one was interested in me.

In Pipalnagar, people wanted to know each other, or at least to know about one another. In Delhi, no one cared who you were or where you came from. Like big cities almost everywhere, it was prosperous but without a heart.

After a day and a night of loneliness, I found myself wishing that Suraj had accompanied me; wishing that I was back in Pipalnagar. But when the job was offered to me — at a starting salary of three hundred rupees per month, a princely sum, compared to what I had been making on my own — I did not have the courage to refuse it. After accepting the job — which was to commence in a week's time — I spent the day wandering through the bazaars, down the wide shady roads of the capital, resting under the *jamun* trees, and thinking all the time of what I would do in the months to come.

I slept at the railway waiting-room and all night long I heard the shunting and whistling of engines which conjured up visions of places with sweet names like Kumbakonam, Krishnagiri, Polonnarurawa. I dreamt of palm-fringed beaches and inland lagoons, of the echoing chambers of deserted cities, red sandstone and white marble; of temples in the sun, and elephants crossing wide slow-moving rivers . . .

XVI

Pitamber was on the platform when the train steamed into the Pipalnagar station in the early hours of a damp September morning. I waved to him from the carriage window, and shouted that everything had gone well.

But everything was not well here. When I got off the train, Pitamber told me that Suraj had been ill — that he'd a fit on a lonely stretch of road the previous afternoon and had lain in the sun for over-an-hour. Pitamber had found him, suffering from heat-stroke, and brought him home. When I saw him, he was sitting up on the string-bed drinking hot tea. He looked pale and weak, but his smile was reassuring.

'Don't worry,' he said. 'I will be all right.'

'He was bad last night, 'said Pitamber. 'He had a fever and kept talking, as in a dream. But what he says is true — he is better this morning.'

'Thanks to Pitamber,' said Suraj. 'It is good to have friends.'

'Come with me to Delhi, Suraj ,' I said. 'I have got a job now. You can live with me and attend a school regularly.'

'It is good for friends to help each other,' said Suraj, 'but only after I have passed my exam will I join you in Delhi. I made myself this promise. Poor Pipalnagar — nobody wants to stay here. Will you be sorry to leave?'

'Yes, I will be sorry. A part of me will still be here.'

XVII

Deep Chand was happy to know that I was leaving. 'I'll follow you soon,' he said. 'There is money to be made in Delhi, cutting hair. Girls are keeping it short these days.'

'But men are growing it long.'

'True. So I shall open a Barber Shop for Ladies and a Beauty Salon for Men! Ramu can attend to the ladies.'

Ramu winked at me in the mirror. He was still at the stage of teasing girls on their way to school or college.

The snip of Deep Chand's scissors made me sleepy, as I sat in his chair. His fingers beat a rhythmic tatto on my scalp. It was my last hair-cut in Pipalnagar, and Deep Chand did not charge me for it. I promised to write as soon as I had settled down in Delhi.

The next day when Suraj was stronger, I said, 'Come, let us go for a walk and visit our crooked tree. Where is your flute, Suraj?'

'I don't know. Let us look for it.'

We searched the room and our belongings for the flute but could not find it.

'It must have been left on the roadside,' said Suraj. 'Never mind, I will make another.'

I could picture the flute lying in the dust on the roadside and somehow this made me feel sad. But Suraj was full of high spirits as we walked across the railway-lines and through the fields.

'The rains are over,' he said, kicking off his *chappals* and lying down on the grass. 'You can smell the autumn in the air. Somehow, it makes me feel light-hearted. Yesterday I was sad, and tomorrow I might be sad again, but today I know that I am happy. I want to live on and on. One lifetime cannot satisfy my heart.'

'A day in a lifetime,' I said 'I'll remember this day — the way the sun touches us, the way the grass bends, the smell of this leaf as I crush it . . .'

XVIII

At six every morning the first bus arrives, and the passengers alight, looking sleepy and dishevelled, and rather discouraged by their first sight of Pipalnagar. When they have gone their various ways, the bus is driven into the shed. Cows congregate at the dustbin, and the pavement dwellers come to life, stretching their tired limbs on the hard stone steps. I carry the bucket up the steps to my room, and bathe for the last time on the open balcony. In the villages, the buffaloes are wallowing in green ponds, while naked urchins sit astride them, scrubbing their backs, and a crow or water-bird perches on their glistening necks. The parrots are busy in the crooked tree, and a slim green snake basks in the sun on our island near the brick-kiln. In the hills, the mists have lifted and the distant mountains are fringed with snow.

It is autumn, and the rains are over. The earth meets the sky in one broad, bold sweep.

A land of thrusting hills. Terraced hills, wood-covered and wind-swept. Mountains where the Gods speak gently to the lonely. Hills of green grass and grey rock, misty at dawn, hazy at noon, molten at sunset, where fierce fresh torrents rush to the valleys below. A quiet land of fields and ponds, shaded by ancient trees and ringed with palms, where sacred rivers are touched by temples, where temples are touched by southern seas.

This is the land I should write about. Pipalnagar should be forgotten: I should turn aside from it to sing instead of the splendours of exotic places.

But only yesterdays are truly splendid . . . And there are other singers, sweeter than I, to sing of tomorrow. I can only write of today, of Pipalnagar, where I have lived and loved.

The Garlands on His Brow

Fame has but a fleeting hold
on the reins in our fast-paced society ;
so many of yesterday's
heroes crumble.

Shortly after my return from England, I was walking down the main
road of my old home town of Dehra, gazing at the shops and
passers-by to see what changes, if any, had taken place during my
absence. I had been away three years. Still a boy when I went
abroad, I was twenty-one when I returned with some mediocre
qualifications to flaunt in the faces of my envious friends.(I did not
tell them of the loneliness of those years in exile; it would not have
impressed them). I was nearing the clock tower when I met a
beggar coming from the opposite directon. In one respect, Dehra
had not changed. The beggars were as numerouś as ever, though I
must admit they looked healthier.

This beggar had a straggling beard, a hunch, a cavernous chest,
and unsteady legs on which a number of purple sores were fester-
ing. His shoulders looked as though they had once been powerful,
and his hands thrusting a begging-bowl at me,were still strong.

He did not seem sufficiently decrepit to deserve of my charity,
and I was turning away when I thought I discerned a gleam of
recognition in his eyes. There was something slightly familiar about
the man; perhaps he was a beggar who remembered me from earlier years. He was even attempting a smile; showing me a few
broken yellow fangs; and to get away from him, I produced a coin,

dropped it in his bowl, and hurried away.

I had gone about a hundred yards when, with a rush of memory, I knew the identity of the beggar. He was the hero of my childhood, Hassan, the most magnificent wrestler in the entire district.

I turned and retraced my steps, half hoping I wouldn't be able to catch up with the man; and he had indeed been lost in the bazaar crowd. Well, I would doubtless be confronted by him again in a day or two . . . Leaving the road, I went into the Municipal gardens and stretching myself out on the fresh green February grass, allowed my memory to journey back to the days when I was a boy of ten, full of health and optimism, when my wonder at the great game of living had yet to give way to disillusionment at its shabbiness.

On those precious days when I played truant from school — and I would have learnt more had I played truant more often— I would sometimes make my way to the *akhara* at the corner of the gardens to watch the wrestling-pit. My chin cupped in my hands, I would lean against a railing and gaze in awe at their rippling muscles, applauding with the other watchers whenever one of the wrestlers made a particularly clever move or pinned an opponent down on his back.

Amongst these wrestlers the most impressive and engaging young man was Hassan, the son of a kite-maker. He had a magnificent build, with great wide shoulders and powerful legs, and what he lacked in skill he made up for in sheer animal strength and vigour. The idol of all small boys, he was followed about by large numbers of us, and I was a particular favourite of his. He would offer to lift me on to his shoulders and carry me across the *akhara* to introduce me to his friends and fellow-wrestlers.

From being Dehra's champion, Hassan soon became the outstanding representative of his art in the entire district, His technique improved, he began using his brain in addition to his brawn, and it was said by everyone that he had the making of a national champion.

It was during a large fair towards the end of the rains that destiny took a hand in the shaping of his life. The Rani of — was visiting the fair, and she stopped to watch the wrestling bouts. When she saw Hassan stripped and in the ring, she began to take more more than a casual interest in him. It has been said that she was a woman of a passionate and amoral nature, who could not be satisfied by her weak and ailing husband. She was struck by Hassan's perfect manhood, and through an official offered him the post of her personal bodyguard.

The Rani was rich and, in spite of having passed her fortieth summer,was a warm and attractive woman. Hassan did not find it difficult to make love according tothe bidding, and on the whole he was happy in her service. True, he did not wrestle as often as in the past; but when he did enter a competition, his reputation and his physique combined to overawe his opponents, and they did not put up much resistance. One or two well-known wrestlers were invited to the district. The Rani paid them liberally, and they permitted Hassan to throw them out of the ring. Life in the Rani's house was comfortable and easy, and Hassan, a simple man, felt himself secure. And it is to the credit of the Rani (and also of Hassan) that she did not tire of him as quickly as she had of others.

But Ranis, like washerwomen, are mortal; and when a long-standing and neglected disease at last took its toll, robbing her at once of all her beauty, she no longer struggled against it, but allowed it to poison and consume her once magnificent body.

It would be wrong to say that Hassan was heart-broken when she died. He was not a deeply emotional or sensitive person. Though he could attract the sympathy of others, he had difficulty in producing any of his own. His was a kindly but not compassionate nature.

He had served the Rani well, and what he was most aware of now was that he was without a job and without any money. The Raja had his own personal amusements and did not want a wrestler who was beginning to sag a little about the waist.

Times had changed. Hassan's father was dead, and there was no longer a living to be had from making kites; so Hassan returned to doing what he had always done: wrestling. But there was no money to be made at the *akhara*. It was only in the professional arena that a decent living could be made. And so, when a travelling circus of professionals — a Negro, a Russian, a Cockney-Chinese and a giant Sikh — came to town and offered a hundred rupees and a contract to the challenger who could stay five minutes in the ring with any one of them, Hassan took up the challenge.

He was pitted against the Russian, a bear of a man, who wore a black mask across his eyes; and in two minutes Hassan's Dehra supporters saw their hero slung about the ring, licked in the head and groin, and finally flung unceremoniously through the ropes.

After this humiliation, Hassan did not venture into competitive bouts again. I saw him sometimes at the *akhara*, where he made a few rupees giving lessons to children. He had a paunch, and folds were beginning to accumulate beneath his chin.I was no longer a small boy, but he always had a smile and a hearty back-slap reserved for me.

I remember seeing him a few days before I went abroad. He was moving heavily about the *akhara*; he had lost the lightning swiftness that had once made him invincible. Yes, I told myself.

The garlands wither on your brow;
Then boast no more your mighty deeds . . .

That had been over three years ago. And for Hassan to have been reduced to begging was indeed a sad reflection of both the passing of time and the changing times. Fifty years ago a popular local wrestler would never have been allowed to fall into a state of poverty and neglect.He would have been fed by his old friends and stories would have been told of his legendary prowess. He would not have been forgotten. But those were more leisurely times, when the individual had his place in society,when a man was praised for his past achievements and his failures were tolerated and forgiven. But life had since become fast and cruel and unreflective, and people were too busy counting their gains to bother about the idols of their youth.

It was a few days after my last encounter with Hassan that I found a small crowd gathered at the side of the road, not far from the clock tower. They were staring impassively at something in the drain, at the same time keeping at a discreet distance. Joining the group, I saw that the object of their disinterested curiosity was a corpse, its head hidden under a culvert, legs protruding into the open drain. It looked as though the man had crawled into the drain to die, and had done so with his head in the culvert so the world would not witness his last unavailing struggle.

When the municipal workers came in their van, and lifted the body out of the gutter, a cloud of flies and bluebottles rose from the corpse with an angry buzz of protest. The face was muddy, but I recognized the beggar who was Hassan.

In a way, it was a consolation to know that he had been forgotten, that no one present could recognize the remains of the man who had once looked like a young God. I did not come forward to identify the body. Perhaps I saved Hassan from one final humiliation.

A Guardian Angel

I can still picture the little Dilaram bazaar as I first saw it 20 years ago. Hanging on the hem of Aunt Mariam's *sari*, I had followed her along the sunlit length of the dusty road and up the wooden staircase to her rooms above the barber's shop.

There were number of children playing in the road, and they all stared at me. They must have wondered what my dark, black haired aunt was doing with a strange child who was fairer than most. She did not bother to explain my presence, and it was several weeks before the bazaar people learned something of my origins.

Aunt Mariam, my mother's younger sister, was at that time about 30. She came from a family of Christian converts, originally Muslims of Rampur. My mother had married an Englishman, who died while I was still a baby, she herself was not a strong woman, and fought a losing battle with tuberculosis while bringing me up.

My sixth birthday was approaching when she died, in the middle of the night, without my being aware of it, and I woke up to experience, for a day, all the terrors of abandonment.

But that same evening Aunt Mariam arrived. Her warmth, worldliness and carefree chatter gave me the reassurance I needed so badly. She slept beside me that night and next morning, after the funeral, took me with her to her rooms in the bazaar. This small flat was to be my home for the next year-and-a-half.

Before my mother's death I had seen very little of my aunt. From the remarks I occasionally overheard, it appeared that Aunt Mariam had, in some indefinable way, disgraced the family. My mother was cold towards her, and I could not help wondering why because a more friendly and cheerful extrovert than Aunt Mariam could hardly be encountered.

There were other relatives, but they did not come to my rescue with the same readiness. It was only later, when the financial issues became clearer, that innumerable uncle and aunts appeared on the scene.

The age of six is the beginning of an interesting period in the life of a day, and the months I spent with Aunt Mariam are not difficult to recall. She was a joyous, bubbling creature — a force of nature rather than a woman — and every time I think of her I am tempted to put down on paper some aspect of her conversation, or her gestures, or her magnificent physique.

She was a strong woman, taller than most men in the bazaar, but this did not detract from her charms. Her voice was warm and deep, her face was a happy one, broad and unlined, and her teeth gleamed white in the dark brilliance of her complexion.

She had large soft breasts, long arms and broad thighs. She was majestic, and at the same time she was graceful. Above all, she was warm and full of understanding, and it was this tenderness of hers that overcame resentment and jealousy in other women.

She called me *Ladla*, her darling, and told me she had always wanted to look after me. She had never married. I did not, at that age, ponder the reasons for her single state. At six, I took all things for granted and accepted Mariam for what she was — my benefactress and gaurdian angel.

Her rooms were untidy compared with the neatness of my mother's house. Mariam reveled in untidiness. I soon grew accustomed to the topsy-turviness of her rooms and found them comfortable. Beds (hers a very large and soft one) were usually left unmade, while clothes lay draped over chairs and tables.

A large watercolour hung on a wall, but Mariam's bodice and knickers were usually suspended from it, and I cannot recall the subject of the painting. The dressing table was a fascinating place, crowded with all kinds of lotions, mascaras, paints, oil and ointments.

Mariam would spend much time sitting in front of the mirror running a comb through her long black hair, or preferably having young Mulia, a servant girl, comb it for her. Though a Christian, my aunt retained several Muslim superstitions, and never went into the open with her hair falling loose.

Once Mulia came into the rooms with her own hair open. 'You ought not to leave your hair open. Better knot it,' said Aunt Mariam.

'But I have not yet oiled it, Aunty,' replied Mulia. 'How can I put it up?'

'You are too young to understand. There are *jinns* — aerial spirits — who are easily attracted by long hair and pretty black eyes like yours.'

'Do *jinns* visit human beings, Aunty?'

'Learned people say so. Though I have never seen a *jinn* myself, I have seen the effect they can have on one.'

'Oh, do tell about them,' said Mulia.

'Well, there was once a lovely girl like you, who had a wealth of black hair,' said Mariam. 'Quite unaccountably she fell ill, and in spite of every attention and the best medicines, she kept getting worse. She grew as thin as a whipping post, her beauty decayed, and all that remained of it till her dying day was her wonderful head of hair.'

It did not take me long to make friends in the Dilaram bazaar. At first I was an object of curiosity, and when I came down to play in the street both women and children would examine me as though, I was a strange marine creature.

'How fair he is,' observed Mulia.

'And how black his aunt,' commented the washerman's wife, whose face was fiddled with the marks of smallpox.

'His skin is very smooth,' pointed out Mulia, who took considerable pride in having been the first to see me at close quarters. She pinched my cheeks with obvious pleasure.

'His hair and eyes are black,' remarked Mulia's aging mother.

'Is it true that his father was an Englishman?'

'Mariam-*bi* says so,' said Mulia. 'She never lies.'

'True,' said the washerman's wife, 'Whatever her faults — and they are many — she has never been known to lie.'

My aunt's other 'faults' were a deep mystery to me; nor did anyone try to enlighten me about them.

Some nights she had me sleep with her, other nights (I often wondered why) she gave me a bed in an adjoining room, although I much preferred remaining with her — especially since, on cold January nights, she provided me with considerable warmth.

I would curl up into a ball just below her soft tummy. On the other side, behind her knees, slept Leila, an enchanting Siamese cat given to her by an American businessman whose house she would sometimes visit. Every night, before I fell asleep, Mariam would kiss me, very softly, on my closed eyelids. I never fell asleep until I had received this phantom kiss.

At first I resented the nocturnal visitors that Aunt Mariam frequently received; their arrival meant that I had to sleep in the spare room with Leila. But when I found that these people were impermanent creatures, mere ships that passed in the night, I learned to put up with them.

I seldom saw those men, though occasionally I caught a glimpse of a beard or an expensive waistcoat or white pyjamas. They did not interest me very much, though I did have a vague idea that they provided Aunt Mariam with some sort of income, thus enabling her to look after me.

Once, when one particular visitor was very drunk, Mariam had to force him out of the flat. I glimpsed this episode through a crack in the door. The man was big, but no match for Aunt Mariam.

She thrust him out onto the landing, and then he lost his footing and went tumbling downstairs. No damage was done, and the man called on Mariam again a few days later, very sober and contrite, and was re-admitted to my aunt's favours.

Aunt Mariam must have begun to worry about the effect these comings and goings might have on me, because after a few months she began to make arrangements for sending me to a boarding school in the hills.

I had not the slightest desire to go to school and raised many objections. We had long arguments in which she tried vainly to impress upon me the desirability of receiving an education.

'To make a living, my *Ladla*,' she said, 'you must have an education.'

'But you have no education,' I said, 'and you have no difficulty in making a living!'

Mariam threw up her arms in mock despair. 'Ten years from now I will not be able to make such a living. Then who will support and help me? An illiterate young fellow, or an educated gentleman? When I am old, my son, when I am old . . .'

Finally I succumbed to her arguments and agreed to go to a boarding school. And when the time came for me to leave, both Aunt Mariam and I broke down and wept at the railway station.

I hung out of the window as the train moved away from the

platform, and saw Mariam, her bosom heaving, being helped from the platform by Mulia and some of our neighbours.

My incarceration in a boarding school was made more unbearable by the absence of any letters from Aunt Mariam. She could write little more than her name.

I was looking forward to my winter holidays and my return to Aunt Mariam and the Dilaram bazaar, but this was not to be. During my absence there had been some litigation over my custody, and my father's relatives claimed that Aunt Mariam was not a fit person to be a child's guardian.

And so when I left school, it was not to Aunt Mariam's place that I was sent, but to a strange family living in a railway colony near Moradabad. I remained with these relatives until I finished school; but that is a different story.

I did not see Aunt Mariam again. The Dilaram bazaar and my beautiful aunt and the Siamese cat all became part of the receding world of my childhood.

I would often think of Mariam, but as time passed she became more remote and inaccessible in my memory. It was not until many years later, when I was a young man, that I visited the Dilaram bazaar again. I knew from my foster parents that Aunt Mariam was dead. Her heart, it seemed, had always been weak.

I was anxious to see the Dilaram bazaar and its residents again, but my visit was a disappointment. The place had disappeared; or rather, it had been swallowed up by a growing city.

It was lost in the complex of a much larger market which had sprung up to serve a new government colony. The older people had died, and the young ones had gone to colleges or factories or offices in different towns. Aunt Mariam's rooms had been pulled down.

I found her grave in the little cemetery on the town's outskirts. One of her more devoted admirers had provided a handsome gravestone, surmounted by a sculptured angel. One of the wings had broken off, and the face was chipped, which gave the angel a slightly crooked smile.

But in spite of the broken wing and the smile, it was a very ordinary stone angel and could not hold a candle to my Aunt Mariam, the very special gaurdian angel of my childhood.

Death of a Familiar

When I learnt from a mutual acquaintance that my friend Sunil had been killed, I could not help feeling a little surprised, even shocked. Had Sunil killed somebody, it would not have surprised me in the least; he did not greatly value the lives of others. But for him to have been the victim was a sad reflection of his rapid decline.

He was twenty-one at the time of his death. Two friends of his had killed him, stabbing him several times with their knives. Their motive was said to have been revenge: apparently he had seduced their wives. They had invited him to a bar in Meerut, had plied him with country liquor, and had then accompanied him out into the cold air of a December night. It was drizzling a little. Near the bridge over the canal, one of his companions seized him from behind, while the other plunged a knife first into his stomach and then into his chest. When Sunil slumped forward, the other friend stabbed him in the back. A passing cyclist saw the little group, heard a cry and a groan, saw a blade flash in the light from his lamp. He pedalled furiously into town, burst into the *kotwali*, and roused the sergeant on duty. Accompanied by two constables, they ran to the bridge but found the area deserted. It was only as the rising sun drew an open wound across the sky that they found Sunil's body on the canal-bank, his head and shoulders on the sand, his legs in running water.

The bar-keeper was able to describe Sunil's companions, and they were arrested that same morning in their homes. They had not found time to get rid of their blood-soaked clothes. As they were not known to me, I took very little interest in the proceedings against them; but I understand that they have appealed against their sentences of life imprisonment.

I was in Delhi at the time of the murder, and it was almost a year since I had last seen Sunil. We had both lived in Shahganj and had left the place for jobs; I to work in a newspaper office, he in a paper factory owned by an uncle. It had been hoped that he would in time acquire a sense of responsibility and some stability of character; but I had known Sunil for over two years, and in that time it had been made abundantly clear that he had not been torn to fit in with the conventions. And as for character, his had the stability of a grasshopper. He was forever in search of new adventures and sensations, and this appetite of his for every novelty led him into some awkward situations.

He was a product of Partition, of the frontier provinces, of Anglo-Indian public schools, of films Indian and American, of medieval India, knights in armour, hippies, drugs, sex-magazines and the subtropical Terai. Had he lived in the time of the Moghuls, he might have governed a province with saturnine and spectacular success. Being born into the 20th century, he was but a juvenile delinquent.

It must be said to his credit that he was a delinquent of charm and originality. I realised this when I first saw him, sitting on the wall of the football stadium, his long legs — looking even longer and thinner because of the tight trousers he wore —dangling over the wall, his *chappals* trailing in the dust of the road, while his white bush-shirt lay open, unbuttoned, showing his smooth brown chest. He had a smile on his long face, which, with its high cheekbones, gave his cheeks a cavernous look, an impression of unrequited hunger.

We were both watching the wrestling. Two practice bouts were in progress — one between two thin, undernourished boys, and the other between the master of the *akhara* and a bearded Sikh who drove trucks for a living. They struggled in the soft mud of the wrestling pit, their well-oiled bodies glistening in the sunlight that filtered through a massive banyan tree. I had been standing near the *akhara* for a few minutes when I became conscious of the young man's gaze. When I turned round to look at him, he smiled satanically.

'Are you a wrestler, too?' he asked.

'Do I look like one?' I countered.

'No, you look more like an athlete' he said. 'I mean a long-distance runner. Very thin.'

'I'm a writer. Like long-distance runners, most writers are very thin.'

'You're an Anglo-Indian, aren't you?'

'My family history is very complicated, otherwise I'd be delighted to give you all the details.'

'You could pass for a European, you know. You're quite fair. But you have an Indian accent.'

'An Indian accent is very similar to a Welsh accent,' I observed. 'I might pass for Welsh, but not many people in India have met Welshmen!'

He chuckled at my answer; then stared at me speculatively. 'I say,' he said at length, as though an idea of great weight and importance had occurred to him. 'Do you have any magazines with pictures of dames?'

'Well, I may have some old Playboys. You can have them if you like.'

'Thanks,' he said, getting down from the wall. 'I'll come and fetch them. This wrestling is boring, anyway.'

He slipped his hand into mine (a custom of no special significance), and began whistling snatches of Hindi film tunes and the latest American hits.

I was living at the time in a small flat above the town's main shopping centre. Below me there were shops, restaurants and a cinema. Behind the building lay a junkyard littered with the framework of vintage cars and broken-down *tongas*. I was paying thirty rupees a month for my two rooms, and sixty to the Punjabi restaurant where I took my meals. My earnings as a freelance writer were something like a hundred and fifty rupees a month, sufficient to enable me to make both ends meet, provided I remained in the back-water, that was Shahganj.

Sunil (I had learnt his name during our walk from the stadium), made himself at home in my flat as soon as he entered it. He went through all my magazines, books and photographs with the thoroughness of an executor of a will. In India, it is customary for people to try and find out all there is to know about you, and Sunil went through the formalities with considerable thoroughness. While he spoke, his roving eyes made a mental inventory of all my belongings. These were few — a typewriter, a small radio, and a

90

cupboard-full of books and clothes, besides the furniture that went with the flat. I had no valuables. Was he disappointed? I could not be sure. He wore good clothes and spoke fluent English, but good clothes and good English are no criterion of honesty. He was a little too glib to inspire confidence. Apparently, he was still at college. His father owned a cloth shop; a strict man who did not give his son much spending money.

But Sunil was not seriously interested in money, as I was shortly to discover. He was interested in experience, and searched for it in various directions.

'You have a nice view,' he said, leaning over my balcony and looking up and down the street. 'You can see everyone on parade. Girls! They're becoming quite modern now. Short hair and small blouses. Tight salwars. Maxis, minis. Falsies. Do you like girls?'

'Well . . .' I began, but he did not really expect an answer to his question.

'What are little girls made of? That's an English poem, isn't it?' 'Sugar, and spice and everything nice . . .,' 'and I don't remember the rest.' He lowered his voice to a confidential undertone. 'Have you had any girls?'

'Well . . .'

'I had fun with a girl, you know, my cousin. She came to stay with us last summer. Then there's a girl in college who's stuck on me. But this is such a backward country. We can't be seen together in public, and I can't invite her to my house. Can I bring her here some day?'

'Well, I don't know . . .' I hadn't lived in a small town like Shah-ganj for some time, and wasn't sure if morals had changed along with the fashions.

'Oh, not now,' he said. 'There's no hurry. I'll give you plenty of warning, don't worry.' He put an arm around my shoulders and looked at me with undisguised affection. 'We are going to be great friends, you and I.'

After that I began to receive almost daily visits from Sunil. His college classes gave over at three in the afternoon, and though it was seldom that he attended them, he would stop at my place after putting in a brief appearance at the study hall. I could hardly blame him for neglecting his books: Shakespeare and Chaucer were pres-cribed for students who had but a rudimentary knowledge of Mod-ern English usage. Vast numbers of graduates were produced every year, and most of them became clerks or bus-conductors or, perhaps, school-teachers. But Sunil's father wanted the best for his son. And in Shahganj that meant as many degrees as possible.

Sunil would come stamping into my rooms, waking me from the siesta which had become a habit during summer afternoons. When he found that I did not relish being woken up, he would leave me to sleep while he took a bath under the tap. After making liberal use of my hair-cream and after-shave lotion (he had just begun shaving, but used the lotion on his body), he would want to go to a picture or restaurant, and would sprinkle me with cold water so that I leapt off the bed.

One afternoon he felt more than usually ebullient, and poured a whole bucket of water over me, soaking the sheets and mattress. I retaliated by flinging the water-jug at his head. It missed him and shattered itself against the wall. Sunil then went berserk and started splashing water all over the room, while I threatened and shouted. When I tried restraining him by force, we rolled over on the ground, and I banged my head against the bedstead and almost lost consciousness. He was then full of contrition, and massaged the lump on my head with hair-cream and refused to borrow any money from me that day.

Sunil's 'borrowing' consisted of extracting a few rupee-notes from my wallet, saying he needed the money for books or a tailor's bill or a shopkeeper who was threatening him with violence, and then spending it on something quite different. Before long I gave up asking him to return anything, just as I had given up asking him to stop seeing me.

Sunil was one of those people best loved from a distance. He was born with a special talent for trouble. I think it pleased his vanity when he was pursued by irate creditors, shopkeepers, brothers whose sisters he had insulted, and husbands whose wives he had molested. My association with him did nothing to improve my own reputation of Shahganj.

My landlady, a protective, motherly, Punjabi widow, said: 'Son, you are in bad company. Do you know that Sunil has already been expelled from one school for stealing, and from another for sexual offences?'

'He's only a boy,' I said. 'And he's taking longer than most boys to grow up. He doesn't realise the seriousness of what he does. He will learn as he grows older.'

'If he grows older,' said my landlady darkly. 'Do you know that he nearly killed a man last year? When a fruit-seller who had been cheated threatened to report Sunil to the police, he threw a brick at the man's head. The poor man was in hospital for three weeks. If Sunil's father did not have political influence, the boy would be in jail now, instead of climbing your stairs every afternoon.'

Once again I suggested to Sunil that he come to see me less often. He looked hurt and offended.

'Don't you like me any more?'

'I like you immensely. But I have work to do . . .'

'I know. You think I am a crook. Well, I am a crook.' He spoke with all the confidence of a young man who has never been hurt or disillusioned; he had romantic notions about swindlers and gangsters. 'I'll be a big crook one day, and people will be scared of me. But don't worry, old boy, you're my friend. I wouldn't harm you in any way. In fact, I'll protect you.'

'Thank you, but I don't require protection, I want to be left alone. I have work, and you are a worry and a distraction.'

'Well, I'm not going to leave you alone,' he said, assuming the posture of a spoilt child. 'Why should you be left alone? Who do you think you are? If we're friends now, it's your fault. I'm not going to buzz off just to suit your convenience.'

'Come less often, that's all.'

'I'll come more often, you old snob! I know, you're thinking of your reputation — as if you had any. Well, you don't have to worry, *mon ami* — as they say in Hollywood. I'll be very discreet, *daddyji!*'

Whenever I complained or became querulous, Sunil would call me daddy or uncle or sometimes mum, and make me feel more ridiculous. If he was in a good mood, he would use the Hindi word *chacha* (uncle). All it did was to make me feel much older than my twenty-five years.

Sunil turned up one afternoon with blood streaming from his nose and from a gash across his forehead. He sat down at the foot of the bed, and began dabbling his face with the bedsheet.

'What have you done to yourself?' I asked in some alarm.

'Some fellows beat me up. There were three of them. They followed me on their cycles.'

'Who were they?' I asked, looking for iodine on the dressing-table.

'Just some fellows . . .'

'They must have had a reason.'

'Well, a sister of one of them had been talking to me.'

'Well, that isn't a reason, even in Shahganj. You must have said or done something to offend her.'

'No, she likes me,' he said, wincing as I dabbed iodine on his forehead 'We went to the guava orchard near my uncle's farm.'

'She went out there alone with you?'

'Sure. I took her on my bike. They must have followed us. Anyway, we weren't doing much except kissing and fooling around. But some people seem to think that's worse than . . .'

Both he and the other boys of Shahganj had grown up to look upon girls as strange, exotic animals, who must be seized at the first opportunity. Experimenting in sex was like playing a surreptitious game of marbles.

Sunil produced a clasp-knife from his pocket, opened it, and held the blade against the flat of his hand.

'Don't worry, uncle, I can look after myself. The next fellow who tries to interfere with me will get this in his guts.'

'Don't be silly,' I said. 'You will go to prison for ten years. Listen, I'm going up to Simla for a couple of weeks, just for a change. Why don't you come with me? It will be a pleasant change from Shahganj, and in the meantime all this fuss will die down.'

It was one of those invitations which I make so readily and instantly regret. As soon as I had made the suggestion, I realised that Sunil in Simla might be even more of a problem than Sunil in Shahganj. But it was too late for me to back out.

'Simla! Why not? The college is closing for the summer holidays, and my father won't mind my going with you. He believes you're the only respectable friend I've got. Boy! we'll have a good time in Simla.'

'You'll have to behave yourself there, if you want to come with me. No girls, Sunil.'

'No girls, sir. I'll be very good, *chachaji*. Please take me to Simla.'

'I think two hundred rupees should be enough for a fortnight for both of us,' I said.

'Oh, too much,' said Sunil modestly.

And a week later we were actually in Simla, putting up at a moderately priced, middle-class hotel.

Our first few days in the hill-station were pleasant enough. We went for long walks, tired ourselves out, and acquired enormous appetites. Sunil, in the hills for the first time in his life, declared that they were wonderful, and thanked me a score of times for bringing him up. He took a genuine interest in exploring remote valleys, forests and waterfalls, and seemed to be losing some of his self-centredness. I believe that mountains do affect one's personality, if one can remain among them long enough; and if Sunil had grown up in the hills instead of in a refugee township, I have no doubt he would have been a completely different person.

There was one small waterfall I rather liked. It was down a ravine, in a rather inaccessible spot, where very few people ever went. The water fell about thirty feet into a small pool. We bathed here on two occasions, and Sunil quite forgot the attractions of the town. And we would have visited the spot again had I not slipped and sprained my ankle. This accident confined me to the hotel balcony for several days, and I was afraid that Sunil, for want of companionship, would go in search of more mundane distractions. But though he went out often enough, he came back dusty and sunburnt; and the fact that he asked me for very little money was evidence enough of his fondness for the outdoors. Striding through forests of oak and pine, with all the world stretched out far below, was no doubt a new and exhilarating experience for him. But how long would it be before the spell was broken?

'Don't you need any money?' I asked him uneasily, on the third day of his Thoreau-like activities.

'What for, uncle? Fresh air costs nothing. And besides, I don't owe money to anyone in Simla. We haven't been here long enough.'

'Then perhaps we should be going,' I said.

'Shahganj is a miserable little dump.'

'I know, but it's your home. And for the time being, it's mine.'

'Listen, uncle,' he said, after a moment of reflection. 'Yesterday, on one of my walks, I met a school-teacher. She's over thirty, so don't get nervous. She doesn't have any brothers or relatives who will come chasing after me. And she's much fairer than you, uncle. Is it all right if I'm friendly with her?'

'I suppose so,' I said uncertainly. School teachers can usually take care of themselves (if they want to), and, besides, an older woman might have had a sobering influence on Sunil.

He brought her over to see me that same evening, and seemed quite proud of his new acquisition. She was indeed fair, perhaps insipidly so, with blonde hair and light blue eyes. She had a young face and a healthy body, but her voice was peculiarly toneless and flat, giving an impression of boredom, of lassitude. I wondered what she found attractive in Sunil apart from his obvious animal charm. They had hardly anything in common; but perhpas the absence of similar interests was an attraction in itself. In six or seven years of teaching Maureen must have been tired of the usual scholastic types. Sunil was refreshingly free from all classroom associations.

Maureen let her hair down at the first opportunity. She switched on the bedroom radio and found Ceylon. Soon she was teaching Sunil to dance. This was amusing, because Sunil, with his long legs, had great difficulty in taking small steps; nor could Maureen cope with his great strides. But he was very earnest about it all, and inserting an unlighted cigarette between his lips, did his best to move rhythmically around the bedroom. I think he was convinced that by learning to dance he would reach the high-water mark of western culture. Maureen stood for all that was remote and romantic, and for all the films that he had seen. To conquer her would, for Sunil, be a voyage of discovery, not a mere gratification of his senses. And for Maureen, this new unconventional friendship must have been a refreshing diversion from the dreariness of her school routine. She was old enough to realise that it was only a diversion. The intensity of emotional attachments had faded with her early youth, and love could wound her heart no more. But for Sunil, it was only the beginning of something that stirred him deeply, moved him inexorably towards manhood.

It was unfortunate that I did not then notice this subtle change in my friend. I had known him only as a shallow creature, and was certain that this new infatuation would disappear as soon as the novelty of it wore off. As Maureen had no encumbrances, no relations that she would speak of, I saw no harm in encouraging the friendship and seeing how it would develop.

'I think we'd better have something to drink,' I said, and ringing the bell for the room-bearer, ordered several bottles of beer.

Sunil gave me an odd, whimsical look. I had never before encouraged him to drink. But he did not hesitate to open the bottles; and, before long, Maureen and he were drinking from the same glass.

'Let's make love,' said Sunil, putting his arm round Maureen's shoulders and gazing adoringly into her dreamy blue eyes.

They seemed unconcerned by my presence; but I was embarrassed, and getting up, said I would be going for a walk.

'Enjoy yourself,' said Sunil, winking at me over Maureen's shoulder.

'You ought to get yourself a girl friend,' said the young woman in a conciliatory tone.

'True,' I said, and moved guiltily out of the room I was paying for.

Our stay in Simla lasted several days longer than we had planned. I saw little of Sunil and Maureen during this time. As Sunil had no desire to return to Shahganj any earlier than was absolutely necessary, he avoided me during the day; but I managed to stay awake late enough one night to confront him when he crept quietly into the room.

'Dear friend and familiar,' I said. 'I hate to spoil your beautiful romance, but I have absolutely no money left, and unless you have resources of your own — or if Maureen can support you — I suggest that you accompany me back to Shahganj the day after tomorrow.'

'How mean you are, *chachaji*. This is something serious. I mean Maureen and me. Do you think we should get married?'

'No.'

'But why not?'

'Because she cannot support you on a teacher's salary. And she probably isn't interested in a permanent relationship — like ours.'

'Very funny. And you think I'd let my wife slave for me?'

'I do. And besides . . .'

'And besides,' he interrupted, grinning, 'she's old enough to be my mother.'

'Are you really in love with her?' I asked him. 'I've never known you to be serious about anything.'

'Honestly, uncle.'

'And what about her?'

'Oh, she loves me terribly, really she does. She's ready to come down with us if it's possible. Only I've told her that I'll first have to break the news to my father, otherwise he might kick me out of the house.'

'Well, then,' I said shrewdly, 'the sooner we return to Shahganj and get your father's blessings, the sooner you and Maureen can get married, if that's what both of you really want.'

Early next morning Sunil disappeared, and I knew he would be gone all day. My foot was better, and I decided to take a walk on my own to the waterfall I had liked so much. It was almost noon when I reached the spot and began descending the steep path to the ravine. The stream was hidden by dense foliage, giant ferns and dahlias, but the water made a tremendous noise as it tumbled over the rocks. When I reached a sharp promontory, I was able to look down on the pool. Two people were lying on the grass.

I did not recognise them at first. They looked very beautiful together, and I had not expected Sunil and Maureen to look so beautiful. Sunil, on whom no surplus flesh had as yet gathered, possessed all the sinuous grace and power of a young God; and the woman, her white flesh pressed against young grass, reminded me of a painting by Titian that I had seen in a gallery in Florence. Her full, mature body was touched with a tranquil intoxication, her breasts rose and fell slowly, and waves of muscle merged into the shadows of her broad thighs. It was as though I had stumbled into another age, and had found two lovers in a forest glade. Only a fool would have wished to disturb them. Sunil had for once in his life risen above mediocrity, and I hurried away before the magic was lost.

The human voice often shatters the beauty of the most tender passions; and when we left Simla next day, and Maureen and Sunil used all the stock cliches to express their love, I was a little disappointed. But the poetry of life was in their bodies, not in their tongues.

Back in Shahganj, Sunil actually plucked up courage to speak to his father. This, to me, was a sign that he took the affair very seriously, for he seldom approached his father for anything. But all the sympathy that he received was a box on the ears. I received a curt note suggesting that I was having a corrupting influence on the boy and that I should stop seeing him. There was little I could do in the matter, because it had always been Sunil who had insisted on seeing me.

He continued to visit me, bring me Maureen's letters (strange, how lovers cannot bear that the world should not know their love), and his own to her, so that I could correct his English!

It was at about this time that Sunil began speaking to me about his uncle's paper factory, and the possibility of working in it. Once he was getting a salary, he pointed out, Maureen would be able to leave her job and join him.

Unfortunately Sunil's decision to join the paper factory took months to crystallise into a definite course of action, and in the meantime he was finding a panacea for love-sickness in rum and sometimes cheap country spirits. The money that he now borrowed was used not to pay his debts, or to incur new ones, but to drink himself silly. I regretted having been the first person to have offered him a drink: I should have known that Sunil was a person who could do nothing in moderation.

He pestered me less often now, but the purpose of his occasional visits became all too obvious. I was having a little success, and thoughtlessly gave Sunil the few rupees he usually demanded. At the same time I was beginning to find other friends, and I no longer found myself worrying about Sunil, as I had so often done in the past. Perhaps this was treachery on my part . . .

When finally I decided to leave Shahganj for Delhi. I went in search of Sunil to say goodbye. I found him in a small bar, alone at a table with a bottle of rum. Though barely twenty, he no longer looked a boy. He was a completely different person from the handsome, cocksure youth I had met at the wrestling-pit a year previously. His cheeks were hollow and he had not shaved for days. I knew that when I had first met him he had been without scruples, a shallow youth, the product of many circumstances. He was no longer so shallow and he had stumbled upon love, but his character was too weak to sustain the weight of disillusionment. Perhaps I should have left him severely alone from the beginning. Before me sat a ruin, and I had helped to undermine the foundations. None of us can really avoid seeing the outcome of our smallest actions . . .

'I'm off to Delhi, Sunil.'

He did not look up from the table.

'Have a good time,' he said.

'Have you heard from Maureen?' I asked, certain that he had not. He nodded, but for once he did not offer to show me the letter.

'What's wrong?' I asked.

'Oh, nothing,' he said, looking up and forcing a smile. 'These dames are all the same, uncle. We shouldn't take them too seriously, you know.'

'Why, what has she done, got married to someone else?'

'Yes,' he said scornfully. 'To a bloody teacher.'

'Well, she wasn't young,' I said. 'She couldn't wait for you for ever, I suppose.'

'She could if she had really loved me. But there's no such thing as love, is there, uncle?'

I made no reply. Had he really broken his heart over a woman? Were there, within him, unsuspected depths of feeling and passion? You find love when you least expect to; and lose it, when you are sure that it is in your grasp.

'You're a lucky beggar,' he said. 'You're a philosopher. You find a reason for every stupid thing, and so you are able to ignore all stupidity.'

I laughed. 'You're becoming a philosopher yourself. But don't think too hard, Sunil, you might find it painful.'

'Not I, *chachaji*,' he said, emptying his glass. 'I'm not going to think. I'm going to work in a paper factory. I shall become respectable. What an adventure that will be!'

And that was the last time I saw Sunil.

He did not become respectable. He was still searching like a great discoverer for something new, someone different, when he met his pitiful end in the cold rain of a December night.

Though murder cases usually get reported in the papers, Sunil was a person of such little importance that his violent end was not considered newsworthy. It went unnoticed, and Maureen could not have known about it. The case has already been forgotten, for in the great human mass that is India, hundreds of people disappear every day and are never heard of again. Sunil will be quickly forgotten by all except those to whom he owed money.

The Kitemaker

There was but one tree in the street known as Gali Ram Nath — an ancient banyan that had grown through the cracks of an abandoned mosque — and little Ali's kite had caught in its branches. The boy, barefoot and clad only in a torn shirt, ran along the cobbled stones of the narrow street to where his grandfather sat nodding dreamily in the sunshine of their back courtyard.

'Grandfather,' shouted the boy. 'My kite has gone!'

The old man woke from his daydream with a start, and raising his head, displayed a beard that would have been white, had it not been dyed red with *mehndi* leaves.

'Did the twine break?' he asked. 'I know that kite twine is not what it used to be.'

'No, grandfather, the kite is stuck in the banyan tree.'

The old man chuckled. 'You have yet to learn how to fly a kite properly, my child. And I am too old to teach you, that's the pity of it. But you shall have another.'

He had just finished making a new kite from bamboo paper and thin silk, and it lay in the sun, firming up. It was a pale pink kite, with a small green tail. The old man handed it to Ali, and the boy raised himself on his toes and kissed his grandfather's hollowed-out cheek.

'I will not lose this one,' he said. 'This kite will fly like a bird.' And he turned on his heels and skipped out of the courtyard.

The old man remained dreaming in the sun. His kite shop was gone, the premises long since sold to a junk dealer; but he still made kites, for his own amusement and for the benefit of his grand-

101

son, Ali. Not many people bought kites these days. Adults disdained them, and children preferred to spend their money at the cinema. Moreover, there were not many open spaces left for the flying of kites. The city had swallowed up the open grassland that had stretched from the old fort's walls to the river bank.

But the old man remembered a time when grown men flew kites, and great battles were fought, the kites swerving and swooping in the sky, tangling with each other until the string of one was severed. Then the defeated but liberated kite would float away into the blue unknown. There was a good deal of betting, and money frequently changed hands.

Kite-flying was then the sport of kings, and the old man remembered how the Nawab himself would come down to the riverside with his retinue to participate in this noble pastime. There was time, then, to spend an idle hour with a gay, dancing strip of paper. Now everyone hurried, hurried in a heat of hope, and delicate things like kites and daydreams were trampled underfoot.

He, Mehmood the kite-maker, had in the prime of his life been well-known throughout the city. Some of his more elaborate kites once sold for as much as three or four rupees each.

At the request of the Nawab he had once made a very special kind of kite, unlike any that had been seen in the district. It consisted of a series of small, very light paper disks, trailing on a thin bamboo frame. To the end of each disk he fixed a sprig of grass, forming a balance on both sides.

The surface of the foremost disk was slightly convex, and a fantastic face was painted on it, having two eyes made of small mirrors. The disks, decreasing in size from head to tail, assumed an undulatory form, and gave the kite the appearance of a crawling serpent. It required great skill to raise this cumbersome device from the ground, and only Mehmood could manage it.

Everyone had heard of the 'Dragon Kite' that Mehmood had built, and word went round that it possessed supernatural powers. A large crowd assembled in the open to watch its first public launching in the presence of the Nawab.

At the first attempt it refused to leave the ground.

The disks made a plaintive, protesting sound, and the sun was trapped in the little mirrors, and made of the kite a living, complaining creature. And then the wind came from the right direction, and the Dragon Kite soared into the sky, wriggling its way higher and higher, with the sun still glinting in its devil-eyes. And when it went very high, it pulled fiercely on the twine, and Mehmood's young sons had to help him with the reel; but still the kite pulled, determined to be free, to break loose, to live a life of its own. And eventually it did so.

The twine snapped, the kite leaped away toward the sun, sailed on heavenward until it was lost to view. It was never found again, and Mehmood wondered afterwards if he had made too vivid, too living a thing of the great kite. He did not make another like it, and instead he presented to the Nawab a musical kite, one that made a sound like a violin when it rose in the air.

Those were more leisurely, more spacious days. But the Nawab had died years ago, and his descendants were almost as poor as Mehmood himself. Kite-makers, like poets, once had their patrons; but no one knew Mehmood, simply because there were too many people in the *Gali*, and they could not be bothered with their neighbours.

When Mehmood was younger and had fallen sick, everyone in the neighbourhood had come to ask after his health; but now, when his days were drawing to a close, no one visited him. True, most of his old friends were dead and his sons had grown up: one was working in a local garage, the other had been in Pakistan at the time of Partition and had not been able to rejoin his relatives.

The children who had bought kites from him 10 years ago were now grown men, struggling for a living; they did not have time for the old man and his memories. They had grown up in a swiftly changing and competitive world, and they looked at the old kite-maker and the banyan tree with the same indifference.

Both were taken for granted — permanent fixtures that were of no concern to the raucous, sweating mass of humanity that surrounded them. No longer did people gather under the banyan tree to discuss their problems and their plans: only in the summer months did a few seek shelter from the fierce sun.

But there was the boy, his grandson; it was good that Mehmood's son worked close by, for it gladdened the old man's heart to watch the small boy at play in the winter sunshine, growing under his eyes like a young and well-nourished sapling putting forth new leaves each day. There is a great affinity between trees and men. We grow at much the same pace, if we are not hurt or starved or cut down. In our youth we are resplendent creatures, and in our declining years we stoop a little, we remember, we stretch our brittle limbs in the sun, and then, with a sigh, we shed our last leaves.

Mehmood was like the banyan, his hands gnarled and twisted like the roots of the ancient tree. Ali was like the young mimosa planted at the end of the courtyard. In two years both he and the tree would acquire the strength and confidence of their early youth.

The voices in the street grew fainter, and Mehmood wondered if he was going to fall asleep and dream, as he so often did, of a kite so beautiful and powerful that it would resemble the great white bird of the Hindus, Garuda, God Vishnu's famous steed. He would like to make a wonderful new kite for little Ali. He had nothing else to leave the boy.

He heard Ali's voice in the distance, but did not realise that the boy was calling him. The voice seemed to come from very far away.

Ali was at the courtyard door, asking if his mother had as yet returned from the bazaar. When Mehmood did not answer, the boy came forward repeating his question. The sunlight was slanting across the old man's head, and a small white butterfly rested on his flowing beard. Mehmood was silent; and when Ali put his small brown hand on the old man's shoulder, he met with no response. The boy heard a faint sound, like the rubbing of marbles in his pocket.

Suddenly afraid, Ali turned and moved to the door, and then ran down the street shouting for his mother. The butterfly left the old man's beard and flew to the mimosa tree, and a sudden gust of wind caught the torn kite and lifted it into the air, carrying it far above the struggling city into the blind blue sky.

The Monkeys

I couldn't be sure, next morning, if I had been dreaming or if I had really heard dogs barking in the night and had seen them scampering about on the hillside below the cottage. There had been a Golden Cocker, a Retriever, a Peke, a Dachshund, a black Labrador, and one or two nondescripts. They had woken me with their barking shortly after midnight, and made so much noise that I got out of bed and looked out of the open window. I saw them quite plainly in the moonlight, five or six dogs rushing excitedly through the bracket and long monsoon grass.

It was only because there had been so many breeds among the dogs that I felt a little confused. I had been in the cottage only a week, and I was already on nodding or speaking terms with most of my neighbours. Colonel Fanshawe, retired from the Indian Army, was my immediate neighbour. He did keep a Cocker, but it was black. The elderly Anglo-Indian spinsters who lived beyond the deodars kept only cats. (Though why cats should be the prerogative of spinsters, I have never been able to understand) The milkman kept a couple of mongrels. And the Punjabi industrialist who had bought a former prince's palace — without ever occupying it — left the property in charge of a watchman who kept a huge Tibetan mastiff.

None of these dogs looked like the ones I had seen in the night.

'Does anyone here keep a Retriever?' I asked Colonel Fanshawe, when I met him taking his evening walk.

'No one that I know of,' he said, and he gave me a swift, penetrating look from under his bushy eyebrows. 'Why, have you seen one around?'

'No, I just wondered. There are a lot of dogs in the area, aren't there?'

'Oh, yes. Nearly everyone keeps a dog here. Of course every now and then a panther carries one off. Lost a lovely little terrier myself, only last winter.'

Colonel Fanshawe, tall and red-faced, seemed to be waiting for me to tell him something more — or was he just taking time to recover his breath after a stiff uphill climb?

That night I heard the dogs again. I went to the window and looked out. The moon was at the full, silvering the leaves of the oak trees.

The dogs were looking up into the trees, and barking. But I could see nothing in the trees, not even an owl.

I gave a shout, and the dogs disappeared into the forest.

Colonel Fanshawe looked at me expectantly when I met him the following day. He knew something about those dogs, of that I was certain; but he was waiting to hear what I had to say. I decided to oblige him.

'I saw at least six dogs in the middle of the night,' I said. 'A Cocker, a Retriever, a Peke, a Dachshund, and two mongrels. Now, Colonel, I'm sure you must know whose they are.'

The Colonel was delighted. I could tell by the way his eyes glinted that he was going to enjoy himself at my expense.

'You've been seeing Miss. Fairchild's dogs,' he said with smug satisfaction.

'Oh, and where does she live?'

'She doesn't, my boy. Died fifteen years ago.'

'Then what are her dogs doing here?'

'Looking for monkeys,' said the Colonel. And he stood back to watch my reactions.

'I'm afraid I don't understand,' I said.

'Let me put it this way,' said the Colonel. 'Do you believe in ghosts?'

'I've never seen any,' I said.

'But you have, my boy, you have. Miss. Fairchild's dogs died years ago — a Cocker, a Retriever, a Dachshund, a Peke, and two mongrels. They were buried on a litle knoll under the oaks. Nothing odd about their deaths, mind you. They were all quite old, and didn't survive their mistress very long. Neighbours looked after them until they died.'

'And Miss. Fairchild lived in the cottage where I stay? Was she young?'

'She was in her mid-forties, an athletic sort of woman, fond of the outdoors. Didn't care much for men. I thought you knew about her.'

'No, I haven't been here very long, you know. But what was it you said about monkeys? Why were the dogs looking for monkeys?'

'Ah, that's the interesting part of the story. Have you seen the *langur* monkeys that sometimes come to eat oak leaves?'

'No.'

'You will, sooner or later. There has always been a band of them roaming these forests. They're quite harmless really, except that they'll ruin a garden if given half a chance . . . Well, Miss. Fairchild fairly loathed those monkeys. She was very keen on her dahlias — grew some prize specimens — but the monkeys would come at night, dig up the plants, and eat the dahlia-bulbs. Apparently they found the bulbs much to their liking. Miss. Fairchild would be furious. People who are passionately fond of gardening often go off balance when their best plants are ruined — that's only human, I suppose. Miss. Fairchild set her dogs at the monkeys, whenever she could, even if it was in the middle of the night. But the monkeys simply took to the trees and left the dogs barking.'

'Then one day — or rather, one night — Miss. Fairchild took desperate measures. She borrowed a shotgun, and sat up near a window. And when the monkeys arrived, she shot one of them dead.'

The Colonel paused and looked out over the oak trees which were shimmering in the warm afternoon sun.

'She shouldn't have done that,' he said.

'Never shoot a monkey. It's not only that they're sacred to Hindus — but they are rather human, you know. Well, I must be getting on. Good-day!' And the Colonel, having ended his story rather abruptly, set off at a brisk pace through the deodars.

I didn't hear the dogs that night. But next day I saw the monkeys — the real ones, not ghosts. There were about twenty of them, young and old, sitting in the trees munching oak leaves. They didn't pay much attention to me, and I watched them for some time.

They were handsome creatures, their fur a silver-grey, their tails long and sinuous. They leapt gracefully from tree to tree, and were very polite and dignified in their behaviour towards each other —

unlike the bold, rather crude red monkeys of the plains. Some of the younger ones scampered about on the hillside, playing and wrestling with each other like schoolboys.

There were no dogs to molest them — and no dahlias to tempt them into the garden.

But that night, I heard the dogs again. They were barking more furiously than ever.

'Well, I'm not getting up for them this time' I mumbled, and pulled the blankets over my ears.

But the barking grew louder, and was joined by other sounds, a squealing and a scuffling.

Then suddenly the piercing shriek of a woman rang through the forest. It was an unearthly sound, and it made my hair stand up.

I leapt out of bed and dashed to the window.

A woman was lying on the ground, and three or four huge monkeys were on top of her, biting her arms and pulling at her throat. The dogs were yelping and trying to drag the monkeys off, but they were being harried from behind by others. The woman gave another bloodcurdling shriek, and I dashed back into the room, grabbed hold of a small axe, and ran into the garden.

But everyone — dogs, monkeys and shrieking woman — had disappeared, and I stood alone on the hillside in my pyjamas, clutching an axe and feeling very foolish.

The Colonel greeted me effusively the following day.

'Still seeing those dogs?' he asked in a bantering tone.

'I've seen the monkeys too,' I said.

'Oh, yes, they've come around again. But they're real enough, and quite harmless.'

'I know — but I saw them last night with the dogs.'

'Oh, did you really? That's strange, very strange.'

The Colonel tried to avoid my eye, but I hadn't quite finished with him.

'Colonel,' I said. 'You never did get around to telling me how Miss. Fairchild died.'

'Oh, didn't I? Must have slipped my memory. I'm getting old, don't remember people as well as I used to. But of course I remember about Miss. Fairchild, poor lady. The monkeys killed her. Didn't you know? They simply tore her to pieces . . .'

His voice trailed off, and he looked thoughtfully at a caterpillar that was making its way up his walking-stick.

'She shouldn't have shot one of them,' he said. 'Never shoot a monkey — they're rather human, you know . . .'

The Prospect of Flowers

Fern Hill, The Oaks, Hunter's Lodge, The Parsonage, The Pines, Dumbarnie, Mackinnon's Hall and Winqermere. These are the names of some of the old houses that still stand on the outskirts of one of the smaller Indian hill stations. Most of them have fallen into decay and ruin. They are very old, of course — built over a hundred years ago by Britishers who sought relief from the searing heat of the plains. Today's visitors to the hill stations prefer to live near the markets and cinemas and many of the old houses, set amidst oak and maple and deodar, are inhabited by wild cats, bandicoots, owls, goats, and the occasional charcoal-burner or mule-driver.

But amongst these neglected mansions stands a neat, white-washed cottage called Mulberry Lodge. And in it, up to a short time ago, lived an elderly English spinster named Miss. Mackenzie.

In years Miss Mackenzie was more than 'elderly,' being well over eighty. But no one would have guessed it. She was clean, sprightly, and wore old-fashioned but well-preserved dresses. Once a week, she walked the two miles to town to buy butter and jam and soap and sometimes a small bottle of *eau-de-Col'ogne*.

She had lived in the hill station since she had been a girl in her teens, and that had been before the First World War. Though she had never married, she had experienced a few love affairs and was far from being the typical frustrated spinster of fiction. Her parents had been dead thirty years; her brother and sister were also dead. She had no relatives in India, and she lived on a small pension of forty rupees a month and the gift parcels that were sent out to her from New Zealand by a friend of her youth.

Like other lonely old people, she kept a pet, a large black cat with bright yellow eyes. In her small garden she grew dahlias, chrysanthemums, gladioli and a few rare orchids. She knew a great deal about plants, and about wild flowers, trees, birds. and insects. She had never made a serious study of these things, but, having lived with them for so many years, had developed an intimacy with all that grew and flourished around her.

She had few visitors. Occasionally the padre from the local church called on her, and once a month the postman came with a letter from New Zealand or her pension papers. The milkman called every second day with a litre of milk for the lady and her cat. And sometimes she received a couple of eggs free, for the egg-seller remembered a time when Miss. Mackenzie, in her earlier prosperity, bought eggs from him in large quantities. He was a sentimental man. He remembered her when she was a ravishing beauty in her twenties and he had gazed at her in round-eyed, nine-year-old wonder and consternation.

Now it was September and the rains were nearly over and Miss. Mackenzie's chrysanthemums were coming into their own. She hoped the coming winter wouldn't be too severe because she found it increasingly difficult to bear the cold.

One day, as she was pottering about in her garden, she saw a schoolboy plucking wild flowers on the slope about the cottage.

'Who's that?' she called. 'What are you up to, young man?'

The boy was alarmed and tried to dash up the hillside, but he slipped on pine needles and came slithering down the slope into Miss. Mackenzie's nasturtium bed.

When he found there was no escape, he gave a bright disarming smile and said, 'Good morning, Miss.'

He belonged to the local English-medium school, and wore a bright red blazer and a red-and-black-striped tie. Like most polite Indian schoolboys, he called every woman 'Miss.'

'Good morning,' said Miss. Mackenzie severely. 'Would you mind moving out of my flower-bed?'

The boy stepped gingerly over the nasturtiums and looked up at Miss. Mackenzie with dimpled cheeks and appealing eyes. It was impossible to be angry with him.

'You're trespassing,' said Miss Mackenzie.

'Yes, Miss.'

'And you ought to be in school at this hour.'

'Yes, Miss.'

'Then what are you doing here?'

'Picking flowers, Miss.' And he held up a bunch of ferns and wild flowers.

'Oh,' Miss Mackenzie was disarmed. It was a long time since she had seen a boy taking an interest in flowers, and, what was more, playing truant from school in order to gather them.

'Do you like flowers?' she asked.

'Yes, Miss. I'm going to be a botan — a botantist?'

'You mean a botanist.'

'Yes, Miss.'

'Well, that's unusual. Most boys at your age want to be pilots or soldiers or perhaps engineers. But you want to be a botanist. Well, well. There's still hope for the world, I see. And do you know the names of these flowers?'

'This is a *Bukhilo* flower,' he said, showing her a small golden flower. 'That's a *Pahari* name. It means *Puja*, or prayer. The flower is offered during prayers. But I don't know what this is . . .'

He held out a pale pink flower with a soft, heart-shaped leaf.

'It's a wild begonia,' said Miss Mackenzie. 'And that purple stuff is salvia, but it isn't wild, it's a plant that escaped from my garden. Don't you have any books on flowers?'

'No, Miss.'

'All right, come in and I'll show you a book.'

She led the boy into a small front room, which was crowded with furniture and books and vases and jam-jars, and offered him a chair. He sat awkwardly on its edge. The black cat immediately leapt on to his knees, and settled down on them, purring loudly.

'What's your name?' asked Miss Mackenzie, as she rummaged among her books.

'Anil, Miss.'

'And where do you live?'

'When school closes, I go to Delhi. My father has a business.'

'Oh, and what's that?'

'Bulbs, Miss.'

'Flower bulbs?'

'No, electric bulbs.'

'Electric bulbs! You might send me a few, when you get home. Mine are always fusing, and they're so expensive, like everything else these days. Ah, here we are!' She pulled a heavy volume down from the shelf and laid it on the table. '*Flora Himaliensis*, published in 1892, and probably the only copy in India. This is a very valuable book, Anil. No other naturalist has recorded so many wild Himalayan flowers. And let me tell you this, there are many flowers and plants which are still unknown to the fancy botanists who spend all their time at microscopes instead of in the mountains. But perhaps, *you'll* do something about that, one day.'

'Yes, Miss.'

They went through the book together, and Miss. Mackenzie pointed out many flowers that grew in and around the hill station, while the boy made notes of their names and seasons. She lit a stove, and put the kettle on for tea. And then the old English lady and the small Indian boy sat side by side over cups of hot sweet tea, absorbed in a book of wild flowers.

'May I come again?' asked Anil, when finally he rose to go.

'If you like,' said Miss Mackenzie. 'But not during school hours. You mustn't miss your classes.'

After that, Anil visited Miss. Mackenzie about once a week, and nearly always he brought a wildflower for her to identify. She found herself looking forward to the boy's visits — and sometimes, when more than a week passed and he didn't come, she was disappointed and lonely and would grumble at the black cat.

Anil reminded her of her brother, when the latter had been a boy. There was no physical resemblance. Andrew had been fair-haired and blue-eyed. But it was Anil's eagerness, his alert bright look and the way he stood — legs apart, hands on hips, a picture of confidence — that reminded her of the boy who had shared her own youth in these same hills.

And why did Anil come to see her so often?

Partly because she knew about wild flowers, and he really did want to become a botanist. And partly because she smelt of freshly baked bread, and that was a smell his own grandmother had possessed. And partly because she was lonely and sometimes a boy of twelve can sense loneliness better than an adult. And partly because he was a little different from other children.

By the middle of October, when there was only a fortnight left for the school to close, the first snow had fallen on the distant mountains. One peak stood high above the rest, a white pinnacle against the azure-blue sky. When the sun set, this peak turned from orange to gold to pink to red.

'How high is that mountain?' asked Anil.

'It must be over 12,000 feet,' said Miss. Mackenzie. 'About thirty miles from her, as the crow flies. I always wanted to go there, but there was no proper road. At that height, there'll be flowers that you don't get here — the blue gentian and the purple columbine, the anemone and the edelweiss.'

'I'll go there one day,' said Anil.

'I'm sure you will, if you really want to.'

The day before his school closed, Anil came to say goodbye to Miss. Mackenzie.

'I don't suppose you'll be able to find many wild flowers in Delhi,' she said. 'But have a good holiday.'

'Thank you, Miss.'

As he was about to leave, Miss Mackenzie, on an impulse, thrust the *Flora Himaliensis* into his hands.

'You keep it,' she said. 'It's a present for you.'

'But I'll be back next year, and I'll be able to look at it then. It's so valuable.'

'I know it's valuable and that's why I've given it to you. Otherwise it will only fall into the hands of the junk-dealers.'

'But, Miss . . .'

'Don't argue. Besides, I may not be here next year.'

'Are you going away?'

'I'm not sure. I may go to England.'

She had no intention of going to England; she had not seen the country since she was a child, and she knew she would not fit in with the life of post-war Britain. Her home was in these hills, among the oaks and maples and deodars. It was lonely, but at her age it would be lonely anywhere.

The boy tucked the book under his arm, straightened his tie, stood stiffly to attention, and said, 'Goodbye, Miss. Mackenzie.'

It was the first time he had spoken her name.

Winter set in early, and strong winds brought rain and sleet, and soon there were no flowers in the garden or on the hillside. The cat stayed indoor, curled up at the foot of Miss. Mackenzie's bed.

Miss. Mackenzie wrapped herself up in all her old shawls and mufflers, but still she felt the cold. Her fingers grew so stiff that she took almost an hour to open a can of baked beans. And then, it snowed, and for several days the milkman did not come. The postman arrived with her pension papers, but she felt too tired to take them up to town to the bank.

She spent most of the time in bed. It was the warmest place. She kept a hot-water bottle at her back, and the cat kept her feet warm. She lay in bed, dreaming of the spring and summer months. In three months' time the Primroses would be out and with the coming of spring the boy would return.

One night the hot water bottle burst and the bedding was soaked through. As there was no sun for several days, the blanket remained damp. Miss. Mackenzie caught a chill and had to keep to her cold, uncomfortable bed. She knew she had a fever but there was no thermometer with which to take her temperature. She had difficulty in breathing.

A strong wind sprang up one night, and the window flew open and kept banging all night. Miss. Mackenzie was too weak to get up and close it, and the wind swept the rain and sleet into the room. The cat crept into the bed and snuggled close to its mistress's warm body. But towards morning that body had lost its warmth and the cat felt the bed and started scrathing about on the floor.

As a shaft of sunlight streamed through the open window, the milkman arrived. He poured some milk into the cat's saucer on the doorstep and the cat leapt down from the window-sill and made for the milk.

The milkman called a greeting to Miss. Mackenzie, but received no answer. Her window was open and he had always known her to be up before sunrise. So he put his head in at the window and called again. But Miss. Mackenzie did not answer. She had gone away to the mountain where the blue gentian and purple columbine grew.

A Case for Inspector Lal

I met Inspector Keemat Lal about two years ago, while I was living in the hot, dusty town of Shahpur in the plains of northern India.

Keemat Lal had charge of the local police station. He was a heavily built man, slow and rather ponderous, and inclined to be lazy; but, like most lazy people, he was intelligent. He was also a failure. He had remained an Inspector for a number of years, and had given up all hope of further promotion. His luck was against him, he said. He should never have been a policeman. He had been born under the sign of Capricorn and should really have gone into the restaurant business; but now it was too late to do anything about it.

The Inspector and I had little in common. He was nearing forty, and I was twenty-five. But both of us spoke English, and in Shahpur there were very few people who did. In addition, we were both fond of beer. There were no places of entertainment in Shahpur. The searing heat, the dust that came whirling up from the east, the mosquitoes (almost as numerous as the flies), and the general monotony gave one a thirst for something more substantial than stale lemonade.

My house was on the outskirts of the town, where we were not often disturbed. On two or three evenings in the week, just as the sun was going down and making it possible for one to emerge from the *khas*-cooled confines of a dark, high-ceilinged bedroom, Inspector Keemat Lal would appear on the verandah steps, mopping the sweat from his face with a small towel, which he used instead of a handkerchief. My only servant, excited at the prospect of serving an Inspector of Police, would hurry out with glasses, a bucket of ice and several bottles of the best Indian beer.

One evening, after we had overtaken out fourth bottle, I said, 'You must have had some interesting cases in your career, Inspector.'

'Most of them were rather dull,' he said. 'At least the successful ones were. The sensational cases usually went unsolved — otherwise I might have been a Superintendent by now. I suppose you are talking of murder cases. Do you remember the shooting of the Minister of the Interior? I was on that one, but it was a political murder and we never solved it.'

'Tell me about a case you solved,' I said. 'An intersting one.' When I saw him looking uncomfortable, I added, 'You don't have to worry, Inspector. I'm a very discreet person, in spite of all the beer I consume.'

'But how can you be discreet? You are a writer.'

I protested: 'Writers are usually very discreet. They always change the names of people and places.'

He gave me one of his rare smiles. 'And how would you describe me, if you were to put me into a story?'

'Oh, I'd leave you as you are. No one would believe in you, anyway.'

He laughed indulgently and poured out more beer. 'I suppose I can change names, too . . . I will tell you of a very interesting case. The victim was an unusual person, and so was the killer. But you must promise not to write this story.'

'I promise,' I lied.

'Do you know Panauli?'

'In the hills? Yes, I have been there once to twice.'

'Good, then you will follow me without my having to be too descriptive. This happened about three years ago, shortly after I had been stationed at Panauli. Nothing much ever happened there. There were a few cases of theft and cheating, and an occasional fight during the summer. A murder took place about once every ten years. It was therefore quite an event when the Rani of — was found dead in her sitting-room, her head split open by an axe. I knew that I would have to solve the case if I wanted to stay in Panauli.'

'The trouble was, anyone could have killed the Rani, and there were some who made no secret of their satisfaction that she was dead. She had been an unpopular woman. Her husband was dead, her children were scattered, and her money — for she had never been a very wealthy Rani — had been dwindling away. She lived alone in an old house on the outskirts of the town, ruling the locality with the stern authority of a matriarch. She had a servant, and he was the man who found the body and came to the police, dithering and tongue-tied. I arrested him at once, of course. I knew he was probably innocent, but a basic rule is to grab the first man on the scene of the crime, especially if he happens to be a servant. But we let him go after a beating. There was nothing much he could tell us, and he had a sound alibi.'

'The axe with which the Rani had been killed must have been a small woodcutter's axe — so we deduced from the wound. We couldn't find the weapon. It might have been used by a man or a woman, and there were several of both sexes who had a grudge against the Rani. There were bazaar rumours that she had been supplementing her income by trafficking in young women: she had the necessary connections. There were also rumours that she possessed vast wealth, and that it was stored away in her godowns. We did not find any treasure. There were so many rumours darting about like battered shuttlecocks that I decided to stop wasting my time in trying to follow them up. Instead I restricted my enquiries to those people who had been close to the Rani — either in their personal relationships or in actual physical proximity.'

'To begin with, there was Mr. Kapur, a wealthy businessman from Bombay who had a house in Panauli. He was supposed to be an old admirer of the Rani's. I discovered that he had occasionally lent her money, and that, in spite of his professed friendship for her, he had charged a high rate of interest.'

'Then there were her immediate neighbours — an American missionary and his wife, who had been trying to convert the Rani to Christianity; an English spinster of seventy who made no secret of the fact that she and the Rani had hated each other with great enthusiasm; a local councillor and his family, who did not get on well with their aristocratic neighbour; and a tailor, who kept his shop close by. None of these people had any powerful motive for killing the Rani — or none that I could discover. But the tailor's daughter interested me.'

'Her name was Kusum. She was twelve or thirteen years old — a thin dark girl, with lovely black eyes and a swift, disarming smile. While I was making my routine enquiries in the vicinity of the Rani's house, I noticed that the girl always tried to avoid me. When I questioned her about the Rani, and about her own movements on the day of the crime, she pretended to be very vague and stupid.'

'But I could see she was not stupid, and I became convinced that she knew something unusual about the Rani. She might even know something about the murder. She could have been protecting someone, and was afraid to tell me what she knew. Often, when I spoke to her of the violence of the Rani's death, I saw fear in her eyes. I began to think the girl's life might be in danger, and I had a close watch kept on her. I liked her. I liked her youth and freshness. and the innocence and wonder in her eyes. I spoke to her whenever I could, kindly and paternally, and though I knew she rather liked me and found me amusing — the ups and downs of Panauli always left me panting for breath — and though I could see that she *wanted* to tell me something, she always held back at the last moment.'

'Then, one afternoon while I was in the Rani's house going through her effects, I saw something glistening in a narrow crack near the door-step. I would not have noticed it if the sun had not been pouring through the window, glinting off the little object. I stooped and picked up a piece of glass. It was part of a broken bangle.'

'I turned the fragment over in my hand. There was something familiar about its colour and design. Didn't Kusum wear similar glass bangles? I went to look for the girl but she was not at her father's shop. I was told that she had gone down the hill, to gather firewood.'

'I decided to take the narrow path down the hill. It went round some rocks and cactus, and then disappeared into a forest of oak trees. I found Kusum sitting at the edge of the forest, a bundle of twigs beside her.'

'You are always wandering about alone,' I said. 'Don't you feel afraid?'

'It is safer when I am alone,' she replied. 'Nobody comes here.'

'I glanced quickly at the bangles on her wrist, and noticed that their colour matched that of broken piece. I held out the bit of broken glass and said, 'I found it in the Rani's house. It must have fallen . . .'

'She did not wait for me to finish what I was saying. With a look of terror, she sprang up from the grass and fled into the forest.'

'I was completely taken aback. I had not expected such a reaction.

Of what significance was the broken bangle? I hurried after the girl, slipping on the smooth pine needles that covered the slopes. I was searching amongst the trees when I heard someone sobbing behind me. When I turned round, I saw the girl standing on a boulder, facing me with an axe in her hands.'

'When Kusum saw me staring at her, she raised the axe and rushed down the slope towards me.'

'I was too bewildered to be able to do anything but stare with open mouth as she rushed at me with the axe. The impetus of her run would have brought her right up against me, and the axe, coming down, would probably have crushed my skull, thick though it is. But while she was still six feet from me, the axe flew out of her hands. It sprang into the air as though it had a life of its own and came curving towards me.'

'In spite of my weight, I moved swiftly aside. The axe grazed my shoulder and sank into the soft bark of the tree behind me. And Kusum dropped at my feet, weeping hysterically.'

Inspector Keemat Lal paused in order to replenish his glass. He took a long pull at the beer, and the froth glistened on his moustache.

'And then what happened?' I prompted him.

'Perhaps it could only have happened in India — and to a person like me,' he said. 'This sudden compassion for the person you are supposed to destroy. Instead of being furious and outraged, instead of seizing the girl and marching her off to the police station, I stroked her head and said silly comforting things.'

'And she told you that she had killed the Rani?'

'She told me how the Rani had called her to her house and given her tea and sweets. Mr. Kapur had been there. After some time he began stroking Kusum's arms and squeezing her knees. She had drawn away, but Kapur kept pawing her. The Rani was telling Kusum not to be afraid, that no harm would come to her. Kusum slipped away from the man and made a rush for the door. The Rani caught her by the shoulders and pushed her back into the room. The Rani was getting angry. Kusum saw the axe lying in a corner of the room. She seized it, raised it above her head and threatened Kapur. The man realised that he had gone too far, and, valuing his neck, backed away. But the Rani, in a great rage, sprang at the girl. And Kusum, in desperation and panic, brought the axe down across the Rani's head.'

'The Rani fell to the ground. Without waiting to see what Kapur might do, Kusum fled from the house. Her bangle must have broken when she stumbled against the door. She ran into the forest and, after concealing the axe amongst some tall ferns, lay weeping on the grass until it grew dark. But such was her nature, and such the resilience of youth, that she recovered sufficiently to be able to return home looking her normal self. And during the following days she managed to remain silent about the whole business.'

'What did you do about it?' I asked.

Keemat lal looked me straight in my berry eye.

'Nothing,' he said. 'I did absolutely nothing. I couldn't have the girl put away in a remand home. It would have crushed her spirit.'

'And what about Kapur?'

'Oh, he had his own reasons for remaining quiet, as you may guess. No, the case was closed — or perhaps I should say the file was put in my pending tray. My promotion, too, went into the pending tray.'

'It didn't turn out very well for you,' I said.

'No. Here I am in Shahpur, and still an Inspector. But, tell me, what would you have done if you had been in my place?'

I considered his question carefully for a moment or two, then said, 'I suppose it would have depended on how much sympathy the girl evoked in me. She had killed in innocence . . .'

'Then you would have put your personal feelings above your duty to uphold the law?'

'Yes. But I would not have made a very good policeman.'

'Exactly.'

'Still, it's a pity that Kapur got off so easily.'

'There was no alternative if I was to let the girl go. But he didn't get off altogether. He found himself in trouble later on for swindling some manufacturing concern, and went to jail for a couple of years.'

'And the girl — did you see her again?'

'Well, before I was transferred from Panauli, I saw her occasionally on the road. She was usually on her way to school. She would greet me with joined palms, and call me Uncle.'

The beer bottles were all empty, and Inspector Keemat Lal got up to leave. His final words to me were, 'I should never have been a policeman.'

A Face in the Night

It may give you some idea of rural humour if I begin this tale with an anecdote that concerns me. I was walking alone through a village at night when I met an old man carrying a lantern. I found, to my surprise, that the man was blind. 'Old man,' I asked, 'if you cannot see, why do you carry a lantern?'

I carry this,' he replied, 'so that fools do not stumble against me in the dark.'

This incident has only a slight connection with the story that follows, but I think it provides the right sort of tone and setting. Mr. Oliver, an Anglo-Indian teacher, was returning to his school late one night, on the outskirts of the hill station of Simla. The school was conducted on English public school lines and the boys, most of them from well-to-do Indian families, wore blazers, caps and ties. Life magazine, in a feature on India, had once called this school the 'Eton of the East'. Mr. Oliver had been teaching in the school for several years. (He is no longer there). The Simla bazaar, with its cinemas and restaurants, was about two miles from the school; and Mr. Oliver, a bachelor, usually strolled into the town in the evening, returning after dark, when he would take a short cut through a pine forest.

When there was a strong wind, the pine trees made sad, eerie sounds that kept most people to the main road. But Mr. Oliver was not a nervous or imaginative man. He carried a torch and, on the night I write of, its pale gleam — the batteries were running down — moved fitfully over the narrow forest path. When its flickering light fell on the figure of a boy, who was sitting alone on a rock, Mr.

Oliver stopped. Boys were not supposed to be out of school after 7 p.m., and it was now well past nine.

'What are you doing out here, boy?' asked Mr. Oliver sharply, moving closer so that he could recognise the miscreant. But even as he approached the boy, Mr. Oliver sensed that something was wrong. The boy appeared to be crying. His head hung down, he held his face in his hands, and his body shook convulsively. It was a strange, soundless weeping, and Mr. Oliver felt distinctly uneasy.

'Well — what's the matter?' he asked, his anger giving way to concern. 'What are you crying for?' The boy would not answer or look up. His body continued to be racked with silent sobbing. 'Come on, boy, you shouldn't be out here at this hour. Tell me the trouble. Look up!' The boy looked up. He took his hands from his face and looked up at his teacher. The light from Mr. Oliver's torch fell on the boy's face — if you could call it a face.

He had no eyes, ears, nose or mouth. It was just a round smooth head — with a school cap on top of it. And that's where the story should end — as indeed it has, for several people who have had similar experiences and dropped dead of inexplicable heart attacks. But for Mr. Oliver it did not end there.

The torch fell from his trembling hand. He turned and scrambled down the path, running blindly through the trees and calling for help. He was still running towards the school buildings when he saw a lantern swinging in the middle of the path. Mr. Oliver had never before been so pleased to see the night-watchman. He stumbled up the watchman, gasping for breath and speaking incoherently. 'What is it, *Sahib*?' asked the watchman. 'Has there been an accident? Why are you running?'

'I saw something — something horrible — a boy weeping in the forest — and he had no face!' 'No face, Sahib?' 'No eyes, nose, mouth — nothing.' 'Do you mean it was like this, *Sahib*?' asked the watchman, and raised the lamp to his own face. The watchman had no eyes, no ears, no features at all — not even an eyebrow! The wind blew the lamp out, and Mr. Oliver had his heart attack.

A Job Well done

Dhuki, the gardener, was clearing up the weeds that grew in profusion around the old disused well. He was an old man, skinny and bent and spindly-legged; but he had always been like that; his strength lay in his wrists and in his long, tendril-like fingers. He looked as frail as a petunia, but he had the tenacity of a vine.

'Are you going to cover the well?' I asked. I was eight, a great favourite of Dhuki. He had been the gardener long before my birth; had worked for my father, until my father died, and now worked for my mother and step-father.

'I must cover it, I suppose,' said Dhuki. 'That's what the 'Major *sahib*' wants. He'll be back any day, and if he finds the well still uncoverd he'll get into one of his raging fits and I'll be looking for another job!'

The 'Major *sahib*' was my step-father, Major Summerskill. A tall, hearty, back-slapping man, who liked polo and pig-sticking. He was quite unlike my father. My father had always given me books to read. The Major said I would become a dreamer if I read too much, and took the books away. I hated him; and did not think much of my mother for marrying him.

'The boy's too soft,' I heard him tell my mother. 'I must see that he gets riding lessons.'

But, before the riding lessons could be arranged, the Major's regiment was ordered to Peshawar. Trouble was expected from some of the frontier tribes. He was away for about two months. Before leaving, he had left strict instructions for Dhuki to cover up the old well.

'Too damned dangerous having an open well in the middle of the garden,' my step-father had said. 'Make sure that it's completely covered by the time I get back.'

Dhuki was loth to cover up the old well. It had been there for over 50 years, long before the house had been built. In its walls lived a colony of pigeons. Their soft cooing filled the garden with a lovely sound. And during the hot, dry, summer months, when taps ran dry, the well was always a dependable source of water. The *bhisti* still used it, filling his goatskin bag with the cool clear water and sprinkling the paths around the house to keep the dust down.

Dhuki pleaded with my mother to let him leave the well uncovered.

'What will happen to the pigeons?' he asked.

'Oh, surely they can find another well,' said my mother. 'Do close it up soon, Dhuki. I don't want the *Sahib* to come back and find that you haven't done anything about it.'

My mother seemed just a little bit afraid of the Major. How can we be afraid of those we love? It was a question that puzzled me then, and puzzles me still.

The Major's absence made life pleasant again. I returned to my books, spent long hours in my favourite banyan tree, ate buckets of mangoes, and dawdled in the garden talking to Dhuki.

Neither he nor I were looking forward to the Major's return. Dhuki had stayed on after my mother's second marriage only out of loyalty to her and affection for me; he had really been my father's man. But my mother had always appeared deceptively frail and helpless, and most men, Major Summerskill included, felt protective towards her. She liked people who did things for her.

'Your father liked this well,' said Dhuki. 'He would often sit here in the evenings, with a book in which he made drawings of birds and flowers and insects.'

I remembered those drawings, and I remembered how they had all been thrown away by the Major when he had moved into the house. Dhuki knew about it too. I didn't keep much from him.

'It's a sad business closing this well,' said Dhuki again. 'Only a fool or a drunkard is likely to fall into it.'

But he had made his preparations. Planks of *sal* wood, bricks and cement were neatly piled up around the well.

'Tomorrow,' said Dhuki. 'Tomorrow I will do it. Not today. Let the birds remain for one more day. In the morning, *baba*, you can help me drive the birds from the well.'

On the day my step-father was expected back, my mother hired a *tonga* and went to the bazaar to do some shopping. Only a few people had cars in those days. Even colonels went about in *tongas*. Now, a clerk finds it beneath his dignity to sit in one.

As the Major was not expected before evening, I decided I would make full use of my last free morning, I took all my favourite books and stored them away in an outhouse, where I could come for them from time to time. Then, my pockets bursting with mangoes, I climbed into the banyan tree. It was the darkest and coolest place on a hot day in June.

From behind the screen of leaves that concealed me, I could see Dhuki moving about near the well. He appeared to be most unwilling to get on with the job of covering it up.

'*Baba!*' he called, several times; but I did not feel like stirring from the banyan tree. Dhuki grasped a long plank of wood and placed it across one end of the well. He started hammering. From my vantage point in the banyan tree, he looked very bent and old.

A jingle of *tonga* bells and the squeak of unoiled wheels told me that a *tonga* was coming in at the gate. It was too early for my mother to be back. I peered through the thick, waxy leaves of the tree, and nearly fell off my branch in surprise. It was my step-father, the Major! He had arrived earlier than expected.

I did not come down from the tree. I had no intention of confronting my step-father until my mother returned.

The Major had climbed down from the *tonga* and was watching his luggage being carried on to the verandah. He was red in the face and the ends of his handlebar moustache were stiff with brilliantine. Dhuki approached with a half-hearted *salaam*.

'Ah, so there you are, you old scoundrel!' exclaimed the Major, trying to sound friendly and jocular. 'More jungle than garden, from what I can see. You're geting too old for this sort of work, Dhuki. Time to retire! And where's the *Memsahib*?'

'Gone to the bazaar,' said Dhuki.

'And the boy?'

Dhuki shrugged. 'I have not seen the boy, today, *Sahib*.'

'Damn!' said the Major. 'A fine homecoming, this. Well, wake up the cook-boy and tell him to get some sodas.'

'Cook-boy's gone away,' said Dhuki.

'Well, I'll be double-damned,' said the major.

The *tonga* went away, and the Major started pacing up and down the garden path. Then he saw Dhuki's unfinished work at the well. He grew purple in the face, strode across to the well, and started ranting at the old gardener.

Dhuki began making excuses. He said something about a shortage of bricks; the sickness of a niece; unsatisfactory cement; unfavourable weather; unfavourable gods. When none of this seemed to satisfy the Major, Dhuki began mumbling about something bubbling up from the bottom of the well, and pointed down into its depths. The Major stepped on to the low parapet and looked down. Dhuki kept pointing. The Major leant over a little.

Dhuki's hand moved swiftly, like a conjurer's making a pass. He did not actually push the Major. He appeared merely to tap him once on the bottom. I caught a glimpse of my step-father's boots as he disappeared into the well. I couldn't help thinking of Alice in Wonderland, of Alice disappearing down the rabbit hole.

There was a tremendous splash, and the pigeons flew up, circling the well thrice before settling on the roof of the bungalow.

By lunch time — or tiffin, as we called it then — Dhuki had the well covered over with the wooden planks.

'The Major will be pleased,' said my mother, when she came home. 'It will be quite ready by evening, won't it, Dhuki?'

By evening, the well had been completely bricked over. It was the fastest bit of work Dhuki had ever done.

Over the next few weeks, my mother's concern changed to anxiety, her anxiety to melancholy, and her melancholy to resignation. By being gay and high-spirited myself, I hope I did something to cheer her up. She had written to the Colonel of the Regiment, and had been informed that the Major had gone home on leave a fortnight previously. Somewhere, in the vastness of India, the Major had disappeared.

It was easy enough to disappear and never be found. After several months had passed without the Major turning up, it was presumed that one of two things must had happened. Either he had been murdered on the train, and his corpse flung into a river; or, he had run away with a tribal girl and was living in some remote corner of the country.

Life had to carry on for the rest of us. The rains were over, and the guava season was approaching.

My mother was receiving visits from a colonel of His Majesty's

32nd Foot. He was an elderly, easy-going, seemingly absent-minded man, who didn't get in the way at all, but left slabs of chocolate lying around the house.

'A good *Sahib*,' observed Dhuki, as I stood beside him behind the bougainvillaea, watching the colonel saunter up the verandah steps. 'See how well he wears his *sola topee*! It covers his head completely.'

'He's bald underneath,' I said.

'No matter. I think he will be all right.'

'And if he isn't,' I said, 'we can always open up the well again.'

Dhuki dropped the nozzle of the hose pipe, and water gushed out over our feet. But he recovered quickly, and taking me by the hand, led me across to the old well, now surmounted by a three-tiered cement platform which looked rather like a wedding cake.

'We must not forget our old well,' he said. 'Let us make it beautiful, *baba*. Some flower pots, perhaps.'

And together we fetched pots, and decorated the covered well with ferns and geraniums. Everyone congratulated Dhuki on the fine job he'd done. My only regret was that the pigeons had gone away.

The Story of Madhu

I met little Madhu several years ago, when I lived alone in an obscure town near the Himalayan foothills. I was in my late twenties then, and my outlook on life was still quite romantic; the cynicism that was to come with the thirties had not yet set in.

I preferred the solitude of the small district town to the kind of social life I might have found in the cities; and in my books, my writing and the surrounding hills, there was enough for my pleasure and occupation.

On summer mornings I would often sit beneath an old mango tree, with a notebook or a sketch pad on my knees. The house which I had rented (for a very nominal sum) stood on the outskirts of the town; and a large tank and a few poor houses could be seen from the garden wall. A narrow public pathway passed under the low wall.

One morning, while I sat beneath the mango tree, I saw a young girl of about nine, wearing torn clothes, darting about on the pathway and along the high banks of the tank.

Sometimes she stopped to look at me; and, when I showed that I noticed her, she felt encouraged and gave me a shy, fleeting smile. The next day I discovered her leaning over the garden wall, following my actions as I paced up and down on the grass.

In a few days an acquaintance had been formed. I began to take the girl's presence for granted, and even to look for her; and she, in turn, would linger about on the pathway until she saw me come out of the house.

One day, as she passed the gate, I called her to me.

'What is your name?' I asked. 'And where do you live?'

'Madhu,' she said, brushing back her long untidy black hair and smiling at me from large black eyes. She pointed across the road: 'I live with my grandmother.'

'Is she very old?' I asked.

Madhu nodded confidingly and whispered: 'A hundred years . . .'

'We will never be that old,' I said. She was very slight and frail, like a flower growing in a rock, vulnerable to wind and rain.

I discovered later that the old lady was not her grandmother but a childless woman who had found the baby girl on the banks of the tank. Madhu's real parentage was unknown; but the wizened old woman had, out of compassion, brought up the child as her own.

My gate once entered, Madhu included the garden in her circle of activities. She was there every morning, chasing butterflies, stalking squirrels and mynahs, her voice brimming with laughter, her slight figure flitting about between the trees.

Sometimes, but not often, I gave her a toy or a new dress; and one day she put aside her shyness and brought me a present of a nose-gay, made up of marigolds and wild blue-cotton flowers.

'For you,' she said, and put the flowers in my lap.

'They are very beautiful,' I said, picking out the brightest marigold and putting it in her hair. 'But they are not as beautiful as you.'

More than a year passed before I began to take more than a mildly patronizing interest in Madhu.

It occurred to me after some time that she should be taught to read and write, and I asked a local teacher to give her lessons in the garden for an hour every day. She clapped her hands with pleasure at the prospect of what was to be for her a fascinating new game.

In a few weeks Madhu was surprising us with her capacity for absorbing knowledge. She always came to me to repeat the lessons of the day, and pestered me with questions on a variety of subjects. How big was the world? And were the stars really like our world? Or were they the sons and daughters of the Sun and the Moon?

My interest in Madhu deepened, and my life, so empty till then, became imbued with a new purpose. As she sat on the grass beside me, reading aloud, or listening to me with a look of complete trust and belief, all the love that had been lying dormant in me during my years of self-exile surfaced in a sudden surge of tenderness.

Three years glided away imperceptibly, and at the age of 13 Madhu was on the verge of blossoming into a woman. I began to feel a certain responsibility towards her.

It was dangerous, I knew, to allow a child so pretty to live almost alone and unprotected, and to run unrestrained about the grounds. And in a censorious society she would be made to suffer if she spent too much time in my company.

She could see no need for any separation; but I decided to send her to a mission school in the next district, where I could visit her from time to time.

'But why?' said Madhu. 'I can learn more from you, and from the teacher who comes. I am so happy here.'

'You will meet other girls and make many friends,' I told her. 'I will come to see you. And, when you come home, we will be even happier. It is good that you should go.'

It was the middle of June, a hot and oppressive month in the Siwaliks. Madhu had expressed her readiness to go to school, and when, one evening, I did not see her as usual in the garden, I thought nothing of it; but the next day I was informed that she had fever and could not leave the house.

Illness was something Madhu had not known before, and for this reason I felt afraid. I hurried down the path which led to the old woman's cottage. It seemed strange that I had never once entered it during my long friendship with Madhu.

It was a humble mud hut, the ceiling just high enough to enable me to stand upright, the room dark but clean. Madhu was lying on a string cot exhausted by fever, her eyes closed, her long hair unkempt, one small hand hanging over the side.

It struck me then how little, during all this time, I had thought of her physical comforts. There was no chair; I knelt down, and took her hand in mine. I knew, from the fierce heat of her body, that she was seriously ill.

She recognized my touch, and a smile passed across her face before she opened her eyes. She held on to my hand, then laid it across her cheek.

I looked round the little room in which she had grown up. It had scarcely an article of furniture apart from two string cots, on one of which the old woman sat and watched us, her white, wizened head nodding like a puppet's.

In a corner lay Madhu's little treasures. I recognized among them the presents which during the past four years I had given her. She had kept everything. On her dark arm she still wore a small piece of ribbon which I had playfully tied there about a year ago. She had given her heart, even before she was conscious of possessing one, to a stranger unworthy of the gift.

As the evening drew on, a gust of wind blew open the door of the dark room, and a gleam of sunshine streamed in, lighting up a portion of the wall. It was the time when every evening she would join me under the mango tree. She had been quiet for almost an hour, and now a slight pressure of her hand drew my eyes back to her face.

'What will we do now?' she said. 'When will you send me to school?'

'Not for a long time. First you must get well and strong. That is all that matters.'

She didn't seem to hear me. I think she knew she was dying, but she did not resent its happening.

'Who will read to you under the tree?' she went on. 'Who will look after you?' she asked, with the solicitude of a grown woman.

'You will, Madhu. You are grown up now. There will be no one else to look after me.'

The old woman was standing at my shoulder. A hundred years — and little Madhu was slipping away. The woman took Madhu's hand from mine, and laid it gently down. I sat by the cot a little longer, and then I rose to go, all the loneliness in the world pressing upon my heart.

The Cherry Tree

One day, when Rakesh was six, he walked home from the Mussoorie bazaar eating cherries. They were a little sweet, a little sour; small, bright red cherries, which had come all the way from the Kashmir Valley.

Here in the Himalayan foothills where Rakesh lived, there were not many fruit trees. The soil was stony, and the dry cold winds stunted the growth of most plants. But on the more sheltered slopes there were forests of oak and deodar.

Rakesh lived with his grandfather on the outskirts of Mussoorie, just where the forest began. His father and mother lived in a small village fifty miles away, where they grew maize and rice and barley in narrow terraced fields on the lower slopes of the mountain. But there were no schools in the village, and Rakesh's parents were keen that he should go to school. As soon as he was of school-going age, they sent him to stay with his grandfather in Mussoorie.

Grandfather was a retired forest ranger. He had a little cottage outside the town.

Rakesh was on his way home from school when he bought the cherries. He paid fifty paise for the bunch. It took him about half-an-hour to walk home, and by the time he reached the cottage there were only three cherries left.

'Have a cherry, Grandfather,' he said, as soon as he saw his grandfather in the garden.

Grandfather took one cherry and Rakesh promptly ate the other two. He kept the last seed in this mouth for some time, rolling it round and round on his tongue until all the tang had gone. Then he

133

placed the seed on the palm of his hand and studied it.

'Are cherry seeds lucky?' asked Rakesh.

'Of course.'

'Then I'll keep it.'

'Nothing is lucky if you put it away. If you want luck, you must put it to some use.'

'What can I do with a seed?'

'Plant it.'

So Rakesh found a small spade and began to dig up a flower-bed.

'Hey, not there,' said Grandfather. 'I've sown mustard in that bed. Plant it in that shady corner, where it won't be disturbed.'

Rakesh went to a corner of the garden where the earth was soft and yielding. He did not have to dig. He pressed the seed into the soil with his thumb and it went right in.

Then he had his lunch, and ran off to play cricket with his friends, and forgot all about the cherry seed.

When it was winter in the hills, a cold wind blew down from the snows and went *whoo-whoo-whoo* in the deodar trees, and the garden was dry and bare. In the evenings Grandfather and Rakesh sat over a charcoal fire, and Grandfather told Rakesh stories — stories, about people who turned into animals, and ghosts who lived in trees, and beans that jumped and stones that wept — and in turn Rakesh would read to him from the newspaper, Grandfather's eyesight being rather weak. Rakesh found the newspaper very dull — especially after the stories — but Grandfather wanted all the news . . .

They knew it was spring when the wild duck flew north again, to Siberia. Early in the morning, when he got up to chop wood and light a fire, Rakesh saw the V. shaped formation streaming northwards, the calls of the birds carrying clearly through the thin mountain air.

One morning in the garden he bent to pick up what he thought was a small twig and found to his surprise that it was well rooted. He stared at it for a moment, then ran to fetch Grandfather, calling, 'Dada, come and look, the cherry tree has come up!'

'What cherry tree?' asked Grandfather, who had forgotten about it.

'The seed we planted last year — look, it's come up!'

Rakesh went down on his haunches, while Grandfather bent almost double and peered down at the tiny tree. It was about four inches high.

'Yes, it's a cherry tree,' said Grandfather. 'You should water it now and then.'

Rakesh ran indoors and came back with a bucket of water.

'Don't drown it!' said Grandfather.

Rakesh gave it a sprinkling and circled it with pebbles.

'What are the pebbles for?' asked Grandfather.

'For privacy,' said Rakesh.

He looked at the tree every morning but it did not seem to be growing very fast. So he stopped looking at it — except quickly, out of the corner of his eye. And, after a week or two, when he allowed himself to look at it properly, he found that it had grown — at least an inch!

That year the monsoon rains came early and Rakesh plodded to and from school in raincoat and gum boots. Ferns sprang from the trunks of trees, strange-looking lilies came up in the long grass, and even when it wasn't raining the trees dripped and mist came curling up the valley. The cherry tree grew quickly in this season.

It was about two feet high when a goat entered the garden and ate all the leaves. Only the main stem and two thin branches remained.

'Never mind,' said Grandfather, seeing that Rakesh was upset. 'It will grow again, cherry trees are tough.'

Towards the end of the rainy season new leaves appeared on the tree. Then a woman cutting grass scrambled down the hillside, her scythe swishing through the heavy monsoon foliage. She did not try to avoid the tree: one sweep, and the cherry tree was cut in two.

When Grandfather saw what had happened, he went after the woman and scolded her; but the damage could not be repaired.

'Maybe it will die now,' said Rakesh.

'Maybe,' said Grandfather.

But the cherry tree had no intention of dying.

By the time summer came round again, it had sent out several new shoots with tender green leaves. Rakesh had grown taller too He was eight now, a sturdy boy with curly black hair and deep black eyes. 'Blackberry eyes,' Grandfather called them.

That monsoon Rakesh went home to his village, to help his father and mother with the planting and ploughing and sowing. He was thinner but stronger when he came back to Grandfather's house at the end of the rains, to find that the cherry tree had grown another foot. It was now up to his chest.

Even when there was rain, Rakesh would sometimes water the

tree. He wanted it to know that he was there.

One day he found a bright green praying-mantis perched on a branch, peering at him with bulging eyes. Rakesh let it remain there. It was the cherry tree's first visitor.

The next visitor was a hairy caterpillar, who started making a meal of the leaves. Rakesh removed it quickly and dropped it on a heap of dry leaves.

'Come back when you're a butterfly,' he said.

Winter came early. The cheery tree bent low with the weight of snow. Field-mice sought shelter in the roof of the cottage. The road from the valley was blocked, and for several days there was no newspaper, and this made Grandfather quite grumpy. His stories began to have unhappy endings.

In February it was Rakesh's birthday. He was nine — and the tree was four, but almost as tall as Rakesh.

One morning, when the sun came out, Grandfather came into the garden to 'let some warmth get into my bones,' as he put it. He stopped in front of the cherry tree, stared at it for a few moments, and then called out, 'Rakesh! Come and look! Come quickly before it falls!'

Rakesh and Grandfather gazed at the tree as though it had performed a miracle. There was a pale pink blossom at the end of a branch.

The following year there were more blossoms. And suddenly the tree was taller than Rakesh, even though it was less than half his age. And then it was taller than Grandfather, who was older than some of the oak trees.

But Rakesh had grown too. He could run and jump and climb trees as well as most boys, and he read a lot of books, although he still liked listening to Grandfather's tales.

In the cherry free, bees came to feed on the nectar in the blossoms, and tiny birds pecked at the blossoms and broke them off. But the tree kept blossoming right through the spring, and there were always more blossoms than birds.

That summer there were small cherries on the tree. Rakesh tasted one and spat it out.

'It's too sour,' he said.

'They'll be better next year,' said Grandfather.

But the birds liked them — especially the bigger birds, such as the bulbuls and scarlet minivets — and they flitted in and out of the foliage, feasting on the cherries.

On a warm sunny afternoon, when even the bees looked sleepy, Rakesh was looking for Grandfather without finding him in any of his favourite places around the house. Then he looked out of the bedroom window and saw Grandfather reclining on a cane chair under the cherry tree.

'There's just the right amount of shade here,' said Grandfather. 'And I like looking at the leaves.'

'They're pretty leaves,' said Rakesh. 'And they are always ready to dance. If there's breeze.'

After Grandfather had come indoors. Rakesh went into the garden and lay down on the grass beneath the tree. He gazed up through the leaves at the great blue sky; and turning on his side, he could see the mountain striding away into the clouds. He was still lying beneath the tree when the evening shadows crept across the garden. Grandfather came back and sat down beside Rakesh, and they waited in silence until the stars came out and the nightjar began to call. In the forest below, the crickets and cicadas began tuning up; and suddenly the trees were full of the sound of insects.

'There are so many trees in the forest,' said Rakesh. 'What's so special about this tree? Why do we like it so much?'

'We planted it ourselves,' said Grandfather. That's why it's special.'

'Just one small seed,' said Rakesh, and he touched the smooth bark of the tree that had grown. He ran his hand along the trunk of the tree and put his finger to the tip of a leaf. 'I wonder,' he whispered. 'Is this what it feels to be God?

My Father's Trees in Dehra

Our trees still grow in Dehra. This is one part of the world where trees are a match for man. An old *peepul* may be cut down to make way for a new building; two *peepul* trees will sprout from the walls of the building. In Dehra the air is moist, the soil hospitable to seeds and probing roots. The valley of Dehra Dun lies between the first range of the Himalayas and the smaller but older Siwalik range. Dehra is an old town, but it was not in the reign of Rajput prince or Mogul king that it really grew and flourished; it acquired a certain size and importance with the coming of British and Anglo-Indian settlers. The English have an affinity with trees, and in the rolling hills of Dehra they discovered a retreat which, in spite of snakes and mosquitoes, reminded them, just a little bit, of England's green and pleasant land.

The mountains to the north are austere and inhospitable; the plains to the south are flat, dry and dusty. But Dehra is green. I look out of the train window at daybreak, to see the *sal* and *shisham* trees sweep by majestically, while trailing vines and great clumps of bamboo give the forest a darkness and density which add to its mystery. There are still a few tigers in these forests; only a few, and perhaps they will survive, to stalk the spotted deer and drink at forest pools.

I grew up in Dehra. My grandfather built a bungalow on the outskirts of the town, at the turn of the century. The house was sold a few years after independence. No one knows me now in Dehra, for it is over twenty years since I left the place, and my boyhood friends are scattered and lost; and although the India of Kim is no more, and the Grand Trunk Road is now a procession of trucks instead of a slow-moving caravan of horses and camels, India is still a country in which people are easily lost and quickly forgotten.

From the station I take a *tonga*. I can take either a taxi or a snappy little scooter-*rickshaw* (Dehra had neither, before 1950), but, because I am on an unashamedly sentimental pilgrimage, I take a *tonga*, drawn by a lean, listless pony, and driven by a tubercular old Moslem in a shabby green waistcoat. Only two or three *tongas* stand outside the station. There were always twenty or thirty here in the nineteen-forties, when I came home from boarding school to be met at the station by my grandfather; but the days of the *tonga* are nearly over, and in many ways this is a good thing, because most *tonga* ponies are overworked and underfed. Its wheels squeaking from lack of oil and its seat slipping out from under me, the *tonga* drags me through the bazaars of Dehra. A couple of miles at this slow, funereal pace makes me impatient to use my own legs, and I dismiss the *tonga* when we get to the small Dilaram Bazaar.

It is a good place from which to start walking.

The Dilaram Bazaar has not changed very much. The shops are run by a new generation of bakers, barbers and *banias*, but professions have not changed. The cobblers belong to the lower castes, the bakers are Moslems, the tailors are Sikhs. Boys still fly kites from the flat roof-tops, and women wash clothes on the canal steps. The canal comes down from Rajpur and goes underground here, to emerge about a mile away.

I have to walk only a furlong to reach my grandfather's house. The road is lined with eucalyptus, jacaranda and laburnum trees. In the compounds there are small groves of mangoes, *lichis* and papayas. The poinsettia thrusts its scarlet leaves over garden wall. Every verandah has its bougainvillaea creeper, every garden its bed of marigolds. Potted palms, those symbols of Victorian snobbery, are popular with Indian housewives. There are a few houses, but most of the bungalows were built by 'old India hands,' on their retirement from the Army, the police or the railways. Most of the present owners are Indian businessmen or Government officials.

I am standing outside my grandfather's house. The wall has been raised, and the wicket-gate has disappeared; I cannot get a clear view of the house and garden. The nameplate identifies the owner as Major General Saigal; the house has had more than one owner since my grandparents sold it in 1949.

On the other side of the road there is an orchard of *lichi* trees. This is not the season for fruit, and there is no one looking after the garden. By taking a little path that goes through the orchard, I reach higher ground and gain a better view of our old house.

Grandfather built the house with granite rocks taken from the foothills. It shows no sign of age. The lawn has disappeared; but the big jackfruit tree, giving shade to the side verandah, is still there. In this tree I spent my afternoons, absorbed in my Magnets, Champions and Hotspurs, while sticky mango juice trickled down my chin. (One could not eat the jackfruit unless it was cooked into a vegetable curry.) There was a hole in the bole of the tree in which I kept my pocket-knife, top, catapult and any badges or buttons that could be saved from my father's RAF tunics when he came home on leave. There was also an Iron Cross, a relic of the First World War, given to me by my grandfather. I have managed to keep the Iron Cross; but what did I do with my top and catapult? Memory fails me. Possibly they are still in the hole in the jackfruit tree; I must have forgotten to collect them when we went away after my father's death. I am seized by a whimsical urge to walk in at the gate, climb into the branches of the jackfruit tree, and recover my lost possessions. What would the present owner, the Major General (retired), have to say if I politely asked permission to look for a catapult left behind more than twenty years ago?

An old man is coming down the path through the *lichi* trees. He is not a Major General but a poor street vendor. He carries a small tin trunk on his head, and walks very slowly. When he sees me he stops and asks me if I will buy something. I can think of nothing I need, but the old man looks so tired, so very old, that I am afraid he will collapse if he moves any further along the path without resting. So I ask him to show me his wares. He cannot get the box off his head by himself, but together we manage to set it down in the shade, and the old man insists on spreading its entire contents on the grass;: bangles, combs, shoelaces, safety-pins, cheap stationery, buttons, pomades, elastic and scores of other household necessities.

When I refuse buttons because there is no one to sew them on for me, he piles me with safety-pins. I say no; but as he moves from one article to another, his querulous, persuasive voice slowly wears down my resistance, and I end up by buying envelopes, a letter-pad (pink roses on bright blue paper), a one-rupee fountain pen guaranteed to leak and several yards of elastic. I have no idea what I will do with the elastic, but the old man convinces me that I cannot live without it.

Exhausted by the effort of selling me a lot of things I obviously do not want, he closes his eyes and leans back against the trunk of a *lichi* tree. For a moment I feel rather nervous. Is he going to die sitting here beside me? He sinks to his haunches and his chin on his hands. He only wants to talk.

'I am very tired, *hazoor*,' he says. 'Please do not mind if I sit here for a while.'

'Rest for as long as you like,' I say. 'That's a heavy load you've been carrying.'

He comes to life at the chance of a conversation, and says, 'When I was a young man, it was nothing. I could carry my box up from Rajpur to Mussoorie by the bridle-path — seven steep miles! But now I find it difficult to cover the distance from the station to the Dilaram Bazaar.'

'Naturally. You are quite old.'

'I am seventy, *sahib*.'

'You look very fit for your age.' I say this to please him; he looks frail and brittle. 'Isn't there someone to help you?' I ask.

'I had a servant boy last month, but he stole my earnings and ran off to Delhi. I wish my son was alive — he would not have permitted me to work like a mule for a living — but he was killed in the riots in forty-seven.'

'Have you no other relatives?'

'I have outlived them all. That is the curse of a healthy life. Your friends, your loved ones, all go before you, and at the end you are left alone. But I must go too, before long. The road to the bazaar seems to grow longer every day. The stones are harder. The sun is hotter in the summer, and the wind much colder in the winter. Even some of the trees that were there in my youth have grown old and have died. I have outlived the trees.'

He has outlived the trees. He is like an old tree himself, gnarled and twisted. I have the feeling that if he falls asleep in the orchard, he will strike root here, sending out crooked branches. I can imagine a small bent tree wearing a black waist-coat; a living scarecrow.

He closes his eyes again, but goes on talking.

'The English *memsahibs* would buy great quantities of elastic. Today it is ribbons and bangles for the girls, and combs for the boys.

141

But I do not make much money. Not because I cannot walk very far. How many houses do I reach in a day? Ten, fifteen. But twenty years ago I could visit more than fifty houses. *That* makes a difference.'

'Have you always been here?'

'Most of my life, *hazoor*. I was here before they built the motor road to Mussoorie, I was here when the *sahibs* had their own carriages and ponies and the *memsahibs* their own *rickshaws*. I was here before there were any cinemas. I was here when the Prince of *Wales* came to Dehra Dun . . . Oh, I have been here a long time, *hazoor*. I was here when *that* house was built,' he says, pointing with his chin towards my grandfather's house. 'Fifty, sixty years ago it must have been. I cannot remember exactly. What is ten years when you have lived seventy? But it was a tall, red-bearded *sahib* who built that house. He kept many creatures as pets. A *kachwa*, a turtle, was one of them. And there was a python, which crawled into my box one day and gave me a terrible fright. The *sahib* used to keep it hanging from his shoulders, like a garland. His wife, the *burra-mem*, always bought a lot from me — lots a elastic. And there were sons, one a teacher, another in the Air Force, and there were always children in the house. Beautiful children. But they went away many years ago. Everyone has gone away.'

I do not tell him that I am one of the 'beautiful children,' I doubt if he would believe me. His memories are of another age, another place, and for him there are no strong bridges into the present.

'But others have come,' I say.

'True, and that is as it should be. That is not my complaint. My complaint — should God be listening — is that I have been left behind.'

He gets slowly to his feet and stands over his shabby tin box, gazing down at it with a mixture of disdain and affection. I help him to lift and balance it on the flattened cloth on his head. He does not have the energy to turn and make a salutation of any kind; but, setting his sights on the distant hills, he walks down the path with steps that are shaky and slow but still wonderfully straight.

I wonder how much longer he will live. Perhaps a year or two, perhaps a week, perhaps an hour. It will be an end of living, but it will not be death. He is too old for death; he can only sleep; he can only fall gently, like an old, crumpled brown leaf.

I leave the orchard. The bend in the road hides my grandfather's house. I reach the canal again. It emerges from under a small culvert, where ferns and maidenhair grow in the shade. The water, coming from a stream in the foot-hills, rushes along with a familiar sound; it does not lose its momentum until the canal has left the gently sloping streets of the town.

There are new buildings on this road, but the small police station is housed in the same old limewashed bungalow. A couple of off-duty policemen, partly uniformed but with their pyjamas on, stroll hand in hand on the grass verge. Holding hands (with persons of the same sex of course) is common practice in northern India, and denotes no special relationship.

I cannot forget this little police station. Nothing very exciting ever happened in its vicinity until, in 1947, communal riots broke out in Dehra. Then, bodies were regularly fished out of the canal and dumped on a growing pile in the station compound. I was only a boy, but when I looked over the wall at that pile of corpses, there was no one who paid any attention to me. They were too busy to send me away; at the same time they knew that I was perfectly safe. While Hindu and Moslem were at each other's throats, a white boy could walk the streets in safety. No one was any longer interested in the Europeans.

The people of Dehra are not violent by nature, and the town has no history of communal discord. But when refugees from the parti tioned Punjab poured into Dehra in their thousands, the atmos-phere became charged with tension. These refugees, many of them Sikhs, had lost their homes and livelihoods; many had seen their loved ones butchered. They were in a fierce and vengeful frame of mind. The clam, sleepy atmosphere of Dehra was shattered during two months of looting and murder. Those Moslems who could get away fled. The poorer members of the community remained in a refugee camp until the holocaust was over; then they returned to their former occupation, frightened and deeply mistrustful. The old boxman was one of them.

I cross the canal and take the road that will lead me to the river-bed. This was one of my father's favourite walks. He, too, was a walking man. Often, when he was home on leave, he would say, 'Ruskin, let's go for a walk,' and we would be slip off together and walk down to the river-bed or into the sugar-cane fields or across the railway lines and into the jungle.

On one of these walks (this was before Independence), I remember him saying, 'After the war is over, we'll be going to

England. Would you like that?'

'I don't know,' I said. 'Can't we stay in India?'

'It won't be ours any more.'

'Has it always been ours?' I asked.

'For a long time,' he said. 'Over two hundred years. But we have to give it back now.'

'Give it back to whom?' I asked. I was only nine.

'To the Indians,' said my father.

The only Indians I had known till then were my *ayah* and the cook and the gardener and their children, and I could not imagine them wanting to be rid of us. The only other Indian who came to the house was Dr. Ghose, and it was frequently said of him that he was more English than the English. I could understand my father better when he said, 'After the war, there'll be a job for me in England. There'll be nothing for me here.'

The war had at first been a distant event; but somehow it kept coming closer. My aunt, who lived in London with her two children, was killed with them during an air-raid; then my father's younger brother died of dysentery on the long walk out from Burma. Both these tragic events depressed my father. Never in good health (he had been prone to attacks of malaria), he looked more worn and wasted every time he came home. His personal life was far from being happy, as he and my mother had separated, she to marry again. I think he looked forward a great deal to the days he spent with me; far more than I could have realized at the time. I was someone to come back to; someone for whom things could be planned; someone who could learn from him.

Dehra suited him. He was always happy when he was among trees, and this happiness communicated itself to me. I felt like drawing close to him. I remember sitting beside him on the verandah steps one that was trailing near my feet. As we sat there, doing nothing in particular — in the best gardens, time has no meaning —I found that the tendril was moving almost imperceptibly away from me and towards my father. Twenty minutes later it had crossed the verandah steps and was touching my father's feet. This, in India, is the sweetest of salutations.

There is probably a scientific explanation for the plant's behaviour — something to do with the light and warmth on the verandah steps — but I like to think that its movements were motivated simply by an affection for my father. Sometimes, when I sat alone beneath a tree, I felt a little lonely or lost. As soon as my father joined me, the atmosphere lightened, the tree itself became more friendly.

Most of the fruit trees round the house were planted by father; but he was not content with planting trees in the garden. On rainy days we would walk beyond the river-bed, armed with cuttings and saplings, and then we would amble through the jungle, planting flowering shrubs betweeen the *sal* and *shisham* trees.

'But no one ever comes here,' I protested the first time. 'Who is going to see them?'

'Some day,' he said, '*someone* may come this way . . . If people keep cutting trees, instead of planting them, there'll soon be no forests left at all, and the world will be just one vast desert.'

The prospect of a world without trees became a sort of nightmare for me (and one reason why I shall never want to live on a treeless moon), and I assisted my father in his tree-planting with great enthusiasm.

'One day the trees will move again,' he said. 'They've been standing still for thousands of years. There was a time which they could walk about like people, but someone cast a spell on them and rooted them to one place. But they're always trying to move — see how they reach out with their arms!'

We found an island, a small rocky island in the middle of a dry river-bed. It was one of those river-beds, so common in the foot-hills, which are completely dry in the summer but flooded during the monsoon rains. The rains had just begun, and the stream could still be crossed on foot, when we set out with a number of tamarind, laburnum and coral-tree saplings and cuttings. We spent the day planting them on the island, then ate our lunch there, in the shelter of a wild plum.

My father went away soon after that tree-planting. Three months later, in Calcutta, he died.

I was sent to boarding-school. My grandparents sold the house and left Dehra. After school, I went to England. The years passed, my grandparents died, and when I returned to India I was the only member of the family in the country.

And now I am in Dehra again, on the road to the river-bed.

The houses with their trim gardens are soon behind me, and I am walking through fields of flowering mustard, which make a carpet of yellow blossom stretching away towards the jungle and the foothills.

The river-bed is dry at this time of the year. A herd of skinny cattle graze on the short brown grass at the edge of the jungle. The *sal* trees have been thinned out. Could our trees have survived? Will our island be there, or has some flash-flood during a heavy monsoon washed it away completely?

As I look across the day water-course, my eye is caught by the spectacular red plumes of the coral blossom. In contrast with the dry, rocky river-bed, the little island is a green oasis. I walk across to the trees and notice that a number of parrots have come to live in them. A koel-bird challenges me with a rising *who-are-you, who-are-you* . . .

But the trees seem to know me. They whisper among themselves and beckon me nearer. And looking round, I find that other trees and wild plants and grasses have sprung up under the protection of the trees we planted.

They have multiplied. They are moving. In this small forgotten corner of the world, my father's dreams are coming true, and the trees are moving again.

Panther's Moon

I

In the entire village, he was the first to get up. Even the dog, a big hill mastiff called Sheroo, was asleep in a corner of the dark room, curled up near the cold embers of the previous night's fire. Bisnu's tousled head emerged from his blanket. He rubbed the sleep from his eyes, and sat up on his haunches; then, gathering his wits, he crawled in the direction of the loud ticking that came from the battered little clock which occupied the second most honoured place in a niche in the wall. The most honoured place belonged to a picture of Ganesh, the god of learning, who had an elephant's head and a fat boy's body.

Bringing his face close to the clock, Bisnu could just make out the dial-hands. It was five o'clock. He had half-an-hour in which to get ready and leave.

He got up, in vest and underpants, and moved quietly towards the door. The soft tread of his bare feet woke Sheroo, and the big black dog rose silently and padded behind the boy. The door opened and closed, and then the boy and the dog were outside in the early dawn. The month was June, and nights were warm, even in the Himalayan valleys; but there was fresh dew on the grass. Bisnu felt the dew beneath his feet. He took a deep breath and began walking down to the stream.

The sound of the stream filled the small valley. At that early hour of the morning, it was the only sound; but Bisnu was hardly conscious of it. It was a sound he lived with and took for granted. It was only when he was over the hill, on his way to the distant town — and the sound of the stream grew distant — that he really began to notice it. And it was only when the stream was too far away to be heard that he really missed its sound.

He slipped out of his underclothes, gazed for a few moments at the goose-pimples rising on his flesh, and then dashed into the shallow stream. As he went further in, the cold mountain water reached his loins and navel, and he gasped with shock and pleasure. He drifted slowly with the current, swam across to a small inlet which formed a fairly deep pool, and plunged beneath the water. Sheroo hated cold water at this early hour. Had the sun been up, he would not have hesitated to join Bisnu. Now he contented himself with sitting on a smooth rock and gazing placidly at the slim brown boy splashing about in the clear water, in the widening light of dawn.

Bisnu did not stay long in the water. There wasn't time. When he returned to the house, he found his mother up, making tea and *chapatties*. His sister, Puja, was still asleep. She was a little older than Bisnu, a pretty girl with large black eyes, good teeth and strong arms and legs. During the day, she helped her mother in the house and in the fields. She did not go the school with Bisnu. But when he came home in the evenings, he would try teaching her some of the things he had learnt. Their father was dead. Bisnu, at twelve, considered himself the head of the family.

He ate two *chapatties*, after spreading butter-oil on them. He drank a glass of hot sweet tea. His mother gave two thick *chapatties* to Sheroo, and the dog wolfed them down in a few minutes. Then she wrapped two *chapatties* and a gourd-curry in some big green leaves, and handed these to Bisnu. This was his lunch-packet. His mother and Puja would take their meal afterwards.

When Bisnu was dressed, he stood with folded hands before the picture of Ganesh. Ganesh is the god who blesses all beginnings. The author who begins to write a new book, the banker who opens a new ledger, the traveller who starts on a journey, all invoke the kindly help of Ganesh. And as Bisnu made a journey every day, he never left without the goodwill of the elephant-headed god.

How, one might ask, did Ganesh get his elephant's head?

When born, he was a beautiful child. Parvati, his mother, was so proud of him that she went about showing him to everyone. Unfortunately she made the mistake of showing the child to that envious planet, Saturn, who promptly burnt off poor Ganesh's head. Parvati in despair went to Brahma, the Creator, for a new head for her son.

He had no head to give her; but he advised her to search for some man or animal caught in a sinful or wrong act. Parvati wandered about until she came upon an elephant sleeping with its head the wrong way, that is, to the south. She promptly removed the elephant's head and planted it on Ganesh's shoulders, where it took root.

Bisnu knew this story. He had heard it from his mother.

Wearing a white shirt and black shorts, and a pair of worn white keds, he was ready for his long walk to school, five miles up the mountain.

His sister woke up just as he was about to leave. She pushed the hair away from her face, and gave Bisnu one of her rare smiles.

'I hope you have not forgotten,' she said.

'Forgotten?' said Bisnu, pretending innocence. 'Is there anything I am supposed to remember?'

'Don't tease me. You promised to buy me a pair of bangles, remember? I hope you won't spend the money on sweets, as you did last time.'

'Oh, yes, your bangles,' said Bisnu. 'Girls have nothing better to do than waste money on trinkets. Now, don't lose your temper! I'll get them for you. Red and gold are the colours you want?'

'Yes, brother,' said Puja gently, pleased that Bisnu had remembered the colours. 'And for your dinner tonight we'll make you something special. Won't we, mother?'

'Yes. But hurry up and dress. There is some ploughing to be done today. The rains will soon be here, if the gods are kind.'

'The monsoon will be late this year,' said Bisnu. 'Mr. Nautiyal, our teacher, told us so. He said it had nothing to do with the gods.'

'Be off, you are getting late,' said Puja, before Bisnu could begin an argument with his mother. She was diligently winding the old clock. It was quite light in the room. The sun would be up any minute.

Bisnu shouldered his school-bag, kissed his mother, pinched his sister's cheeks, and left the house. He started climbing the steep path up the mountain-side. Sheroo bounded ahead; for he, too, always went with Bisnu to school.

Five miles to school. Everyday, except Sunday, Bisnu walked five miles to school; and in the evening, he walked home again. There was no school in his own small village of Manjari, for the village consisted of only five families. The nearest school was at Kemptee, a small township on the bus-route through the district of Garhwal. A number of boys walked to school, from distances of two or three miles; their villages were not quite as remote as Manjari. But Bisnu's village lay right at the bottom of the mountain, a drop of over two thousand feet from Kemptee. There was no proper road between the village and the town.

In Kemptee, there was a school, a small mission hospital, a post office and several shops. In Manjari village there were none of these amenities. If you were sick, you stayed at home until you got well; if you were *very* sick, you walded or were carried to the hospital, up the five-mile path. If you wanted to buy something, you went without it; but if you wanted it very badly, you could walk the five miles to Kemptee.

Manjari was known as the Five Mile Village.

Twice a week, if there were any letters, a postman came to the village. Bisnu usually passed the postman on his way to and from school.

There were other boys in Manjari village, but Bisnu was the only one who went to school. His mother would not have fussed if he had stayed at home and worked in the fields. That was what the other boys did; all except lazy Chittru, who preferred fishing in the stream or helping himself to the fruit of other people's trees. But Bisnu went to school. He went because he wanted to. No one could force him to go; and no one could stop him from going. He had set his heart on receiving a good schooling. He wanted to read and write as well as anyone in the big world, the world that seemed to begin only where the mountains ended. He felt cut off from the world in his small valley. He would rather live at the top of a mountain than at the bottom of one. That was why he liked climbing to Kemptee, it took him to the top of the mountain; and from its ridge he could look down on his own valley, to the north, and on the wide endless plains stretching towards the south.

The plainsman looks to the hills for the needs of his spirit; but the hillman looks to the plains for a living.

Leaving the village and the fields below him, Bisnu climbed steadily up the bare hillside, now dry and brown. By the time the sun was up, he had entered the welcome shade of an oak and rhododendron forest: Sheroo went bounding ahead, chasing squirrels and barking at *langoor* monkeys.

A colony of *langoors* lived in the oak forest. They fed on oak leaves, acorns, and other green things, and usually remained in the trees, coming down to the ground only to bask or play in the sun. They were beautiful, supple-limbed animals, with black faces and silver-grey coats and long, sensitive tails. They leapt from tree to tree with great agility. The young ones wrestled on the grass like boys.

A dignified community, the *langoors* did not have the cheekiness or dishonest habits of the red monkeys of the plains; they did not approach dogs or humans. But they had grown used to Bisnu's comings and goings, and did not fear him. Some of the older ones would watch him quietly, a little puzzled. They did not go near the town, because the Kemptee boys threw stones at them; and anyway, the oak forest gave them all the food they required.

Emerging from the trees, Bisnu crossed a small brook. Here he stopped to drink the fresh clean water of a spring. The brook tumbled down the mountain, and joined the river a little below Bisnu's village. Coming from another direction was a second path, and at the junction of the two paths Sarru was waiting for him.

Sarru came from a small village about three miles from Bisnu's and closer to the town. He had two large milk cans slung over his shoulders. Every morning he carried this milk to town, selling one can to the school and the other to Mrs. Taylor, the lady doctor at the small mission hospital. He was a little older than Bisnu but not as well-built.

They hailed each other, and Sarru fell into step beside Bisnu. They often met at this spot, keeping each other company for the remaining two miles to Kemptee.

'There was a panther in our village last night,' said Sarru.

This information interested but did not excite Bisnu. Panthers were common enough in the hills and did not usually present a problem except during the winter months, when their natural prey was scarce; then, occasionally, a panther would take to haunting the outskirts of a village, seizing a careless dog or a stray goat.

'Did you lose any animals?' asked Bisnu.

'No. It tried to get into the cow-shed, but the dogs set up an alarm. We drove it off.'

'It must be the same one which came around last winter. We lost a calf and two dogs in our village.'

'Wasn't that the one the *shikaris* wounded? I hope it hasn't became a cattle-lifter.'

151

'It could be the same. It has a bullet in its leg. These hunters are the people who cause all the trouble. They think it's easy to shoot a panther. It would be better if they missed altogether; but they usually wound it.'

'And then the panther's too slow to catch the barking-deer, and starts on our own animals.'

'We're lucky it didn't become a man-eater. Do you remember the man-eater six years ago? I was very small then. My father told me all about it. Ten people were killed in our valley alone. What happened to it?'

'I don't know. Some say it poisoned itself when it ate the headman of another village.'

Bisnu laughed. 'No one liked that old villian. He must have been a man-eater himself in some previous existence!' They linked arms and scrambled up the stony path. Sheroo began barking and ran ahead. Someone was coming down the path.

It was Mela Ram, the postman.

II

'Any letters for us?' asked Bisnu and Sarru together.

They never received any letters but that did not stop them from asking. It was one way of finding out who had received letters.

'You're welcome to all of them,' said Mela Ram, 'if you'll carry my bag for me.'

'Not today,' said Sarru. 'We're busy today. Is there a letter from Corporal Ghanshyam for his family?'

'Yes, there is a postcard for his people. He is posted on the Ladakh border now, and finds it very cold there.'

Postcards, unlike sealed letters, were considered public property and were read by everyone. The senders knew that, too; and so Corporal Ghanshyam Singh was careful to mention that he expected a promotion very soon. He wanted everyone in his village to know it.

Mela Ram, complaining of sore feet, continued on his way, and the boys carried on up the path. It was eight o'clock when they reached Kemptee. Dr. Taylor's out-patients were just beginning to trickle in at the hospital gate. The doctor was trying to prop up a rose-creeper which had blown down during the night. She liked attending to her plants in the mornings, before starting on her patients. She found this helped her in her work; there was a lot in common between ailing plants and ailing people.

Dr. Taylor was fifty, white-haired but fresh in the face and full of vitality. She had been in India for twenty years; and ten of these had been spent working in the hill regions.

She saw Bisnu coming down the road. She knew about the boy and his long walk to school and admired him for his keenness and sense of purpose. She wished there were more like him.

Bisnu greeted her shyly. Sheroo barked and put his paws up on the gate.

'Yes, there's a bone for you,' said Dr. Taylor. She often put aside bones for the big black dog, for she knew that Bisnu's people could not afford to give the dog a regular diet of meat —though he did well enough on milk and *chapatties*.

She threw the bone over the gate, and Sheroo caught it before it fell. The school bell began ringing, and Bisnu broke into a run. Sheroo loped along behind the boy.

When Bisnu entered the school gate, Sheroo sat down on the grass of the compound. He would remain there until the lunch-break. He knew of various ways of amusing himself during school hours, and had friends among the bazaar dogs. But just then he didn't want company. He had his bone to get on with.

Mr. Nautiyal, Bisnu's teacher, was in a bad mood. He was a keen rose-grower, and only that morning, on getting up and looking out of his bedroom window, had been horrified to see a herd of goats in his garden. He had chased them down the road with a stick, but the damage had already been done. His prize roses had all been consumed.

Mr. Nautiyal had been so upset that he had gone without his breakfast. He had also cut himself whilst shaving. Thus, his mood had gone from bad to worse. Several times during the day he brought down his ruler on the knuckles of any boy who irritated him. Bisnu was one of his best pupils. But even Bisnu irritated him by asking too many questions about a new sum which Mr. Nautiyal didn't feel like explaining.

That was the kind of day it was for Mr. Nautiyal. Most school teachers know similar days.

'Poor Mr. Nautiyal,' thought Bisnu. 'I wonder why he's so upset. It must be because of his pay. He doesn't get much money. But he's a good teacher. I hope he doesn't take another job.'

But after Mr. Nautiyal had taken his lunch, his mood improved (as it always did, after a meal), and the rest of the day passed serenely. Armed with a bundle of homework, Bisnu came out from the school compound at four o'clock, and was immediately joined by Sheroo. He proceeded down the road in the company of several of his class fellows. But he did not linger long in the bazaar. There were five miles to walk, and he did not like to get home too late. Usually he reached his house just as it was beginning to get dark.

Sarru had gone home long ago, and Bisnu had to make the return journey on his own. It was a good opportunity for memorising the words of an English poem he had been set to learn.

Bisnu had reached the little brook when he remembered the bangles he had promised to buy for his sister.

'Oh, I've forgotten them again,' he said aloud. 'Now I'll catch it: and she's probably made something special for my dinner!'

Sheroo, to whom these words were addressed, paid no attention, but bounded off into the oak forest. Bisnu looked around for the monkeys but they were nowhere to be seen.

'Strange,' he thought. 'I wonder why they have disappeared.'

He was startled by a sudden sharp cry, followed by a fierce yelp. He knew at once that Sheroo was in trouble. The noise came from the bushes down the *khud*, into which the dog had rushed but a few seconds previously.

Bisnu jumped off the path and ran down the slope towards the bushes. There was no dog and not a sound. He whistled and called but there was no response. Then he saw something lying on the dry grass. He picked it up. It was a portion of a dog's collar, stained with blood. It was Sheroo's collar, and Sheroo's blood.

Bisnu did not search further. He knew, without a doubt, that Sheroo had been seized by a panther. No other animal could have attacked so silently and swiftly and carried off a big dog without a struggle. Sheroo was dead — must have been dead within seconds of being caught and flung into the air. Bisnu knew the danger that lay in wait for him if he followed the blood-trail through the trees. The panther would attack anyone who interfered with its meal.

With tears starting in his eyes, Bisnu carried on down the path to the village. His fingers still clutched the little bit of bloodstained collar that was all that was left to him of his dog.

III

Bisnu was not a very sentimental boy, but he sorrowed for his dog, who had been his companion on many a hike into the hills and forests. He did not sleep that night, but turned restlessly from side to side, moaning softly. After some time he felt Puja's hand on his head. She began stroking his brow. He took her hand in his own, and the clasp of her rough, warm familiar hand gave him a feeling of comfort and security.

Next morning, when he went down to the stream to bathe, he missed the presence of his dog. He did not stay long in the water. It wasn't so much fun when there was no Sheroo to watch him.

When Bisnu's mother gave him his food, she told him to be careful, and to hurry home that evening. A panther, even if it is only a cowardly lifter of sheep or dogs, is not to be trifled with. And this particular panther had shown some daring by seizing the dog even before it was dark.

Still, there was no question of staying away from school. If Bisnu remained at home every time a panther put in an appearance, he might just as well stop going to school altogether.

He set off even earlier than usual, and reached the meeting of the paths long before Sarru. He did not wait for his friend, because he did not feel like talking about the loss of his dog. It was not the day for the postman, and so Bisnu reached Kemptee without meeting anyone on the way. He tried creeping past the hospital-gate unnoticed, but Dr. Taylor saw him, and the first thing she said was: 'Where's Sheroo? I've got something for him.'

When Dr. Taylor saw the boy's face, she knew at once that something was wrong.

'What is it, Bisnu?' she asked. She looked quickly up and down the road. 'Is it Sheroo?'

He nodded gravely.

'A panther took him,' he said.

'In the village.'

'No, while we were walking home through the forest. I did not see anything — but I heard.'

Dr. Taylor knew that there was nothing she could say that would console him, and she tried to conceal the bone which she had brought out for the dog; but Bisnu noticed her hiding it behind her back, and the tears welled up in his eyes. He turned away and began running down the road.

His schoolfellows noticed Sheroo's absence and questioned Bisnu. He had to tell them everything. They were full of sympathy; but they were also quite thrilled at what had happened, and kept pestering Bisnu for all the details. There was a lot of noise in the classroom, and Mr. Nautiyal had to call for order. When he learnt what had happened, he patted Bisnu on the head and told him that he need not attend school for the rest of the day. But Bisnu did not want to go home. After school, he got into a fight with one of the boys, and that helped him to forget.

IV

The panther that plunged the village into an atomsphere of gloom and terror may not have been the same panther that took Sheroo; there was no way of knowing, and it would have made no difference, because the panther that came by night and struck at the people of Manjari was that most-feared of wild creatures, a man-eater.

Nine-year-old Sanjay, son of Kalam Singh, was the first child to be attacked by the panther.

Kalam Singh's house was the last in the village, and nearest the stream. Like the other houses, it was quite small, just a room above and a stable below, with steps leading up from outside the house. He lived there with his wife, two sons (Sanjay was the youngest) and little daughter Basanti who had just turned three.

Sanjay had brought his father's cows home after grazing them on the hillside in the company of other children. He had also brought home an edible wild plant which his mother cooked into a tasty dish for their evening meal. They had their food at dusk, sitting on the floor of their single room, and soon after settled down for the night. Sanjay curled up in his favourite spot, with his head near the door, where he got a little fresh air. As the nights were warm, the door was usually left a little ajar. Sanjay's mother piled ash on the embers of the fire, and the family was soon asleep.

None heard the stealthy padding of a panther approaching the door, pushing it wider open. But suddenly there were sounds of a frantic struggle, and Sanjay's stifled cries were mixed with the grunts of the panther. Kalam Singh leapt to his feet with a shout. The panther had dragged Sanjay out of the door and was pulling him down the steps when Kalam Singh started battering at the animal with a large stone. The rest of the family screamed in terror, rousing the entire village. A number of men came to Kalam Singh's assistance, and the panther was driven off; but Sanjay lay unconscious.

Someone brought a lantern, and the boy's mother screamed when she saw her small son with his head lying in a pool of blood. It looked as if the side of his head had been eaten off by the panther. But he was still alive; and as Kalam Singh plastered ash on the boy's head to stop the bleeding, he found that though the scalp had been torn off one side of the head, the bare bone was smooth and unbroken.

'He won't live through the night,' said a neighbour. 'We'll have to carry him down to the river in the morning.'

The dead were always cremated on the banks of a small river which flowed past Manjari village.

Suddenly the panther, still prowling about the village, called out in rage and frustration, and the villagers rushed to their homes in a panic, and barricaded themselves in for the night.

Sanjay's mother sat by the boy for the rest of the night, weeping and watching. Towards dawn he started to moan and show signs of coming round. At this sign of returning consciousness, Kalam Singh rose determinedly and looked round for his stick.

He told his elder son to remain behind with the mother and daughter, as he was going to take Sanjay to Dr. Taylor at the hospital.

'See, he is moaning and in pain,' said Kalam Singh. 'That means he has a chance to live if he can be treated at once.'

With a stout stick in his hand, and Sanjay on his back, Kalam Singh set off on the two miles of hard mountain track to the hospital at Kemptee. His son, a blood-stained cloth around his head, was moaning but still unconscious. When at last Kalam Singh climbed up through the last fields below the hospital, he asked for the doctor and stammered out an account of what had happened.

It was a terrible injury, as Dr. Taylor discovered. The bone over almost one-third of the head was bare, and the scalp was torn all round. As the father told his story, the doctor cleaned and dressed the wound, and then gave Sanjay a shot of penicillin to prevent sepsis. Later, Kalam Singh carried the boy home again.

V

After this, the panther went away for some time. But the people of

Manjari could not be sure of its whereabouts. They kept to their houses after dark, and shut their doors. Bisnu had to stop going to school, because there was no one to accompany him and it was dangerous to go alone. This worried him, because his final exam was only a few weeks off, and he would be missing important classwork. When he wasn't in the fields, helping with the sowing of rice and maize, he would be sitting in the shade of a chestnut tree, going through his well-thumbed second-hand school books. He had no other reading, except for a copy of the *Ramayana* (epic of the Hindu gods and heroes) and a Hindi translation of *Alice in Wonderland*. These were well-preserved, read only in fits and starts, and usually kept locked in his mother's old tin trunk.

Sanjay had nightmares for several nights, and woke up screaming; but with the resilience of youth, he quickly recovered. At the end of the week he was able to walk to the hospital, though his father always accompanied him. Even a desperate panther will hesitate to attack a party of two. Sanjay, with his thin little face and huge bandaged head, looked a pathetic figure; but he was getting better and the wound looked healthy.

Bisnu often went to see him, and the two boys spent long hours together near the stream. Sometimes Chittru would join them, and they would try catching fish with a home-made net. They were often successful in taking home one or two mountain trout. Sometimes Bisnu and Chittru wrestled in the shallow water, or on the grassy banks of the stream. Chittru was a chubby boy, with a broad chest, strong legs and thighs, and when he used his weight he got Bisnu under him; but Bisnu was hard and wiry, and had very strong wrists and fingers. When he had Chittru in a vice, the bigger boy would cry out and give up the struggle. Sanjay could not join in these games. He had never been a very strong boy, and he needed plenty of rest if his wounds were to heal well.

The panther had not been seen for over a week, and the people of Manjari were beginning to hope that it might have moved on, over the mountain or further down the valley.

'I think I can start going to school again,' said Bisnu. 'The panther has gone away.'

'Don't be too sure,' said Puja, 'The moon is full these days, and perhaps it is only being cautious.'

'Wait a few days,' said their mother. 'It is better to wait. Perhaps you could go the day after tomorrow, when Sanjay goes to the hospital with his father. Then you will not be alone.'

And so, two days later, Bisnu went up to Kemptee with Sanjay and Kalam Singh. Sanjay's wound had almost healed over. Little islets of flesh had grown over the bone. Dr. Taylor told him that he need come to see her only once a fortnight, instead of every third day.

Bisnu went to his school, and was given a warm welcome by his friends and by Mr. Nautiyal.

'You'll have to work hard,' said his teacher. 'You have to catch up with the others. If you like, I can give you some extra time after classes.'

'Thank you sir, but it will make me late,' said Bisnu. 'I must get home before it is dark, otherwise my mother will worry. I think the panther has gone, but nothing is certain.'

'Well, you mustn't take risks. Do your best, Bisnu. Work hard, and you'll soon catch up with your lessons.'

Sanjay and Kalam Singh were waiting for him outside the school. Together they took the path down to Manjari, passing the postman on the way. Mela Ram said that he had heard that the panther was in another district, and that there was nothing to fear; he was on his rounds again.

Nothing happened on the way. The *langoors* were back in their favourite part of the forest. Bisnu got home just as the kerosene-lamp was being lit. Puja met him at the door with a winsome smile.

'Did you get the bangles?' she asked.

But Bisnu had forgotten again.

VI

There had been a thunderstorm and some rain — a short, sharp shower which gave the villagers hope that the monsoon would arrive on time. It brought out the thunder-lilies — pink, crocus-like flowers which sprang up on the hillsides immediately after a summer shower.

Bisnu, on his way home from school, was caught in the rain. He knew the shower would not last, so he took shelter in a small cave and, to pass the time, began doing sums, scratching figures in the damp earth with end of a stick.

When the rain stopped, he came out from the cave and continued down the path. He wasn't in a hurry. The rain had made everything smell fresh and good. The scent from fallen pine-needles rose from the wet earth. The leaves of the oak trees had been washed clean, and a light breeze turned them about, showing their silver undersides. The birds, refreshed and high-spirited, set up a terrific noise. The worst offenders were the yellow-bottomed bulbuls, who squabbled and fought in the blackberry bushes. A Barbet, high up in the branches of a deodar, set up its querulous, plaintive call. And a flock of bright green parrots came swooping down the hill, to settle in a wild plum tree and feast on the under-ripe fruit. The *langoors*, too, had been revived by the rain; they leapt friskily from tree, greeting Bisnu with little grunts.

He was almost out of the oak forest when he heard a faint bleating. Presently a little goat came stumbling up the path towards him. The kid was far from home, and must have strayed from the rest of the herd. But it was not yet conscious of being lost. It came to Bisnu with a hop, skip and a jump, and started nuzzling against his legs like a cat.

'I wonder who you belong to,' mused Bisnu, stroking the little creature. 'You'd better come home with me until someone claims you.'

He didn't have to take the kid in his arms. It was used to humans and followed close at his heels. Now that darkness was coming on, Bisnu walked a little faster.

He had not gone very far when he heard the sawing grunt of a panther.

The sound came from the hill to the right, and Bisnu judged the distance to be anything from a hundred to two hundred yards. He hesitated on the path, wondering what to do; then he picked the kid up in his arms, and hurried on in the direction of home and safety.

The panther called again, much closer now. If it was an ordinary panther, it would go away on finding that the kid was with Bisnu. If it was the man-eater it would not hesitate to attack the boy, for no man-eater fears a human. There was no time to lose, and there did not seem much point in running. Bisnu looked up and down the hillside. The forest was far behind him, and there were only a few trees in his vicinity. He chose a spruce.

The branches of the Himalayan spruce are very brittle and snap easily beneath a heavy weight. They were strong enough to support Bisnu's light frame. It was unlikely they would take the weight of a full-grown panther. At least that was what Bisnu hoped.

Holding the kid with one arm, Bisnu gripped a low branch and swung himself up into the tree. He was a good climber. Slowly but confidently he climbed half-way up the tree, until he was about twelve feet above the ground. He couldn't go any higher without risking a fall.

He had barely settled himself in the crook of a branch when the panther came into the open, running into the clearing at a brisk trot. This was no stealthy approach, no waring stalking of its prey. It was the man-eater, all right. Bisnu felt a cold shiver run down his spine. He felt a little sick.

The panther stood in the clearing with a slight thrusting forward of the head. This gave it the appearance of gazing intently and rather short-sightedly at some invisible object in the clearing. But there is nothing short-sighted about a panther's vision; its sight and hearing are acute.

Bisnu remained motionless in the tree and sent up a prayer to all the gods he could think of; but the kid began bleating. The panther looked up, and gave its deepthroated, rasping grunt — a fearsome sound, calculated to strike terror into any tree-borne animal. Many a monkey, petrified by a panther's roar, has fallen from its perch to make a meal for Mr. Spots. The man-eater was trying the same technique on Bisnu. But though the boy was trembling with fright, he clung firmly to the base of the spruce tree.

The panther did not make any attempt to leap into the tree. Perhaps it knew instinctively that this was not the type of tree that it could climb. Instead it described a semi-circle round the tree, keeping its face turned towards Bisnu. Then it disappeared into the bushes.

The man-eater was cunning. It hoped to put the boy off his guard, perhaps entice him down from the tree; for a few seconds later, with a half-humorous growl, it rushed back into the clearing and then stopped, staring up at the boy in some surprise. The panther was getting frustrated. It snarled, and putting its forefeet up against the tree-trunk, began scratching at the bark in the manner of an ordinary domestic cat. The tree shook at each thud of the beasts' paw.

Bisnu began shouting for help.

The moon had not yet come up. Down in Manjari village, Bisnu's mother and sister stood in their lighted doorway, gazing anxiously up the pathway. Every now and then.Puja would turn to take a look at the small clock.

Sanjay's father appeared in a field below. He had a kerosene lantern in his hand.

'Sister, isn't your boy home as yet?' he asked.

'No, he hasn't arrived. We are very worried. He should have been home an hour ago. Do you think the panther will be about tonight? There's going to be a moon.'

'True, but it will be dark for another hour. I will fetch the other menfolk, and we will go up the mountain for your boy. There may have been a landslip during the rain. Perhaps the path has been washed away.'

'Thank you, brother. But arm yourselves, just in case the panther is about.'

'I will take my spear,' said Kalam Singh. 'I have sworn to spear that devil when I find him. There is some evil-spirit dwelling in the beast, and it must be destroyed!'

'I am coming with you,' said Puja.

'No, you cannot go,' said her mother. 'It's bad enough that Bisnu is in danger. You stay at home with me. This is work for men.'

'I shall be safe with them,' insisted Puja. 'I am going, mother!' And she jumped down the embankment into the field, and followed Sanjay's father through the village.

Ten minutes later, two men armed with axes had joined Kalam Singh in the courtyard of his house, and the small party moved silently and swiftly up the mountain path. Puja walked in the middle of the group, holding the lantern. As soon as the village lights were hidden by a shoulder of the hill, the men began to shout —both to frighten the panther, if it was about, and to give themselves courage.

Bisnu's mother closed the front door, and turned to the image to Ganesh the God for comfort and help.

Bisnu's calls were carried on the wind, and Puja and the men heard him while they were still half-a-mile away. Their own shouts increased in volume, and, hearing their voices, Bisnu felt strength return to his shaking limbs. Emboldened by the approach of his own people, he began shouting insults at the snarling panther, then throwing twings and small branches at the enraged animal. The kid added its bleats to the boy's shouts, the birds took up the chorus, the *langoors* squealed and grunted, the searchers shouted themselves hoarse, and the panther howled with rage. The forest had never before been so noisy.

As the search-party drew near, they could hear the panther's savage snarls, and hurried, fearing that perhaps Bisnu had been seized.

Puja began to run.

'Don't rush ahead, girl,' said Kalam Singh. 'Stay between us.'

The panther, now aware of the approaching humans, stood still in the middle of the clearing, head thrust forward in a familiar stance. There seemed too many men for one panther. When the animal saw the light of the lantern dancing between the trees, it turned, snarled defiance and hate, and without another look at the boy in the tree, disappeared into the bushes. It was not yet ready for a showdown.

VII

Nobody turned up to claim the little goat, so Bisnu kept it. A goat was a poor substitute for a dog; but, like Mary's lamb, it followed Bisnu wherever he went, and the boy couldn't help being touched by its devotion. He took it down to the stream, where it would skip about in the shallows and nibble the sweet grass that grew on the banks.

As for the panther, frustrated in its attempt on Bisnu's life, it did not wait long before attacking another human.

It was Chittru who came running down the path one afternoon, bobbling excitedly about the panther and the postman.

Chittru, deeming it safe to the gathering ripe bilberries in the daytime, had walded about half-a-mile up the path from the village when he had stumbled across Mela Ram's mail-bag lying on the ground. Of the postman himself there was no sign. But a trail of blood led through the bushes.

Once again, a party of men headed by Kalam Singh and accompanied by Bisnu and Chittru, went out to look for the postman; but though they found Mela Ram's bloodstained clothes, they could not find his body. The panther had made no mistake this time.

It was to be several weeks before Manjari had a new postman.

A few days after Mala Ram's disappearance, an old woman was sleeping with her head near the open door of her house. She had been advised to sleep inside with the door closed; but the nights were hot, and anyway the old woman was a little deaf, and in the middle of the night, an hour before moonrise, the panther seized her by the throat. Her strangled cry woke her grown-up son, and all the men in the village woke up at his shouts and came running.

The panther dragged the old woman out of the house and down the steps but left her when the men approached with their axes and spears, and made off into the bushes. The old woman was still alive, and the men made a rough stretcher of bamboo and vines and started carrying her up the path; but they had not gone far when she began to cough, and because of her terrible throat-wounds her lungs collapsed, and she died.

It was the 'dark of the month' — the week of the new-moon when nights are darkest.

Bisnu, closing the front door and lighting the kerosene lantern, said, 'I wonder where that panther is tonight!'

The panther was busy in another village, Sarru's village.

A woman and her daughter had been out in the evening, bedding the cattle down in the stable. The girl had gone into the house, and the woman was following. As she bent down to go in at the low door, the panther sprang from the bushes. Fortunately, one of its paws hit the door-post and broke the force of the attack, or the woman would have been killed. When she cried out, the men came round shouting, and the panther slunk off. The woman had deep scratches on her back, and was badly shocked.

Next day a small party of villagers presented themselves in front of the magistrate's office at Kemptee, and demanded that something be done about the panther; but the magistrate was away on tour, and there was no one else in Kemptee who had a gun. Mr. Nautiyal met the villagers, and promised to write to a well-known *shikari*, but said that it would be at least a fortnight before he could come.

Bisnu was fretting because he could not go to school. Most boys would be only too happy to miss school; but when you are living in a remote village in the mountains, and having an education is the only way of seeing the world, you look forward to going to school, even if it is five miles from home. Bisnu's exams were only two weeks off, and he didn't want to remain in the same class while the others were promoted. Besides, he knew he could pass even though he had missed a number of lessons. But he had to sit for the exams; he couldn't miss them.

'Cheer up, *Bhaiya*,' said Puja, as they sat drinking glasses of hot tea after their evening meal. 'The panther may go away once the rains break.'

'Even the rains are late this year,' said Bisnu. 'It's so hot and dry. Can't we open the door?'

'And be dragged down the steps by the panther?' said his mother. 'It isn't safe to have the window open, let alone the door.' And she went to the small window — through which a cat could have found difficulty in passing — and bolted it firmly.

With a sigh of resignation Bisnu threw off all his clothes except his underwear, and stretched himself out on the earthen floor.

'We will be rid of the beast soon,' said his mother. 'I know it in my heart. Our prayers will be heard, and you shall go to school and pass your exams.'

To cheer up her children, she told them a humorous story which had been handed down to her by her grandmother. It was all about a tiger, a panther and a bear, the three of whom were made to feel very foolish by a thief hiding in the hollow trunk of a banyan tree. Bisnu was sleepy and did not listen very attentively; he dropped off to sleep before the story was finished.

When he woke, it was dark, and his mother and sister were asleep on the cot. He wondered what it was that had woken him. He would hear his sister's easy breathing, and the steady ticking of the clock. Far away, an owl hooted — an unlucky sign, his mother would have said; but she was asleep, and Bisnu was not superstitious.

And then he heard something scratching at the door, and the hair on his head felt tight and prickly. It was like a cat scratching, only louder. The door creaked a little whenever it felt the impact of the paw — a heavy paw, as Bisnu could tell from the dull sound it made.

'It's the panther,' he muttered under his breath, sitting up on the hard floor.

The door, he felt, was strong enough to resist the panther's weight; and, if he set up an alarm, he could rouse the village. But the middle of the night was no time for the bravest of men to tackle a panther.

In a corner of the room stood a long bamboo stick with a sharp knife tied to one end, which Bisnu sometimes used for spearing fish. Crawling on all fours across the room, he grasped the home-made spear; and then, scrambling on to a cupboard, he drew level with the skylight window. He could get his head and shoulders through the window.

'What are you doing up there?' said Puja, who had woken up at the sound of Bisnu shuffling about the room.

'Be quiet,' said Bisnu. 'You'll wake mother.'

Their mother was awake by now. 'Come down from there, Bisnu. I can hear a noise outside.'

'Don't worry,' said Bisnu, who found himself looking down on the wriggling animal which was trying to get its paw in under the door. With his mother and Puja awake, there was no time to lose. He had got the spear through the window, and though he could not manoeuvre it so as to strike the panther's head, he brought the sharp end down with considerable force on the animal's rump.

With a roar of pain and rage, the man-eater leapt down from the steps and disappeared into the darkness. It did not pause to see what had struck it. Certain that no human could have come upon it in that fashion, it ran fearfully to its lair, howling until the pain subsided.

VIII

A panther is an enigma. There are occasions when he proves himself to be the most cunning animal under the sun, and yet the very next day he will walk into an obvious trap that no self-respecting jackal would ever go near. One day a panther will prove himself to be a complete coward and run like a hare from a couple of dogs, and the very next he will dash in amongst half a dozen men sitting round a camp-fire, and inflict terrible injuries on them.

It is not often that a panther is taken by surprise, as his powers of sight and hearing are very acute. He is a master at the art of camouflage, and his spotted coat is admirably suited for the purpose. He does not need heavy jungle to hide in. A couple of bushes, and the light and shade from surrounding trees, are enough to make him almost invisible.

Because the Manjari panther had been fooled by Bisnu, it did not mean that he was a stupid panther; it simply meant that he had been a little careless. And Bisnu and Puja, growing in confidence since their midnight encounter with the animal, became a little careless themselves.

Puja was hoeing the last field above the house, and Bisnu, at the other end of the same field, was chopping up several branches of green oak, prior to leaving the wood in the loft to dry. It was late afternoon, and the descending sun glinted in patches on the small river. It was a time of day when only the most desperate and daring of man-eaters would be likely to show itself.

Pausing for a moment to wipe the sweat from his brow, Bisnu glanced up at the hillside, and his eye caught sight of a rock on the brown of the hill which seemed unfamiliar to him. Just as he was about to look elsewhere, the round rock began to grow and then alter its shape, and Bisnu, watching in fascination, was at last able to make out the head and forequarters of the panther. It looked enormous from the angle at which he saw it, and for a moment he thought it was a tiger. But Bisnu knew instinctively that it was the man-eater.

Slowly the wary beast pulled itself to its feet and began to walk round the side of the great rock. For a second it disappeared, and Bisnu wondered if it had gone away. Then it reappeared, and the boy was all excitement again. Very slowly and silently the panther walked across the face of the rock until it was in a direct line with that corner of the feild where Puja was working.

With a thrill of horror, Bisnu realised that the panther was stalking his sister. He shook himself free from the spell which had woven itself round him, and shouting hoarsely, ran forward.

'Run, Puja, run!' he called. 'It's on the hill above you!'

Puja turned to see what Bisnu was shouting about. She saw him gesticulate to the hill behind her, looked up just in time to see the panther crouching for his spring.

With great presence of mind, she leapt down the banking of the field, and tumbled into an irrigation ditch.

The springing panther missed its prey, lost its foothold on the slippery shale banking, and somersaulted into the ditch a few feet away from Puja. Before the animal could recover from its surprise, Bisnu was dashing down the slope, swinging his axe and shouting *'Maro, Maro!'* (Kill,Kill!).

Two men came running across the field. They, too, were armed with axes. Together with Bisnu they made a half-circle around the snarling animal, which turned at bay and plunged at them in order to get away. Puja wriggled along the ditch on her stomach. The men aimed their axes at the panther's head, and Bisnu had the satisfaction of getting in a well-aimed blow between the eyes. The animal then charged straight at one of the men, knocked him over, and tried to get at his throat. Just then Sanjay's father arrived with his long spear. He plunged the end of the spear into the panther's neck.

The panther left its victim and ran into the bushes, dragging the spear through the grass and leaving a trail of blood on the ground The men followed cautiously — all except the man who had been wounded and who lay on the ground while Puja and the other womenfolk rushed up to help him.

The panther had made for the bed of the stream, and Bisnu, Sanjay's father, and their companion were able to follow it quite easily. The water was red where the panther had crossed the stream, and the rocks were stained with blood. After they had gone downstream for about a furlong, they found the panther lying still on its side at the edge of the water. It was mortally wounded, but it continued to wave its tail like an angry cat; then even the tail lay still.

'It is dead,' said Bisnu. 'It will not trouble us again in *this* body.'

'Let us be certain,' said Sanjay's father, and he bent down and pulled the panther's tail.

There was no response.

'It is dead,' said Kalam Singh. 'No panther would suffer such an insult were it alive!'

They cut down a long piece of thick bamboo and tied the panther to it by its feet. Then, with their enemy hanging upside down from the bamboo pole, they started back for the village.

'There will be a feast at my house tonight,' said Kalam Singh. 'Everyone in the village must come. And tomorrow we will visit all the villages in the valley, and show them the dead panther, so that they may move about again without fear.'

'We can sell the skin in Kemptee,' said their companion. 'It will fetch a good price.'

'But the claws we will give to Bisnu,' said Kalam singh, putting his arm around the boy's shoulders. 'He has done a man's work today. He deserves the claws.'

A panther's or a tiger's claws are considered to be lucky charms.

'I will take only three claws,' said Bisnu. 'One each for my mother and sister, and one for myself. You may give the others to Sanjay and Chittru and the smaller children.'

As the sun set, a big fire was lit in the middle of the village of Manjari, and the people gathered round it, singing and laughing. Kalam Singh killed his fattest goat, and there was meat for everyone.

IX

Bisnu was on his way home. He had just handed in his first paper, arithmetic, which he had found quite easy. Tomorrow it would be algebra, and when he got home he could have to practise square roots and cube roots and fractional coefficients.

Mr. Nautiyal and the entire class had been happy that he had been able to sit for the exams. He was also a hero to them for his part in killing the panther. The story had spread through the villages with the rapidity of a forest fire, a fire which was now raging in Kemptee town.

When he walked past the hospital, he was whistling cheerfully. Dr. Taylor waved to him from the verandah steps.

'How is Sanjay now?' she asked.

'He is well,' said Bisnu.

'And your mother and sister?'

'They are well,' said Bisnu.

'Are you going to get yourself a new dog?'

'I am thinking about it,' said Bisnu. 'At present I have a baby goat — I am teaching it to swim!'

He started down the path to the valley. Dark clouds had gathered, and there was a rumble of thunder. A storm was imminet.

'Wait for me!' shouted Sarru, running down the path behind Bisnu, his milk-pails clanging against each other. He fell into step beside Bisnu.

'Well, I hope we don't have any more man-eaters for some time,' he said. 'I've lost a lot of money by not being able to take milk up to Kemptee.'

'We should be safe as long as a *shikari* doesn't wound another panther. There was an old bullet-wound in the man-eater's thigh. That's why it couldn't hunt in the forest. The deer were too fast for it.'

'Is there a new postman yet?'

'He starts tomorrow. A cousin of Mela Ram's.'

When they reached the parting of their ways it had begun to rain a little.

'I must hurry,' said Sarru. 'It's going to get heavier any minute.'

'I feel like getting wet,' said Bisnu. 'This time it's the monsoon, I'm sure.'

Bisnu entered the forest on his own, and at the same time the rain came down in heavy opaque sheets. The trees shook in the wind, the *langoors* chattered with excitement.

It was still pouring when Bisnu emerged from the forest, drenched to the skin. But the rain stopped suddenly, just as the village of Manjari came in view. The sun appeared through a rift in the clouds. The leaves and the grass gave out a sweet, fresh smell.

Bisnu could see his mother and sister in the field transplanting the rice seedlings. The menfolk were driving the yoked oxen through the thin mud of the fields, while the children hung on to the oxen's tails, standing on the plain wooden harrows and with weird cries and shouts sending the animals almost at a gallop along the narrow terraces.

Bisnu felt the urge to be with them, working in the fields. He ran down the path, his feet falling softly on the wet earth. Puja saw him coming and waved to him. She met him at the edge of the field.

'How did you find your paper today?' she asked.

'Oh, it was easy.' Bisnu slipped his hand into hers and together they walked across the field. Puja felt something smooth and hard against her fingers, and before she could see what Bisnu was doing, he had slipped a pair of bangles over her wrist.

'I remembered,' he said, with a sense of achievement.

Puja looked at the bangles and burst out: 'But they are blue, *Bhai*, and I wanted red and gold bangles!' And then, when she saw him looking crestfallen, she hurried on: 'But they are very pretty, and you did remember . . . Actually, they're just as nice as red and gold bangles! Come into the house when you are ready. I have made something special for you.'

'I am coming ,' said Bisnu, turning towards the house. 'You don't know how hungry a man gets, walking five miles to reach home!'

The Leopard

I first saw the leopard when I was crossing the small stream at the bottom of the hill.

The ravine was so deep that for most of the day it remained in shadow. This encouraged many birds and animals to emerge from cover during daylight hours. Few people ever passed that way: only milkmen and charcoal-burners from the surrounding villages.

As a result, the ravine had become a little haven of wildlife, one of the few natural sanctuaries left near Mussoorie, a hill station in northern India.

Below my cottage was a forest of oak and maple and Himalayan rhododendron. A narrow path twisted its way down through the trees, over an open ridge where red sorrel grew wild, and then steeply down through a tangle of wild raspberries, creeping vines and slender bamboo.

At the bottom of the hill the path led on to a grassy verge, surrounded by wild dog roses. (It is surprising how closely the flora of the lower Himalayas, between 5,000 to 8,000 feet, resembles that of the English countryside).

The stream ran close by the verge, tumbling over smooth pebbles, over rocks worn yellow with age, on its way to the plains and to the little Song River and finally to the sacred Ganges..

When I first discovered the stream it was early April and the wild roses were flowering — small white blossoms lying in clusters.

I walked down to the stream almost every day, after two or three hours of writing. I had lived in cities too long, and had returned to the hills to renew myself, both physically and mentally. Once you have lived with mountains for any length of time, you belong to them, and must return again and again.

Nearly every morning, and sometimes during the day, I heard the cry of the barking deer. And in the evening, walking through the forest, I disturbed parties of pheasant. The birds went gliding down the ravine on open, motionless wings. I saw pine martens and a handsome red fox, and I recognized the footprints of a bear.

As I had not come to take anything from the forest, the birds and animals soon grew accustomed to my presence; or possibly they recognized my footsteps. After some time, my approach did not disturb them.

The *langurs* in the oak and rhododendron trees, who would at first go leaping through the branches at my approach, now watched me with some curiosity as they munched the tender green shoots of the oak.

The young ones scuffled and wrestled like boys, while their parents groomed each other's coats, stretching themselves out on the sunlit hillside. But one evening, as I passed, I heard them chattering in the trees, and I knew I was not the cause of their excitement.

As I crossed the stream and began climbing the hill, the grunting and chattering increased, as though the *langurs* were trying to warn me of some hidden danger. A shower of pebbles came rattling down the steep hillside, and I looked up to see a sinewy, orange-gold leopard poised on a rock about 20 feet above me.

It was not looking towards me, but had its head thrust attentively forward, in the direction of the ravine. Yet it must have sensed my presence, because it slowly turned its head and looked down at me.

It seemed a little puzzled at my presence there; and when, to give myself courage, I clapped my hands sharply, the leopard sprang away into the thickets, making absolutely no sound as it melted into the shadows.

I had disturbed the animal in its quest for food. But a little after I heard the quickening cry of a barking deer as it fled through the forest. The hunt was still on.

The leopard, like other members of the cat family, is nearing extinction in India, and I was surprised to find one so close to Mussoorie. Probably the deforestation that had been taking place in the surrounding hills had driven the deer into this green valley; and the leopard, naturally, had followed.

It was some weeks before I saw the leopard again, although I was often made aware of its presence. A dry, rasping cough sometimes gave it away. At times I felt almost certain that I was being followed.

Once, when I was late getting home, and the brief twilight gave way to a dark, moonless night, I was startled by a family of porcupines running about in a clearing. I looked around nervously, and saw two bright eyes staring at me from a thicket. I stood still, my heart banging away against my ribs. Then the eyes danced away, and I realized that they were only fireflies.

In May and June, when the hills were brown and dry, it was always cool and green near the stream, where ferns and maidenhair and long grasses continued to thrive.

Downstream I found a small pool where I could bathe, and a cave with water dripping from the roof, the water spangled gold and silver in the shafts of sunlight that pushed through the slits in the cave roof.

'He maketh me to lie down in green pastures: he leadeth me beside the still waters.' Perhaps David had discovered a similar paradise when he wrote those words; perhaps I, too, would write good words. The hill station's summer visitors had not discovered this haven of wild and green things. I was beginning to feel that the place belonged to me, that dominion was mine.

The stream had at least one other regular visitor, a spotted forktail, and though it did not fly away at my approach it became restless if I stayed too long, and then it would move from boulder to boulder uttering a long complaining cry.

I spent an afternoon trying to discover the bird's nest, which I was certain contained young ones, because I had seen the forktail carrying grubs in her bill. The problem was that when the bird flew upstream I had difficulty in following her rapidly enough as the rocks were sharp and slippery.

Eventually I decorated myself with bracken fronds and, after slowly making my way upstream, hid myself in the hollow stump of a tree at a spot where the forktail often disappeared. I had no intention of robbing the bird: I was simply curious to see its home.

By crouching down, I was able to command a view of a small stretch of the stream and the sides of the ravine; but I had done little to deceive the forktail, who continued to object strongly to my presence so near her home.

I summoned up my reserves of patience and sat perfectly still far about ten minutes. The forktail quietened down. Out of sight, out of mind. But where had she gone? Probably into the walls of the ravine where I felt sure, she was guarding her nest.

I decided to take her by surprise, and stood up suddenly, in time to see not the forktail on her doorstep, but the leopard bounding away with a grunt of surprise! Two urgent springs, and it had crossed the stream and plunged into the forest.

I was as astonished as the leopard, and forgot all about the forktail and her nest. Had the leopard been following me again? I decided against this possibility. Only man-eaters follow humans, and, as far as I knew, there had never been a maneater in the vicinity of Mussoorie.

During the monsoon the stream became a rushing torrent, bushes and small trees were swept away, and the friendly murmur of the water became a threatening boom. I did not visit the place too often, as there were leeches in the long grass.

One day I found the remains of a barking deer which had only been partly eaten. I wondered why the leopard had not hidden the rest of his meal, and decided that it must have been disturbed while eating.

Then, climbing the hill, I met a party of hunters resting beneath the oaks. They asked me if I had seen a leopard. I said I had not. They said they knew there was a leopard in the forest.

Leopard skins, they told me, were selling in Delhi at over 1,000 rupees each. Of course there was a ban on the export of skins, but they gave me to understand that there were ways and means . . . I thanked them for their information and walked on, feeling uneasy and disturbed.

The hunters had seen the carcass of the deer, and they had seen the leopard's pug-marks, and they kept coming to the forest. Almost every evening I heard their guns banging away; for they were ready to fire at almost anything.

'There's a leopard about,' they always told me. 'You should carry a gun.'

'I don't have one,' I said.

There were fewer birds to be seen, and even the *langurs* had moved on. The red fox did not show itself; and the pine martens, who had become quite bold, now dashed into hiding, at my approach. The smell of one human is like the smell of any other.

And then the rains were over and it was October; I could lie in the sun, on sweet-smelling grass, and gaze up through a pattern of oak leaves into a blinding blue heaven. And I would praise God for leaves and grass and the smell of things, the smell of mint and bruised clover, and the touch of things — the touch of grass and air and sky, the touch of the sky's blueness.

I thought no more of the men. My attitude towards them was similar to that of the denizens of the forest. These were men, unpredictable, and to be avoided if possible.

On the other side of the ravine rose Pari Tibba, Hill of the Fairies: a bleak, scrub-covered hill where no one lived.

It was said that in the previous century Englishmen had tried building their houses on the hill, but the area had always attracted lightning, due to either the hill's location or due to its mineral deposits; after several houses had been struck by lightning, the settlers had moved on to the next hill, where the town now stands.

To the hillmen it is Pari Tibba, haunted by the spirits of a pair of ill-fated lovers who perished there in a storm; to others it is known as Burnt Hill, because of its scarred and stunted trees.

One day, after crossing the stream, I climbed Pari Tibba — a stiff undertaking, because there was no path to the top and I had to scramble up a preciptious rock-face with the help of rocks and roots that were apt to come loose in my groping hand.

But at the top was a plateau with a few pine trees, their upper branches catching the wind and humming softly. There I found the ruins of what must have been the houses of the first settlers —just a few piles of rubble, now overgrown with weeds, sorrel, dandelions and nettles.

As I walked through the roofless ruins, I was struck by the silence that surrounded me, the absence of birds and animals, the sense of complete desolation.

The silence was so absolute that it seemed to be ringing in my ears. But there was something else of which I was becoming increasingly aware: the strong feline odour of one of the cat family.

I paused and looked about. I was alone. There was no movement of dry leaf or loose stone. The ruins were for the most part open to the sky. Their rotting rafters had collapsed, jamming together to form a low passage like the entrance to a mine; and this dark cavern seemed to lead down into the ground.

The smell was stronger when I approached this spot, so I stopped again and waited there, wondering if I had discovered the lair of the leopard, wondering if the animal was now at rest after a night's hunt.

Perhaps he was crouching there in the dark, watching me, recognizing me, knowing me as the man who walked alone in the forest without a weapon.

I like to think that he was there, that he knew me, and that he acknowledged my visit in the friendliest way: by ignoring me altogether.

Perhaps I had made him confident — too confident, too careless, too trusting of the human in his midst. I did not venture any further; I was not out of my mind. I did not seek physical contact, or even another glimpse of that beautiful sinewy body, springing from rock to rock. It was his trust I wanted, and I think he gave it to me.

But did the leopard, trusting one man, make the mistake of bestowing his trust on others? Did I, by casting out all fear — my own fear, and the leopard's protective fear — leave him defenseless?

Because next day, coming up the path from the stream, shouting and beating drums, were the hunters. They had a long bamboo pole across their shoulders; and slung from the pole, feet up, head down, was the lifeless body of the leopard, shot in the neck and in the head.

'We told you there was a leopard!' they shouted, in great good humour. 'Isn't he a fine specimen?'

'Yes,' I said. 'He was a beautiful leopard.'

I walked home through the silent forest. It was very silent, almost as though the birds and animals knew that their trust had been violated.

I remembered the lines of a poem by D.H. Lawrence; and, as I climbed the steep and lonely path to my home, the words beat out their rhythm in my mind: 'There was room in the world for a mountain lion and me.'

Sita and the River

The Island in the River

In the middle of the river, the river that began in the mountains of the Himalayas and ended in the Bay of Bengal, there was a small island. The river swept round the island, sometimes clawing at its banks but never going right over it. The river was still deep and swift at this point, because the foothills were only forty miles distant. More than twenty years had passed since the river had flooded the island, and at that time no one had lived there. But ten years ago a small family had came to live on the island, and now a small hut stood on it, mud-walled hut with a sloping thatched roof. The hut had been built into a huge rock. Only three of its walls were mud, the fourth was rock.

A few goats grazed on the short grass and the prickly leaves of the thistle. Some hens followed them about. There was a melon patch and a vegetable patch and a small field of marigolds. The marigolds were sometimes made into garlands, and the garlands were sold during weddings or festivals in the nearby town.

In the middle of the islands stood a *peepul* tree. It was the only tree on this tongue of land. But *peepul* trees will grow anywhere — through the walls of old temples, through gravestones, even from rooftops. It is usually the buildings, and not the trees, that give way!

Even during the great flood, which had occured twenty years back, the *peepul* tree had stood firm.

It was an old tree, much older than the old man on the island, who was only seventy. The *peepul* was about three hundred. It also provided shelter for the birds who sometimes visited it from the mainland.

Three hundred years ago, the land on which the *peepul* tree stood had been part of the mainland; but the river had changed its course, and that bit of land with the tree on it had become an island. The tree had lived alone for many years. Now it gave shade and shelter to a small family, who were grateful for its presence.

The people of India love *peepul* trees, especially during the hot summer months when the heart-shaped leaves catch the least breath of air and flutter eagerly, fanning those who sit beneath.

A sacred tree, the *peepul*, the abode of spirits, good and bad.

'Do not yawn when you are sitting beneath the tree,' Grandmother would warn Sita, her ten-year-old granddaughter. 'And if you must yawn always snap your fingers in front of your mouth. If you forget to do that, a demon might jump down your throat!'

'And then what will happen?' asked Sita.

'He will probably ruin your digestion,' said Grandfather, who didn't take demons very seriously.

The *peepul* had beautiful leaf, and Grandmother likened it to the body of the mighty god Krishna — broad at the shoulders, then tapering down to a very slim waist.

The tree attracted birds and insects from across the river. On some nights it was full of fireflies.

Whenever Grandmother saw the fireflies, she told her favourite story.

'When we first came here,' she said, 'we were greatly troubled by mosquitoes. One night your grandfather rolled himself up in his sheet so that they couldn't get at him. After a while he peeped out of his bedsheet to make sure they were gone. He saw a firefly and said, You clever mosquito! You could not see in the dark, so you got a lantern!'

Grandfather was mending a fishing-net. He had fished in the river for ten years, and he was a good fisherman. He knew where to find to slim silver *chilwa* and the big, beautiful *masheer* and the *singhara* with its long whiskers; he knew where the river was deep and where it was shallow; he knew which baits to use — when to use worms and when to use gram. He had taught his son to fish, but his son had gone to work in a factory in a city, nearly a hundred miles away. He had no grandson; but he had a granddaughter, Sita, and she could do all the things a boy could do, and sometimes she could do them better. She had lost her mother when she was two or three. Grandmother had taught her all that a girl should know —

cooking, sewing, grinding spices, cleaning the house, feeding the birds — and Grandfather had taught her other things, like taking a small boat across the river, cleaning a fish, repairing a net, or catching a snake by the tail! And some things she had learnt by herself — like climbing the *peepul* tree, or leaping from rock to rock in shallow water, or swimming in an inlet where the water was calm.

Neither grandparent could read or write, and as a result Sita couldn't read or write.

There was a school in one of the villages across the river, but Sita had never seen it. She had never been further than Shahganj, the small market town near the river. She had never seen a city. She had never been in a train. The river cut her off from many things; but she could not miss what she had never known, and besides, she was much too busy.

While Grandfather mended his net, Sita was inside the hut, pressing her grandmother's forehead which was hot with fever. Grandmother had been ill for three days and could not eat. She had been ill before, but she had never been so bad. Grandfather had brought her some sweet oranges from Shahganj, and she could suck the juice from the oranges, but she couldn't take anything else.

She was younger than Grandfather, but, because she was sick, she looked much older. She had never been very strong. She coughed a lot, and sometimes she had difficulty in breathing.

When Sita noticed that Grandmother was sleeping, she left the bedside and tip-toed out of the room on her bare feet.

Outside, she found the sky dark with monsoon clouds. It had rained all night, and, in a few hours, it would rain again. The monsoon rains had come early, at the end of June. Now it was the end of July, and already the river was swollen. Its rushing sound seemed nearer and more menacing than usual.

Sita went to her grandfather and sat down beside him.

'When you are hungry, tell me,' she said, 'and I will make the bread.'

'Is your grandmother asleep?'

'Yes. But she will wake soon. The pain is deep.'

The old man stared out across the river, at the dark green of the forest, at the leaden sky, and said, 'If she is not better by morning, I will take her to the hospital in Shahganj. They will know how to make her well. Your may be on your own for two or three days. You have been on your own before.'

Sita nodded gravely — she had been alone before; but not in the middle of the rains, with the river so high. But she knew that someone must stay behind. She wanted Grandmother to get well, and she knew that only Grandfather could take the small boat across the river when the current was so strong.

Sita was not afraid of being left alone, but she did not like the look of the river. That morning, when she had been fetching water, she had noticed that the lever suddenly disappeared.

'Grandfather, if the river rises higher, what will I do?'

'You must keep to the high ground.'

'And if the water reaches the high ground?'

'Then go into the hut, and take the hens with you.'

'And if the water comes into the hut?'

'Then climb into the *peepul* tree. It is a strong tree. It will not fall. And the water cannot rise higher than the tree.'

'And the goats, Grandfather?'

'I will be taking them with me. I may have to sell them, to pay for good food and medicine for your grandmother. As for the hens, you can put them on the roof if the water enters the hut. But do not worry too much' — and he patted Sita's head — 'the water will not rise so high. Has it ever done so? I will be back soon, remember that.'

'And won't Grandmother come back?'

'Yes — but they may keep her in the hospital for some time.'

The Sound of the River

That evening it began to rain again. Big pellets of rain, scarring the surface of the river. But it was warm rain, and Sita could move about in it. She was not afraid of getting wet, she rather liked it. In the previous month, when the first monsoon shower had arrived, washing the dusty leaves of the tree and bringing up the good smell of the earth, she had exulted in it, had run about shouting for joy. She was used to it now, even a little tired of the rain, but she did not mind getting wet. It was steamy indoors, and her thin dress would soon dry in the heat from the kitchen fire.

She walked about barefooted, barelegged. She was very sure on her feet; her toes had grown accustomed to gripping all kinds of rocks, slippery of sharp. And though thin, she was surprisingly strong.

Black hair, streaming across her face. Black eyes. Slim brown arms. A scar on her thigh: when she was small, visiting her mother's village, a hyaena had entered the house where she was sleeping, fastened on to her leg and tried to drag her away; but her screams had roused the villagers, and the hyaena had run off.

She moved about in the pouring rain, chasing the hens into a shelter behind the hut. A harmless brown snake, flooded out of its hole, was moving across the open ground. Sita took a stick, picked the snake up with it, and dropped it behind a cluster of rocks. She had no quarrel with snakes. They kept down the rats and the frogs. She wondered how the rats had first come to the island — probably in someone's boat or in a sack of grain.

She disliked the huge black scorpions who left their waterlogged dwellings and tried to take shelter in the hut. It was so easy to step on one, and the sting could be very painful. She had been bitten by a scorpion the previous monsoon, and for a day and a night she had known fever and great pain. Sita had never killed living creatures, but now, whenever she found a scorpion, she crushed it with a rock!

When, finally, she went indoors, she was hungry. She ate some parched gram and warmed up some goats' milk.

Grandmother woke once, and asked for water, and Grandfather held the brass tumbler to her lips.

It rained all night.

The roof was leaking, and a small puddle formed on the floor. Grandfather kept the kerosene-lamps alight. They did not need the light but somehow it made them feel safer.

The sound of the river had always been with them, although they seldom noticed it; but that night they noticed a change in its sound. There was something like a moan, like a wind in the tops of tall trees, and a swift hiss as the water swept round the rocks and carried away pebbles. And sometimes there was a rumble, as loose earth fell into the water. Sita could not sleep.

She had a rag doll, made with Grandmother's help out of bits of old clothing. She kept it by her side every night. The doll was some-one to talk to, when the nights were long and sleep elusive. Her grandparents were often ready to talk; but sometimes Sita wanted to have secrets, and, though there were no special secrets in her life, she made up a few because it was fun to have them. And if you have secrets, you must have a friend to share them with. Since there were no other children on the island, Sita shared her secrets with the rag doll, whose name was Mumta.

Grandfather and Grandmother were asleep, though the sound of Grandmother's laboured breathing was almost as persistent as the sound of the river.

'Mumta,' whispered Sita in the dark, starting one of her private conversations. 'Do you think Grandmother will get well again?'

Mumta always answered Sita's questions, even though the answers were really Sita's answers.

'She is very old,' said Mumta.

'Do you think the river will reach the hut?' asked Sita.

'If it keeps raining like this, and the river keeps rising, it will reach the hut.'

'I am afraid of the river, Mumta. Aren't you afraid?'

'Don't be afraid. The river has always been good to us.'

'What will we do if it comes into the hut?'

'We will climb on the roof.'

'And if it reaches the roof?'

'We will climb the *peepul* tree. The river has never gone higher than the *peepul* tree.'

As soon as the first light showed through the little skylight, Sita got up and went outside. It wasn't raining hard, it was drizzling, but it was the sort of drizzle that could continue for days, and it probably meant that heavy rain was falling in the hills where the river began.

Sita went down to the water's edge. She couldn't find her favourite rock, the one on which she often sat dangling her feet in the water, watching the little *chilwa* fish swim by. it was still there, no doubt, but the river had gone over it.

She stood on the sand, and she could feel the water oozing and bubbling beneath her feet.

The river was no longer green and blue and flecked with white; it was a muddy colour.

She went back to the hut. Grandfather was up now. He was getting his boat ready.

Sita milked the goat, thinking that perhaps it was the last time she would be milking it; but she did not care for the goat in the same way that she cared for Mumta.

The sun was just coming up when Grandfather pushed off in the boat. Grandmother lay in the prow. She was staring hard at Sita, trying to speak, but the words would not come. She raised her hand in a blessing.

Sita bent and touched her grandmother's feet, and then Grandfather pushed off. The little boat — with its two old people and three goats — rode swiftly on the river, edging its way towards the opposite bank. The current was very swift, and the boat would be carried about half-a-mile downstream before Grandfather would be able to get it to dry land.

It bobbed about on the water, getting smaller and smaller, until it was just a speck on the broad river.

And suddenly Sita was alone.

There was a wind, whipping the raindrops against her face; and there was the water, rushing past the island; and there was the distant shore, blurred by rain; and there was the small hut; and there was the tree.

Sita got busy. The hens had to be fed. They weren't concerned about anything except food. Sita threw them handfuls of coarse grain, potato-peels and peanut-shells.

Then she took the broom and swept out the hut; lit the charcoal-burner, warmed some milk, and thought, 'Tomorrow there will be no milk . . .' She began peeling onions. Soon her eyes started smarting, and, pausing for a few moments and glancing round the quiet room, she became aware again that she was alone. Grandfather's *hookah*-pipe stood by itself in one corner. It was a beautiful old *hookah*, which had belonged to Sita's great-grandfather. The bowl was made out of a coconut encased in silver. The long winding stem was at least four feet long. It was their most treasured possession. Grandmother's sturdy *shisham*-wood walking stick stood in another corner.

Sita looked around for Mumta, found the doll beneath the light wooden *charpoy*, and placed her within sight and hearing.

Thunder rolled down from the hills. Boom — boom — boom . . .

'The Gods of the mountains are angry,' said Sita. 'Do you think they are angry with me?'

'Why should they be angry with you?' asked Mumta.

'They don't need a reason for being angry. They are angry with everything, and we are in the middle of everything. We are so small — do you think they know we are here?'

'Who knows what the Gods think?'

'But I made you,' said Sita, 'and I know you are here.'

'And will you save me if the river rises?'

'Yes, of course. I won't go anywhere without you, Mumta.'

The Water Rises

Sita couldn't stay indoors for long. She went out, taking Mumta with her, and stared out across the river, to the safe land on the other side. But was it really safe there? The river looked much wider now. It had crept over its banks and spread far across the flat plain. Far away, people were driving their cattle through waterlogged, flooded fields, carrying their belongings in bundles on their heads or shoulders, leaving their homes, making for high land. It wasn't safe anywhere.

Sita wondered what had happened to Grandfather and Grandmother. If they had reached the shore safely, Grandfather would have to engage a bullock-cart or a pony-drawn *ekka* to get Grandmother to the district hospital, five or six miles away. Shahganj had a market, a court, a jail, a cinema, and a hospital.

She wondered if she would ever see Grandmother again. She had done her best to look after the old lady, remembering the times when Grandmother had looked after her, had gently touched her fevered brow, and had told her stories — stories about the Gods — about the young Krishna, friend of birds and animals, so full of mischief, always causing confusion among the other Gods. He made the God Indra angry by shifting a mountain without permission. Indra was the God of the clouds, who made the thunder and lightning, and when he was angry he sent down a deluge such as this one.

The island looked much smaller now. Some of its mud banks had dissolved quickly, sinking into the river. But in the middle of the island there was rocky ground, and the rocks would never crumble, they could only be submerged.

Sita climbed into the tree to get a better view of the flood. She had climbed the tree many times, and it took her only a few seconds to reach the higher branches. She put her hand to her eyes as a shield from the rain, and gazed upstream.

There was water everywhere. The world had become one vast river. Even the trees on the forested side of the river looked as though they had grown from the water, like mangroves. The sky was banked with massive, moisture-laden clouds. Thunder rolled down from the hills, and the river seemed to take it up with a hollow booming sound.

Something was floating down the river, something big and bloated. It was closer now, and Sita could make out its bulk — a drowned bullock, being carried downstream.

So the water had already flooded the villages further upstream. Or perhaps the bullock had strayed too close to the rising river.

Sita's worst fears were confirmed when, a little later, she saw planks of wood, small trees and bushes, and then a wooden bedstead, floating past the island.

As she climbed down from the tree, it began to rain more heavily. She ran indoors, shooing the hens before her. They flew into the hut and huddled under Grandmother's cot. Sita thought it would be best to keep them together now.

There were three hens and a cockbird. The river did not bother them. They were interested only in food, and Sita kept them content by throwing them a handful of onion-skins.

She would have liked to close the door and shut out the swish of the rain and the boom of the river; but then she would have no way of knowing how fast the water rose.

She took Mumta in her arms and began praying for the rain to stop and the river to fall. She prayed to the God Indra, and, just in case he was busy elsewhere, she prayed to other Gods too. She prayed for the safety of her grandparents and for her own safety. She put herself last — but only after an effort!

Finally Sita decided to make herself a meal. So she chopped up some onions fried them, then added turmeric and red chilli-powder, salt and water, and stirred until she had everything sizzling; and then she added a cup of lentils and covered the pot.

Doing this took her about ten minutes. It would take about half-an-hour for the dish to cook.

When she looked outside, she saw pools of water among the rocks. She couldn't tell if it was rain water or overflow from the river.

She had an idea.

A big tin trunk stood in a corner of the room. In it Grandmother kept an old single-thread sewing-machine. It had belonged once to an English lady, had found its way to a Shahganj junk-yard, and had been rescued by Grandfather who had paid fifteen rupees for it. It was just over a hundred years old, but it could still be used.

The trunk also contained an old sword. This had originally belonged to Sita's great-grandfather, who had used it to help defend his village against marauding Rohilla soldier's more than a century ago. Sita could tell that it had been used to fight with, because there were several small dents in the steel blade.

But there was no time for Sita to start admiring family heirlooms. She decided to stuff the trunk with everything useful or valuable. There was a chance that it wouldn't be carried away by the water.

Grandfather's *hookah* went into the trunk. Grandmother's walking-stick went in, too. So did a number of small tins containing the spices used in cooking — nutmeg, caraway seed, cinnamon, corrainder, pepper — also a big tin of flour and another of molasses. Even if she had to spend several hours in the tree, there would be something to eat when she came down again.

A clean white cotton *dhoti* of Grandfather's, and Grandmother's only spare *sari* also went into the trunk. Never mind if they got stained with curry powder! Never mind if they got the smell of salted fish — some of that went in, too.

Sita was so busy packing the trunk that she paid no attention to the lick of cold water at her heels. She locked the trunk, dropped the key into a crack in the rock wall, and turned to give her attention to the food. It was only then that she discovered that she was walking about on a watery floor.

She stood still, horrified by what she saw. The water was oozing over the door-sill, pushing its way into the room.

In her fright, Sita forgot about her meal and everything else. Darting out of the hut, she ran splashing through ankle-deep water toward the safety of the *peepul* tree. If the tree hadn't been there, such a well-known landmark, she might have floundered into deep water, into the river.

She climbed swiftly into the strong arms of the tree, made herself comfortable on a familiar branch, and thrust the wet hair away from her eyes.

The Tree

She was glad she had hurried. The hut was, now surrounded by water. Only the higher parts of the island could still be seen —a few rocks, the big rock into which the hut was built, a hillock on which some brambles and thorn-apples grew.

The hens hadn't bothered to leave the hut. Instead, they were perched on the wooden bedstead.

'Will the river rise still higher?' wondered Sita. She had never seen it like this before. With a deep, muffled roar it swirled around her, stretching away in all directions.

The most unusual things went by on the water — an aluminium kettle, a cane-chair, a tin of tooth-powder, an empty cigarette packet, a wooden slipper, a plastic doll . . .

A doll!

With a sinking feeling, Sita remembered Mumta.

Poor Mumta, she had been left behind in the hut. Sita, in her hurry, had forgotten her only companion.

She climbed down from the tree and ran splashing through the water towards the hut. Already the current was pulling at her legs. When she reached the hut, she found it full of water. The hens had gone — and so had Mumta.

Sita struggled back to the tree. She was only just in time, for the waters were higher now, the island fast disappearing.

She crouched miserably in the fork of the tree, watching her world disappear.

She had always loved the river. Why was it threatening her now? She remembered the doll, and she thought, 'If I can be so careless with someone I have made, how can I expect the gods to notice me?'

Something went floating past the tree. Sita caught a glimpse of a stiff, upraised arm and long hair streaming behind on the water. The body of a drowned woman. It was soon gone, but it made Sita feel very small and lonely, at the mercy of great and cruel forces. She began to shiver and then to cry.

She stopped crying when she saw an empty kerosene tin, with one of the hens perched on top. The tin came bobbing along on the water and sailed slowly past the tree. The hen looked a bit ruffled but seemed secure on its perch.

A little later Sita saw the remaining hens fly up to the rock-ledge to huddle there in a small recess.

The water was still rising. All that remained of the island was the big rock behind the hut, and the top of the hut, and the *peepul* tree.

She climbed a little higher, into the crook of a branch. A jungle-crow settled in the branches above her. Sita saw the nest, the crow's nest, an untidy platform of twigs wedged in the fork of a branch.

In the nest were four speckled eggs. The crow sat on them and cawed disconsolately. But though the bird sounded miserable its presence brought some cheer to Sita. At least she was not alone.

Better to have a crow for company than no one at all.

Other things came floating out of the hut — a large pumpkin; a red turban belonging to Grandfather, unwinding in the water like a long snake; and then — Mumta!

The doll, being filled with straw and wood shavings moved quite swiftly on the water, too swiftly for Sita to do anything about rescuing it. Sita wanted to call out, to urge her friend to make for the tree; but she knew that Mumta could not swim — the doll could only float, travel with the river, and perhaps be washed ashore many miles downstream.

The trees shook in the wind and the rain. The crow cawed and flew up, circled the tree a few times, then returned to the nest. Sita clung to the branch.

The tree trembled throughout its tall frame. To Sita it felt like an earthquake tremor; she felt the shudder of the tree in her own bones.

The river swirled all around her now. It was almost up to the roof of the hut. Soon the mud walls would crumble and vanish. Except for the big rock and some trees very far away, there was only water to be seen. Water, and grey weeping sky.

In the distance, a boat with several people in it moved sluggishly away from the ruins of a flooded village. Someone looked out across the flooded river and said, 'See, there is a tree right in the middle of the river! How could it have got there? Isn't someone moving in the tree?'

But the others thought he was imagining things it was only a tree carried down by the flood, they said. In worrying about their own distress, they had forgotten about the island in the middle of the river.

The river was very angry now, rampaging down from the hills and thundering across the plain, bringing with it dead animals, uprooted trees, household goods, and huge fish choked to death by the swirling mud.

The *peepul* tree groaned. Its long, winding roots still clung tenaciously to the earth from which it had sprung many, many years ago. But the earth was softening, the stones were being washed away. The roots of the tree were rapidly losing their hold.

The crow must have known that something was wrong because it kept flying up and circling the tree, reluctant to settle in it, yet unwilling to fly away. As long as the nest was there, the crow would remain too.

Sita's wet cotton dress clung to her thin body. The rain streamed down from her long black hair. It poured from every leaf of the tree. The crow, too, was drenched and groggy.

The tree groaned and moved again.

There was a flurry of leaves, then a surge of mud from below. To Sita it seemed as though the river was rising to meet the sky. The tree tilted swinging Sita from side to side. Her feet were in the water but she clung tenaciously to her branch.

And then, she found the tree moving, moving with the river, rocking her about, dragging its roots along the ground as it set out on the first and last journey of its life.

And as the tree moved out on the river and the little island was lost in the swirling waters, Sita forgot her fear and her loneliness. The tree was taking her with it. She was not alone. It was as though one of the gods had remembered her after all.

Taken with the Flood

The branches swung Sita about, but she did not lose her grip. The tree was her friend. it had known her all these years, and now it held her in its old and dying arms as though it were determined to keep her from the river.

The crow kept flying around the moving tree. The bird was in a great rage. Its nest was still up there — but not for long! The tree lurched and twisted, and the nest fell into the water. Sita saw the eggs sink.

The crow swooped low over the water but there was nothing it could do. In a few moments the nest had disappeared.

The bird followed the tree for some time; then, flapping its wings, it rose high into the air and flew across the river until it was out of sight.

Sita was alone once more. But there was no time for feeling lonely. Everything was in motion — up and down and sideways and forwards.

She saw a turtle swimming past — a great big river turtle, the kind that feeds on decaying flesh. Sita turned her face away. In the distance she saw a flooded village and people in flat-bottomed boats; but they were very far.

Because of its great size, the tree did not move very swiftly on the river. Sometimes, when it reached shallow water, it stopped, its roots catching in the rocks; but not for long: the river's momentum soon swept it on.

At one place, where there was a bend in the river, the tree struck a sandbank and was still. It would not move again.

Sita felt very tired. Her arms were aching and she had to cling tightly to her branch to avoid slipping into the water. The rain blurred her vision. She wondered if she should brave the current and try swimming to safety. But she did not want to leave the tree. It was all that was left to her now, and she felt safe in its branches.

Then, above the sound of the river, she heard someone calling. The voice was faint and seemed very far but, looking upriver through the curtain of rain, Sita was able to make out a small boat coming towards her.

There was a boy in the boat. He seemed quite at home on the turbulent river, and he was smiling at Sita as he guided his boat towards the tree. He held on to one of the branches to steady himself, and gave his free hand to Sita.

She grasped the outstretched hand and slipped into the boat beside the boy.

He placed his bare foot against the trunk of the tree and pushed away.

The little boat moved swiftly down the river. Sita looked back and saw the big tree lying on its side on the sandbank, while the river swirled round it and pulled at its branches, carrying away its beautiful slender leaves.

And then the tree grew smaller and was left far behind. A new journey had begun.

The Boy in the Boat

She lay stretched out in the boat, too tried to talk, too tired to move. The boy looked at her but he did not say anything, he just kept smiling. He leant on his two small oars, stroking smoothly, rhythmically, trying to keep from going into the middle of the river. He wasn't strong enough to get the boat right out of the swift current; but he kept trying.

A small boat on a big river — a river that had broken its bounds and reached across the plains in every direction — the boat moved swiftly on the wild brown water, and the girl's home and the boy's home were both left far behind.

The boy wore only a loincloth. He was a slim, wiry boy, with a hard flat belly. He had high cheekbones, strong white teeth. He was a little darker than Sita.

He did not speak until they reached a broader, smoother stretch of river, and then, resting on his oars and allowing the boat to drift a little, he said, 'You live on the island. I have seen you sometimes, from my boat. But where are the others?'

'My grandmother was sick,' said Sita. 'Grandfather took her to the hospital in Shahganj.'

'When did they leave?'

'Early this morning.'

Early that morning — and already Sita felt as though it had been many mornings ago!

'Where are you from?' she asked.

'I am from a village near the foothills. About six miles from your home. I was in my boat, trying to get across the river with the news that our village was badly flooded. The current was too strong. I was swept down and past your island. We cannot fight the river when it is like this, we must go where it takes us.'

'You must be tired,' said Sita. Give me the oars.'

'No. There is not much to do now. The river has gone wherever it wanted to go — it will not drive us before it any more.'

He brought in one oar, and with his free hand felt under the seat, where there was a small basket. He produced two mangoes, and gave one to Sita.

'I was supposed to sell these in Shahganj,' he said. 'My father is very strict. Even if I return home safely, he will ask me what I got for the mangoes!'

'And what will you tell him?'

'I will say they are at the bottom of the river!'

They bit deep into the ripe fleshy mangoes, using their teeth to tear the skin away. The sweet juice trickled down their skins. The good smell — like the smell of the leaves of the cosmos-flower when crushed between the palms — helped to revive Sita. The flavour of the fruit was heavenly — truly the nectar of the gods!

Sita hadn't tasted a mango for over a year. For a few moments she forgot about everything else. All that mattered was the sweet, dizzy flavour of the mango.

The boat drifted, but slowly now, for as they went further downstream, the river gradually lost its power and fury. It was late afternoon when the rain stopped; but the clouds did not break up.

'My father has many buffaloes,' said the boy, 'but several have been lost in the flood.'

'Do you go to school?' asked Sita.

'Yes, I am supposed to go to school. I don't always go, at least, not when the weather is fine! There is a school near our village. I don't think you go to school?'

'No. There is too much work at home.'

'Can you read and write?'

'Only a little...'

'Then you should go to a school.'

'It is too far away.'

'True. But you should know how to read and write. Otherwise you will be stuck on your island for the rest of your life — that is, if your island is still there!'

'But I like the island,' protested Sita.

'Because you are with people you love,' said the boy. 'But your grandparents, they are old, they must die some day — and then you will be alone, and will you like the island then?'

Sita did not answer. She was trying to think of what life would be like without her grandparents. It would be an empty island, that was true. She would be imprisoned by the river.

'I can help you,' said the boy. 'When we get back — if we get back — I will come to see you sometimes, and I will teach you to read and write. All right?'

'Yes,' said Sita, nodding thoughtfully. 'When we get back . . .'

The boy smiled.

'My name is Vijay,' he said.

Towards evening the river changed colour. The sun, low in the sky, broke through a rift in the clouds, and the river changed slowly from grey to gold, from gold to a deep orange, and then, as the sun went down, all these colours were drowned in the river, and the river took the colour of the night.

The moon was almost at the full, and they could see a belt of forest along the line of the river.

'I will try to reach the trees,' said Vijay.

He pulled for the trees, and after ten minutes of strenuous rowing reached a bend in the river and was able to escape the pull of the main current.

Soon they were in a forest, rowing between tall trees, *Sal* and *Shisham*.

The boat moved slowly as Vijay took it in and out of the trees, while the moonlight made a crooked silver path over the water.

'We will tie the boat to tree,' he said. 'Then we can rest. Tomorrow, we will have to find out way out of the forest.'

He produced a length of rope from the bottom of the boat, tied one end to the boat's stern, and threw the other end over a stout branch which hung only a few feet above the water. The boat came to rest against the trunk of the tree.

It was tall, sturdy tree, The Indian mahogany. It was a safe place, for there was no rush of water in the forest; and the trees grew close together, making the earth firm and unyielding.

But those who lived in the forest were on the move. The animals had been flooded out of their holes, caves and lairs, and were looking for shelter and high ground.

Sita and Vijay had just finished tying the boat to the tree when they saw a huge python gliding over the water towards them.

'Do you think it will try to get into the boat?' asked Sita.

'I don't think so,' said Vijay, although he took the precaution of holding an oar ready to fend off the snake.

But the python went past them, its head above water, its great length trailing behind, until it was lost in the shadows.

Vijay had more mangoes in the basket, and he and Sita sucked hungrily at them while they sat in the boat.

A big Sambhur-stag came threshing through the water. He did not have to swim: he was so tall that his head and shoulders remained well above the water. His antlers were big and beautiful.

'There will be other animals,' said Sita. 'Should we climb onto the tree?'

'We are quite safe in the boat,' said Vijay. The animals will not be dangerous tonight. They will not even hunt each other, they are only interested in reaching dry land. For once, the deer are safe from the tiger and the leopard. You lie down and sleep, I will keep watch.'

Sita stretched herself out in the boat and closed her eyes. She was very tired,and the sound of the water lapping against the sides of the boat soon lulled her to sleep.

She woke once, when a strange bird called overhead. She raised herself on one elbow; but Vijay was awake, sitting beside her, his legs drawn up and his chin resting on his knees. He was gazing out across the water. He looked blue in the moonlight, the colour of the young god Krishna, and for a few moments Sita was confused and wondered if the boy was actually Krishna; but when she thought about it, she decided that it wasn't possible, he was just a village boy and she had seen hundreds like him —well, not exactly like him; he was a little different . . .

And when she slept again, she dreamt that the boy and Krishna were one, and that she was sitting beside him on a great white bird, which flew over the mountains, over the snow peaks of the Himalayas, into the cloud-land of the gods. And there was a great rumbling sound, as though the gods were angry about the whole thing, and she woke up to this terrible sound and looked about her, and there in the moonlit glade, up to his belly in water, stood a young elephant, his trunk raised as he trumpeted his predicament to the forest — for he was a young elephant, and he was lost, and was looking for his mother.

He trumpeted again, then lowered his head and listened. And presently, from far away, came the shrill trumpeting of another elephant. It must have been the young one's mother, because he gave several excited trumpet calls, and then went stamping and churning through the flood-water toward a gap in the trees. The boat rocked in the waves made by his passing.

'It is all right,' said Vijay. 'You can go to sleep again.'

'I don't think I will sleep now,' said Sita.

'Then I will play my flute for you and the time will pass quickly.'

He produced a flute from under the seat, and putting it to his lips he began to play. And the sweetest music that Sita had ever heard came pouring from the little flute, and it seemed to fill the forest with its beautiful sound. And the music carried her away again, into the land of dreams, and they were riding on the bird once more, Sita and the blue god, and they were passing through cloud and mist, until suddenly the sun shot through the clouds. And at that moment Sita opened her eyes and saw the sky through the branches of the mahogany tree, the shiny green leaves making a bold pattern against the blinding blue of an open sky.

The forest was drenched with sunshine. Clouds were gathering again, but for an-hour-or-two there would be hot sun on a steamy river.

Vijay was fast asleep in the bottom of the boat. His flute lay in the palm of his half-open hand. The sun came slating across his bare brown legs. A leaf had fallen on his face, but it had not woken him, it lay on his cheek as though it had grown there.

Sita did not move about, as she did not want to wake the boy. Instead she looked around her, and she thought the water level had fallen in the night, but she couldn't be sure.

Vijay woke at last. He yawned, stretched his limbs, and sat up beside Sita.

'I am hungry,' he said.

'So am I,' said Sita.

'The last mangoes,' he said, emptying the basket of its last two mangoes.

After they had finished the fruit, they sucked the big seeds until they were quite dry. The discarded seeds floated well on the water. Sita had always preferred them to paper-boats.

'We had better move on,' said Vijay.

He rowed the boat through the trees, and then for about an hour they were passing through the flooded forest, under the dripping branches of rain washed trees. Sometimes they had to use the oars to push away vines and creepers. Sometimes submerged bushes hampered them. But they were out of the forest before ten o'clock.

The water was no longer very deep, and they were soon gliding over flooded fields. In the distance they saw a village standing on high ground. In the old days, people had built their villages on hill tops as a better defence against bandits and the soldiers of invading armies. This was an old village; and, though its inhabitants had long ago exchanged their swords for pruning-forks, the hill on which it stood gave it protection from the flood waters.

A Bullock-Cart Ride

The people of the village were at first reluctant to help Sita and Vijay.

'They are strangers,' said an old woman. 'They are not of our people.'

'They are of low-caste,' said another. 'They cannot remain with us.'

'Nonsense!' said a tall, turbaned farmer, twirling his long white moustache. 'They are children, not robbers. They will come into my house.'

The people of the village — long-limbed, sturdy men and women of the *Jat* race — were generous by nature, and once the elderly farmer had given them the lead they were friendly and helpful.

Sita was anxious to get to her grandparents; and the farmer, who had business to transact at a village fair some twenty miles distant, offered to take Sita and Vijay with him.

The fair was being held at a place called Karauli, and at Karauli there was a railway station, and a train went to Shahganj.

It was a journey that Sita would always remember. The bullock-cart was so slow on the waterlogged roads that there was plenty of time in which to see things, to notice one another, to talk, to think, to dream.

Vijay couldn't sit still in the cart. He was used to the swift, gliding movements of his boat (which he had had to leave behind in the village), and every now and then he would jump off the cart and walk beside it, often ankle-deep in water.

There were four of them in the cart. Sita and Vijay, Hukam Singh, the *Jat* farmer; and his son, Phambiri, a mountain of a man who was going to take part in the wrestling-matches at the fair.

Hukam Singh, who drove the bullocks, liked to talk. He had been a soldier in the British Indian Army during the First World War, and had been with his regiment to Italy and Mesopotamia.

'There is nothing to compare with soldiering,' he said, 'except, of course, farming. If you can't be a farmer, be a soldier. Are you listening, boy? Which will you be — farmer or soldier?'

'Neither,' said Vijay. 'I shall be an engineer!'

Hukam Singh's long moustaches seemed almost to bristle with indignation.

'An engineer! What next! what does your father do, boy?'

'He keeps buffaloes.'

'Ah! And his son would be an engineer? . . . Well, well, the world isn't what it used to be! No one knows his rightful place any more. Men sent their children to schools, and what is the result? Engineers! And who will look after the buffaloes, while you are engineering?'

'I will sell the buffaloes,' said Vijay, adding rather cheekily: 'Perhaps you will buy one of them, *Subedar-Sahib!*'

He took the cheek out of his remark by adding '*Subedar-Sahib,*' the rank of a non-commissioned officer in the old Army. Hukam Singh, who had never reached this rank, was naturally flattered.

'Fortunately, Phambiri hasn't been to school! He'll be a farmer, and a fine one too.'

Phambiri simply grunted, which could have meant anything. He hadn't studied further than Class six, which was just as well, as he was a man of muscle, not brain.

Phambiri loved putting his strength to some practical and useful purpose. Whenever the cart wheels got stuck in the mud, he would get off, remove his shirt, and put his shoulder to the side of the cart, while his muscles bulged and the sweat glistened on his broad back.

'Phambiri is the strongest man in our district,' said Hukum Singh proudly. 'And clever, too! It takes quick thinking to win a wrestling match.'

'I have never seen one,' said Sita.

'Then stay with us tomorrow morning, and you will see Phambiri wrestle. He has been challenged by the Karauli champion. It will be a great fight!'

'We must see Phambiri win,' said Vijay.

'Will there be time?' asked Sita.

'Why not? The train for Shahganj won't come in till evening. The fair goes on all day, and the wrestling bouts will take place in the morning.'

'Yes, you must see me win!' exclaimed Phambiri, thumping himself on the chest as he climbed back on to the cart after freeing the wheels. 'No one can defeat me!'

'How can you be so certain?' asked Vijay.

'He *has* to be certain,' said Hukam Singh. 'I have taught him to be certain! You can't win anything if you are uncertain . . . Isn't that right, Phambiri? You *know* you are going to win!'

'I know,' said Phambiri, with a grunt of confidence.

'Well, someone has to lose,' said Vijay.

'Very true,' said Hukum Singh smugly. 'After all, what would we do without losers? But for Phambiri, it is win, win, all the time!'

'And *if* he loses?' persisted Vijay.

'Then he will just forget that it happened, and will go on to win his next fight!'

Vijay found Hukum Singh's logic almost unanswerable, but Sita, who had been puzzled by the argument, now saw everything very clearly and said, 'Perhaps he hasn't won any fights as yet. Did he lose the last one?'

'Hush!' said Hukam Singh, looking alarmed. 'You must not let him remember. You do not remember losing a fight, do you, my son?'

'I have never lost a fight,' said Phambiri with great simplicity and confidence.

'How strange,' said Sita. 'If you lose, how can you win?'

'Only a soldier can explain that,' said Hukam Singh. 'For a man who fights , there is no such thing as defeat. You fought against the river, did you not?'

'I went with the river,' said Sita. 'I went where it took me.'

'Yes, and you would have gone to the bottom if the boy had not come along to help you. He fought the river, didn't he?'

'Yes, he fought the river,' said Sita.

'You helped me to fight it,' said Vijay.

'So you both fought,' said the old man with a nod of satisfaction. 'You did not go with the river. You did not leave *everything* to the gods.'

'The gods were with us,' said Sita.

And so they talked, while the bullock-cart trundled along the muddy village roads. Both bullocks were white, and were decked out for the fair with coloured beadnecklaces and bells hanging from their necks. They were patient, docile beasts. But the cart-wheels; which were badly in need of oiling, protested loudly, creaking and groaning as though all the demons in the world had been trapped within them.

Sita noticed a number of birds in the paddy fields. There were black and white curlews, and cranes with pink coat-tails. A good monsoon means plenty of birds. But Hukam Singh was not happy about the cranes.

'They do great damage in the wheat fields,' he said. Lighting up a small hand-held *hookah* pipe, he puffed at it and became philosophical again: 'Life is one long struggle for the farmer. When he has overcome the drought, survived the flood, hunted off the pig, killed the crane, and reaped the crop, then comes that blood-sucking ghoul, the money-lender. There is no escaping him! Is your father in debt to a money-lender, boy?'

'No,' said Vijay.

'That is because he doesn't have daughters who must be married! I have two. As they resemble Phambiri, they will need generous dowries.'

In spite of his grumbling, Hukam Singh seemed fairly content with his lot. He'd had a good maize crop, and the front of his cart was piled high with corn. He would sell the crop at the fair, along with some cucumbers, egg-plants and melons.

The bad road had slowed them down so much that when darkness came they were still far from Karauli. In India there is hardly any twilight. Within a short time of the sun's going down, the stars were out.

'Six miles to go,' said Hukam Singh. 'In the dark our wheels may get stuck again. Let us spend the night here. If it rains, we can pull an old tarpaulin over the cart.'

Vijay made a fire in the charcoal-burner which Hukam Singh had brought along, and they had a simple meal, roasting the corn over the fire and flavouring it with salt and spices and a squeeze of lemon. There was some milk, but not enough for everyone because Phambiri drank three tumblers by himself.

'If I win tomorrow,' he said, 'I will give all of you a feast!'

They settled down to sleep in the bullock-cart, and Phambiri and his father were soon snoring. Vijay lay awake, his arms crossed behind his head, staring up at the stars. Sita was very tired but she couldn't sleep. She was worrying about her grandparents, and wondering when she would see them again.

The night was full of sounds. The loud snoring that came from Phambiri and his father seemed to be taken up by invisible sleepers all around them, and Sita, becoming alarmed, turned to Vijay and asked, 'What is that strange noise?'

He smiled in the darkness, and she could see his white teeth and the glint of laughter in his eyes.

'Only the spirits of lost demons,' he said, and then laughed. 'Can't you recognise the music of the frogs?'

And that was what they heard — a sound more hideous than the wail of demons, a rising crescendo of noise — *wurrk, wurrk, wurrk* —coming from the flooded ditches on either side of the road. All the frogs in the jungle seemed to have gathered at that one spot, and each one appeared to have something to say for himself. The speeches continued for about an hour. Then the meeting broke up, and silence returned to the forest.

A jackal slunk across the road. A puff of wind brushed through the trees. The bullocks, freed from the cart, were asleep beside it. The men's snores were softer now. Vijay slept, a half-smile on his face.

Only Sita lay awake, worried and waiting for the dawn.

At the Fair

Already, at nine o'clock, the fairground was crowded. Cattle were being sold or auctioned. Stalls had opened, selling everything from pins to ploughs. Foodstuffs were on sale — hot food, spicy food, sweets and ices. A merry-go-round, badly oiled, was squeaking and groaning, while a loudspeaker blared popular film music across the grounds.

While Phambiri was preparing for his wrestling match, Hukam Singh was busy haggling over the price of pumpkins. Sita and Vijay wandered on their own among the stalls, gazing at toys and kites and bangles and clothing, at brightly coloured, syruppy sweets. Some of the rural people had transistor-radios dangling by straps from their shoulders, the radio music competing with the louds-peaker. Occasionally a buffalo bellowed, drowning all other sounds.

Various people were engaged in roadside professions. There was the fortune-teller. He had slips of paper, each of them covered with writing, which he kept in little trays along with some grain. He had a tame sparrow. When you gave the fortune-teller your money, he allowed the little bird to hop in and out among the trays until it stopped at one and started pecking at the grain. From this tray the fortune-teller took the slip of paper and presented it to his client. The writing told you what to expect over the next few months or years.

A harrassed, middle-aged man, who was surrounded by six noisy sons and daughters, was looking a little concerned, because his slip of paper said: 'Do not lose hope. You will have a child soon.'

Some distance away sat a barbar, and near him a professional ear-cleaner. Several children clustered around a peepshow, which was built into an old gramophone cabinet. While one man wound up the gramophone and placed a well-worn record on the turn-table, his partner pushed coloured pictures through a slide-viewer.

A young man walked energetically up and down the fairground, beating a drum and announcing the day's attractions. The wrestling-bouts were about to start. The main attraction was going to be the fight between Phambiri, described as a man 'whose thighs had the thickness of an elephant's trunk', and the local champion,

Sher Dil ('Tiger's Heart') — a wild-looking man, with hairy chest and beetling brow. He was heavier than Phambiri but not so tall.

Sita and Vijay joined Hukam Singh at one corner of the *akhara*, the wrestling-pit. Hukam Singh was massaging his son's famous thighs.

A gong sounded and Sher Dil entered the ring, slapping himself on the chest and grunting like a wild boar. Phambiri advanced slowly to meet him.

They came to grips immediately, and stood swaying from side to side, two giants pitting their strength against each other. The sweat glistened on their well-oiled bodies.

Sher Dil got his arms round Phambiri's waist and tried to lift him off his feet; but Phambiri had twined one powerful leg around his opponent's thigh, and they both came down together with a loud squelch, churning up the soft mud of the wrestling-pit. But neither wrestler had been pinned down.

Soon they were so covered with mud that it was difficult to distinguish one from the other. There was a flurry of arms and legs. The crowd was cheering, and Sita and Vijay were cheering too, but the wrestlers were too absorbed in their struggle to be aware of their supporters. Each sought to turn the other on to his back. That was all that mattered. There was no count.

For a few moments Sher Dil had Phambiri almost helpless, but Phambiri wriggled out of a crushing grip and, using his legs once again, sent Sher Dil rocketing across the *akhara*. But Sher Dil landed on his belly, and even with Phambiri on top of him, it wasn't victory.

Nothing happened for several minutes, and the crowd became restless and shouted for more action. Phambiri thought of twisting his opponent's ear; but he realized that he might get disqualified for doing that, so he restrained himself. He relaxed his grip slightly, and this gave Sher Dil a chance to heave himself up and sent Phambiri spinning across the *akhara*. Phambiri was still in a sitting position when the other took a flying leap at him. But Phambiri dived forward, taking his opponent between the legs, and then rising, flung him backwards with a resounding thud. Sher Dil was helpless, and Phambiri sat on his opponent's chest to remove all doubts as to who was the winner. Only when the applause of the spectators told him that he had won did he rise and leave the ring.

Accompanied by his proud father, Phambiri accepted the prize money, thirty rupees, and then went in search of a tap. After he had washed the oil and mud from his body, he put on fresh clothes. Then, putting his arms around Vijay and Sita, he said, 'You have brought me luck, both of you. Now let us celebrate!' And he led the way to the sweet shops.

They ate syruppy *rasgollas* (made from milk and sugar) and almond-filled fudge, and little pies filled with minced meat, and washed everything down with a fizzy orange drink.

'Now I will buy each of you a small present,' said Phambiri.

He bought a bright blue sports' shirt for Vijay. He bought a new *hookah*-bowl for his father. And he took Sita to a stall where dolls were sold, and asked her to choose one.

There were all kinds of dolls — cheap plastic dolls, and beautiful dolls made by hand, dressed in the traditional costumes of different regions of the country. Sita was immediately reminded of Mumta, her own rag doll, who had been made at home with Grandmother's help. And she remembered Grandmother, and Grandmother's sewing-machine, and the home that had been swept away, and the tears started to her eyes.

The dolls seemed to smile at Sita. The shopkeeper held them up one by one, and they appeared to dance, to twirl their wide skirts, to stamp their jingling feet on the counter. Each doll made his own special appeal to Sita. Each one wanted her love.

'Which one will you have?' asked Phambiri. 'Choose the prettiest, never mind the price!'

But Sita could say nothing, she could only shake her head. No doll, no matter how beautiful, could replace Mumta. She would never keep a doll again. That part of her life was over.

So instead of a doll Phambiri bought her bangles coloured glass bangles which slipped easily over Sita's thin wrists. And then he took them into a temporary cinema, a large shed made of corrugated tin sheets.

Vijay had been in a cinema before — the towns were full of cinemas — but for Sita it was another new experience. Many things that were common enough for other boys and girls were strange and new for a girl who had spent nearly all her life on a small island in the middle of a big river.

As they found seats, a curtain rolled up and a white sheet came into view. A babble of talk dwindled into silence. Sita became aware of a whirring noise somewhere not far behind her; but, before she could turn her head to see what it was, the sheet became a rectangle of light and colour. It came to life. People moved and spoke. A story unfolded.

But, long afterwards, all that Sita could remember of her first film was a jumble of images and incidents. A train in danger: the audience murmuring with anxiety: a bridge over a river (but a smaller than hers): the bridge being blown to pieces: the engine plunging into the river: people struggling in the water: a woman rescued by a man who immediately embraced her: the lights coming on again, and the audience rising slowly and drifting out of the theatre, looking quite unconcerned and even satisfied. All those people struggling in the water were now quite safe, back in the little black box in the projection room.

Catching the Train

And now a real engine, a steam-engine belching smoke and fire, was on its way to Sita.

She stood with Vijay on the station platform along with over a hundred other people waiting for the Shahganj train.

The platform was littered with the familiar bedrolls (or hold-alls) without which few people in India ever travel. On these rolls sat women, children, great-aunts and great-uncles, grandfathers, grandmothers and grandchildren, while the more active adults hovered at the edge of the platform, ready to leap onto the train as soon as it arrived and reserve a space for the family. In India, people do not travel alone if they can help it. The whole family must be taken along — especially if the reason for the journey is a marriage, a pilgrimage, or simply a visit to friends or relations.

Moving among the piles of bedding and luggage were coolies, vendors of magazines, sweetmeats, tea, and betal-leaf preparations; also stray dogs, stray people, and sometimes a stray station-master. The cries of the vendors mingled with the general clamour of the station and the shunting of a steam-engine in the yards. 'Tea, hot tea!,' 'Fresh limes!' Sweets, *papads*, hot stuff, cold drinks, mangoes, toothpowder, photos of film stars, bananas, balloons, wooden toys! The platform had become a bazaar. What a blessing for those vendors that trains ran late and that people had to wait, and, waiting, drank milky tea, bought toys for children, cracked peanut shells, munched bananas, and chose little presents for the friends or relations on whom they were going to descend very shortly.

But there came the train!

The signal was down. The crowd surged forward, swamping an assistant station-master. Vijay took Sita by the hand and led her forward. If they were too slow, they would not get a place on the crowded train. In front of them was a tall, burly, bearded Sikh from the Punjab. Vijay decided it would be a wise move to stand behind him and move forward at the same time.

The station bell clanged, and a big, puffing, black steam-engine appeared in the distance. A stray dog, with a lifetime's experience of trains, darted away across the railway lines. As the train came alongside the platform, doors opened, window shutters fell, eager faces appeared in the openings, and, even before the train had come to a stop, people were trying to get in or out.

For a few moments there was chaos. The crowd surged backwards and forwards. No one could get out. No one could get in! Fifty people were leaving the train, a hundred were catching it! No one wanted to give way. But every problem has a solution somewhere, provided one looks for it. And this particular problem was solved by a man climbing out of a window. Others followed his example. The pressure at the doors eased and people started squeezing into their compartments.

Vijay stayed closed to the Sikh who forged a way through the throng. The Sikh reached an open doorway and was through. Vijay and Sita were through! They found somewhere to sit, and were then able to look down at the platform, into the whirlpool, and enjoy themselves a little. The vendors had abandoned the people on the platform and had started selling their wares at the windows. Hukam Singh, after buying their tickets, had given Vijay and Sita a rupee to spend on the way. Vijay bought a freshly split coconut, and Sita bought a comb for her disarranged hair. She had never bothered with her hair before.

They saw a worried man rushing along the platform searching for his family; but they were already in the compartment, having beaten him to it, and eagerly helped him in at the door. A whistle shrilled, and they were off! A couple of vendors made last-minute transactions, then jumped from the slow-moving train. One man did this expertly with a tray of teacups balanced on one hand.

The train gathered speed.

'What will happen to all those people still on the platform?' asked

Sita anxiously. 'Will they all be left behind?'

She put her head out of the window and looked back at the receding platform. It was strangely empty. Only the vendors and the coolies and the stray dogs and the dishevelled railway staff were in evidence. A miracle had happened. No one — absolutely no one — had been left behind!

Then the train was rushing through the night, the engine throwing out bright sparks that danced away like fireflies. Sometimes the train had to slow down, as flood-water had weakened the embankments. Sometimes it stopped at brightly-lit stations.

When the train started again and moved on into the dark countryside, Sita would stare through the glass of the window, at the brightlights of a town or the quiet glow of village lamps. She thought of Phambiri and Hukam Singh, and wondered if she would ever see them again. Already they were like people in a fairy-tale, met briefly on the road and never seen again.

There was no room in the compartment in which to lie down; but Sita soon fell asleep, her head resting against Vijay's shoulder.

A Meeting and a Parting

Sita did not know where to look for her grandfather. For an hour, she and Vijay wandered through the Shahganj bazaar, growing hungrier all the time. They had no money left, and they were hot and thirsty.

Outside the bazaar, near a small temple, they saw a tree in which several small boys were helping themselves to the sour, purple fruit.

It did not take Vijay long to join the boys in the tree. They did not object to his joining them. It wasn't their tree, anyway.

Sita stood beneath the tree, while Vijay threw the *jamuns* down to her. They soon had a small pile of the fruit. They they were on the road again, their faces stained with purple juice.

They were asking the way to the Shahganj hospital when Sita caught a glimpse of her grandfather on the road.

At first the old man did not recognise her. He was walking stiffly down the road, looking straight ahead, and would have walked right past the dusty, dishevelled girl, had she not charged straight at his thin, shaky legs and clasped him round the waist.

'Sita!' he cried, when he had recovered his wind and his balance. 'Why are you here? How did you get off the island? I have been very worried — it has been bad, these last two days . . .'

'Is Grandmother all right?' asked Sita.

But even as she spoke, she knew that Grandmother was no longer with them. The dazed look in the old man's eyes told her as much. She wanted to cry — not for Grandmother, who could suffer no more, but for grandfather, who looked so helpless and bewildered; she did not want him to be unhappy. She forced back her tears, and took his gnarled and trembling hand; and, with Vijay walking beside her, led the old man down the crowded street.

She knew, then, that it would be on her shoulder that Grandfather would lean in the years to come.

They decided to remain in Shahganj for a couple of days, staying at a *Dharamsala* — a wayside rest-house — until the flood-waters subsided. Grandfather still had two of the goats — it had not been necessary to sell more than one — but he did not want to take the risk of rowing a crowded boat across to the island. The river was still fast and dangerous.

But Vijay could not stay with Sita any longer.

'I must go now,' he said. 'My father and mother will be very worried, and they will not know where to look for me. In a day or two the water will go down, and you will be able to go back to your home.'

'Perhaps the island has gone forever,' said Sita.

'It will be there,' said Vijay. 'It is a rocky island. Bad for crops, but good for a house!'

'Will you come?' asked Sita.

What she really wanted to say was, 'Will you come to see me?' but she was too shy to say it; and besides, she wasn't sure if Vijay would want to see her again.

'I will come,' said Vijay. 'That is, if my father gets me another boat!'

As he turned to go, he gave her his flute.

'Keep it for me,' he said. 'I will come for it one day.'

When he saw her hesitate, he smiled and said, 'It is a good flute!'

The Return

There was more rain, but the worst was over, and when Grandfather and Sita returned to the island, the river was no longer in spate.

Grandfather could hardly believe his eyes when he saw that the tree had disappeared — the tree that had seemed as permanent as the island, as much a part of his life as the river itself had been. He marvelled at Sita's escape.

'It was the tree that saved you,' he said.

'And the boy,' said Sita.

Yes, and the boy.

She thought about Vijay and wondered if she would ever see him again. Would he, like Phambiri and Hukam Singh, be one of those people who arrived as though out of a fairy-tale and then disappeared silently and mysteriously? She did not know it then, but some of the moving forces of our lives are meant to touch us briefly and go their way . . .

And because Grandmother was no longer with them, life on the island was quite different. The evenings were sad and lonely.

But there was a lot of work to be done, and Sita did not have much time to think of Grandmother or Vijay or the world she had glimpsed during her journey.

For three nights they slept under a crude shelter made out of gunny-bags. During the day Sita helped Grandfather rebuild the mud-hut. Once again, they used the big rock for support.

The trunk which Sita had packed so carefully had not been swept off the island, but the water had got into it, and the food and clothing had been spoilt. But Grandfather's *hookah* had been saved, and, in the evenings after work was done and they had eaten their light meal which Sita prepared, he would smoke with a little of his old contentment, and tell Sita about other floods which he had experienced as a boy. And he would tell her about the wrestling-matches he had won, and the kites he had flown, for he remembered a time when grown men flew kites, and great battles were fought, the kites swooping and swerving in the sky, tangling with each other until the string of one was cut.

Kite-flying was then the sport of kings, Grandfather remembered how the Raja himself would come down to the river-bank and join in this noble pastime. There was time in those days to spend an hour with a gay, dancing strip of paper. Now everyone hurried, in a heat of hope, and delicate things like kites and daydreams were trampled underfoot.

Grandfather remembered the 'Dragon Kite' that he had built — a great kite with a face painted on it, the eyes made of small mirrors, the tail like a long crawling serpent. A large crowd assembled to watch its launching. At the first attempt it refused to leave the ground. And then the wind came from the right direction, and the Dragon Kite soared into the sky, wriggling its way higher and higher, with the sun still glinting in its eyes. And it went very high, it pulled fiercely on the twine determined to be free, to break loose, to live a life of its own. And eventually it did.

The twine snapped, the kite leapt away toward the sun, sailed on heavenward until it was lost to view. It was never found again, and Grandfather wondered if he had made too vivid, too living a thing of the great kite. He did not make another like it.

It was like her doll, thought Sita.

Mumta had been a real person, not a doll, and now Sita could not make another like her.

Sita planted a mango seed in the same spot where the *peepul* tree had stood. It would be many years before it grew into a big tree, but Sita liked to imagine sitting in the branches one day, picking the mangoes straight from the tree and feasting on the them all day.

Grandfather was more particular about making vegetable garden, putting down peas, carrots, gram and mustard.

One day, when most of the hard work had been done and the new hut was ready, Sita took the flute which had been given to her by Vijay, and walked down to the water's edge and tried to play it. But all she could produce was a few broken notes, and even the goats paid no attention to her music.

Sometimes Sita thought she saw a boat coming down the river, and she would run to meet it; but usually there was no boat, or, if there was, it belonged to a stranger or to another fisherman. And so she stopped looking out for boats.

Slowly, the rains came to an end. The flood-waters had receded, and in the villages people were beginning to till the land again and sow crops for the winter months. There were more cattle fairs and wrestling matches. The days were warm and sultry. The water in the river was no longer muddy, and one evening Grandfather brought home a huge *mahseer*, and Sita made it into a delicious curry.

Deep River

Grandfather sat outside the hut, smoking his *hookah*. Sita was at the far end of the island, spreading clothes on the rocks to dry. One of the goats had followed her. It was the friendlier of the two and often followed Sita about the island. She had made it a necklace of coloured beads.

She sat down on a smooth rock, and, as she did so, she noticed a small bright object in the sand near her feet. She picked it up. It was a little wooden toy — a coloured peacock, the god Krishna's favourite bird — it must have come down on the river and been swept ashore on the island. Some of the paint had been rubbed off; but for Sita, who had no toys, it was a great find.

There was a soft footfall behind her. She looked round, and there was Vijay, barefooted, standing over her and smiling.

'I thought you wouldn't come,' said Sita.

'There was much work in my village. Did you keep my flute?'

'Yes, but I cannot play it properly.'

'I will teach you,' said Vijay.

He sat down beside her, and they cooled their feet in the water, which was clear now, taking in the blue of the sky. You could see the sand and the pebbles of the river-bed.

'Sometimes the river is angry and sometimes it is kind,' said Sita.

'We are part of the river,' said Vijay.

*

It was a good river, deep and strong, beginning in the mountains and ending in the sea.

Along its banks, for hundreds of miles, lived millions of people, and Sita was only one small girl among them, and no one had ever heard of her, no one knew her — except for the old man, and the boy, and the water that was blue and white and wonderful.

Love is a sad Song

I sit against this grey rock, beneath a sky of pristine blueness, and think of you, Sushila. It is November, and the grass is turning brown and yellow. Crushed, it still smells sweet. The afternoon sun shimmers on the oak leaves and turns them a glittering silver. A cricket sizzles its way through the long grass. The stream murmurs at the bottom of the hill — that stream where you and I lingered on a golden afternoon in May.

I sit here and think of you, and try to see your slim brown hand resting against this rock, feeling its warmth. I am aware again of the texture of your skin, the coolness of your feet, the sharp tingle of your finger-tips. And in the pastures of my mind I run my hand through your quivering mouth, and crush your tender breasts. Remembered passion grows sweeter with the passing of time.

You will not be thinking of me now, as you sit in your home in the city, cooking or sewing or trying to study for examinations. There will be men and women and children circling about you, in that crowded house of your grandmother's, and you will not be able to think of me for more than a moment or two. But I know you do think of me sometimes, in some private moment which cuts you off from the crowd. You will remember how I will probably wonder what it is all about, this loving, and why it should cause such an upheaval. You are still a child, Sushila — and yet you found it so easy to quieten my impatient heart.

On the night you came to stay with us, the light from the street lamp shone through the branches of the peach tree and made leaf-patterns on the walls. Through the glass panes of the front door I caught a glimpse of little Sunil's face, bright and questing, and then — a hand — a dark, long-fingered hand that could only have belonged to you.

It was almost a year since I had seen you, my dark and slender girl. And now you were in your sixteenth year. And Sunil was twelve; and your uncle, Dinesh, who lived with me, was twenty-three. And I was almost thirty — a fearful and wonderful age, when life becomes dangerous for dreamers.

I remember that when I left Delhi last year, you cried. At first I thought it was because I was going away; then I realised that it was because you could not go anywhere yourself. Did you envy my freedom — the freedom to live in a poverty of my own choosing, the freedom of the writer? Sunil, to my surprise, did not show much emotion at my going away. This hurt me a little, because during that year he had been particularly close to me, and I felt for him a very special love. But separations cannot be of any significance to small boys of twelve who live for today, tomorrow, and — if they are very serious — the day after.

Before I went away with Dinesh, you made us garlands of marigolds. They were orange and gold, fresh and clean and kissed by the sun. You garlanded me as I sat talking to Sunil. I remember you both as you looked that day — Sunil's smile dimpling his cheeks, while you gazed at me very seriously, your expression very tender. I loved you even then . . .

Our first picnic.

The path to the little stream took us through oak forest, where the flashy Blue Magpies played follow-my-leader with their harsh, creaky calls. Skirting an open ridge (the place where I now sit and write), the path dipped through oak, rhododendron and maple, until it reached a little knoll above the stream. It was a spot unknown to the tourists and summer visitors. Sometimes a milkman or wood-cutter crossed the stream on the way to town or village; but no one lived beside it. Wild roses grew on the banks.

I do not remember much of that picnic. There was a lot of dull conversation with our neighbours, the Kapoors, who had come along too. You and Sunil were rather bored. Dinesh looked preoccupied: he was fed up with college; he wanted to start earning a living; wanted to paint. His restlessness often made him moody, irritable.

Near the knoll the stream was too shallow for bathing, but I told

Sunil about a cave and a pool further downstream, and promised that we would visit the pool another day.

That same night, after dinner, we took a walk along the dark road that goes past the house and leads to the burning-*ghat*. Sunil, who had already sensed the intimacy between us, took my hand put it in yours. An odd, touching little gesture!

'Tell us a story,' you said.

'Yes, tell us,' said Sunil.

I told you the story of the pure in heart. A shepherd boy found a snake in the forest, and the snake told the boy that it was really a princess who had been bewitched and turned into a snake, and that it could only recover its human form if someone who was truly pure in heart gave it three kisses on the mouth. The boy put his lips to the mouth of the snake and kissed it thrice. And the snake was transformed into a beautiful princess. But the boy lay cold and dead.

'You always tell sad stories,' complained Sunil.

'I like sad stories,' you said. 'Tell us another.'

'Tomorrow night. I'm sleepy.'

We were woken in the night by a strong wind, which went whistling round the old house and came rushing down the chimney, humming and hawing and finally choking itself.

Sunil woke up and cried out, 'What's that noise, uncle?'

'Only the wind,' I said.

'Not a ghost?'

'Well, perhaps the wind is made up of ghosts. Perhaps this wind contains the ghosts of all the people who have lived and died in this old house and want to come in again from the cold.'

You told me about a boy who had been fond of you in Delhi. Apparently he had visited the house on a few occasions, and had sometimes met you on the street while you were on your way home from school. At first, he had been fond of another girl but later he switched his affections to you. When you told me that he had written to you recently, and that, before coming up, you had replied to his letter, I was consumed by jealousy — an emotion which I thought I had grown out of long ago. It did not help to be told that you were not serious about the boy, that you were sorry for him because he had already been disappointed in love.

'If you feel sorry for everyone who has been disappointed in love,' I said, 'you will soon be receiving the affections of every young man over ten.'

'Let them give me their affections,' you said, 'and I will give them my *chappal* over their heads.'

'But spare my head,' I said.

'Have *you* been in love before?'

'Many times. But this is the first time.'

'And who is your love?'

'Haven't you guessed?'

Sunil, who was following our conversation with deep interest, seemed to revel in the situation. Probably he fancied himself playing the part of Cupid, or Kamadeva, and delighted in watching the arrows of love strike home. No doubt I made it more enjoyable for him, because I could not hide my feelings. Soon Dinesh would know, too — and then?

A year ago my feelings about you were almost paternal! Or so I thought . . . But you are no longer a child; and I am a little older too. For when, the night after the picnic, you took my hand and held it against your soft warm cheek, it was the first time that a girl had responded to me so readily, so tenderly. Perhaps it was just innocence; but that one action of yours, that acceptance of me, immediately devastated my heart.

Gently, fervently, I kissed your eyes and forehead, your small round mouth, and the lobes of your ears, and your long smooth throat; and I whispered, 'Sushila, I love you, I love you, I love you,' in the same way that millions and millions of love-smitten young men have whispered since time immemorial. What else can one say? I love you, I love you. There is nothing simpler; nothing that can be made to mean anymore than that. And what else did I say? That I would look after you and work for you and make you happy; and that too had been said before, and I was in no way different from anyone. I was a man, and yet I was a boy again.

We visited the stream again, a day or two later, early in the morning. Using the rocks as stepping-stones, we wandered downstream for about a furlong until we reached a pool and a small waterfall and a cool dark cave. The rocks were mostly grey but some were yellow with age and some were cushioned with moss. A forktail stood on a boulder in the middle of the stream, uttering its low pleasant call. Water came dripping down from the sides of the cave, while sunlight filtered through a crevice in the rock-ceiling, dappling your face. A spray of water was caught by a shaft of sunlight, and at intervals it reflected the colours of the rainbow.

'It is a beautiful place,' you said.

'Come, then,' I said, 'Let us bathe.'

Sunil and I removed our clothes and jumped into the pool, while you sat down in the shade of a walnut tree and watched us disport ourselves in the water. Like a frog, Sunil leapt and twisted about in the clear, icy water; his eyes shone, his teeth glistened white, his body glowed with sunshine, youth, and the jewels made by drops of water glistening in the sun.

Then we stretched ourselves out beside you, and allowed the sun to sink deep into our bodies.

Your feet, laved with dew, stood firm on the quickening grass. There was a butterfly between us: red and gold its wings and heavy with dew. It could not move because of the weight of moisture. And as your foot came nearer and I saw that you would crush it, I said, 'Wait. Don't crush the butterfly, Sushila. It has only a few days in the sun, and we have many.'

'And if I spare it,' you said, laughing, 'what will you do for me, what will you pay?'

'Why, anything you say.'

'And will you kiss my foot?'

'Both feet,' I said; and did so willingly. For they were no less than the wings of butterflies.

Later, when you ventured near the water, I dragged you in with me. You cried out, not in alarm but with the shock of the cold water, and then, wrenching yourself from my arms, clambered on to the rocks, your thin dress clinging to your thighs, your feet making long patterns on the smooth stone.

Though we tired ourselves out that day, we did not sleep at night. We lay together, you and Sunil on either side of me. Your head rested on my shoulders, your hair lay pressed against my cheek. Sunil had curled himself up into a ball; but he was far from being asleep. He took my hand, and he took yours, and he placed them together. And I kissed the tender inside of your hand.

I whispered to you, 'Sushila, there has never been anyone I've loved so much. I've been waiting all these years to find you. For a long time I did not even like women. But you are so different. You care for me, don't you?'

You nodded in the darkness. I could see the outline of your face in the faint moonlight that filtered through the skylight. You never replied directly to a question. I suppose that was feminine quality;

coyness, perhaps.

'Do you love me, Sushila?'

No answer.

'Not now. When you are a little older. In a year or two.'

Did she nod in the darkness, or did I imagine it?

'I know it's too early,' I continued. 'You are still too young, you are still at school. But already you are much wiser than me. I am finding too difficult to control myself, but I will, since you wish it so. I'm very impatient, I know that, but I'll wait for as long as you make me — two or three or a hundred years. Yes, Sushila, a hundred years!'

Ah, what a pretty speech I made! Romeo could have used some of it; Majnu, too.

And your answer? Just a nod; a little pressure on my hand.

I took your fingers and kissed them one by one. Long fingers, as long as mine.

After some time I became aware of Sunil nudging me.

'You are not talking to me,' he complained. 'You are only talking to her. You only love her.'

'I'm terribly sorry. I love you too, Sunil.'

Content with this assurance, he fell asleep; but towards morning, thinking himself in the middle of the bed, he rolled over and landed with a thump on the floor. He didn't know how it had happened, and accused me of pushing him out.

'I know you don't want me in the bed,' he said.

It was a good thing, Dinesh, in the next room, didn't wake up.

*

'Have you done any work this week?' asked Dinesh with a look of reproach.

'Not much,' I said.

'You are hardly ever in the house. You are never at your desk. Something seems to have happened to you.'

'I have given myself a holiday, that's all. Can't writers take holidays too?'

'No. You have said so yourself. And anyway, you seem to have taken a permanent holiday.'

'Have you finished that painting of the Tibetan woman?' I asked, trying to change the subject.

'That's the third time you've asked me that question, even though you saw the completed painting a week ago. You're getting very absent-minded.'

There was a letter from your old boy friend; I mean your young boy friend. It was addressed to Sunil, but I recognised the sender's name and knew it was really for you.

I assumed a look of calm detachment and handed the letter to you; but both you and Sunil sensed my dismay. At first you teased me, and showed me the boy's photograph, which had been enclosed (he was certainly good-looking in a flashy way); then, finding that I became gloomier every minute, you tried to make amends, assuring me that the correspondence was one-sided and that you no longer replied to his letters.

And that night, to show me that you really cared, you gave me your hand as soon as the lights were out. Sunil was fast asleep.

We sat together at the foot of your bed. I kept my arm about you, while you rested your head against my chest. Your feet lay in repose upon mine. I kept kissing you. And when we lay down together, I loosened your blouse, and kissed your small firm breasts, and put my lips to your nipples and felt them grow hard against my mouth.

The shy responsiveness of your kisses soon turned to passion. You clung to me. We had forgotten time and place and circumstance. The light of your eyes had been drowned in that lost look of a woman who desires. For a space we both struggled against desire. Suddenly I had become afraid of myself — afraid for you. I tried to free myself from your clasping arms. But you cried in a low voice: 'Love me! Love me! I want you to love me.'

*

Another night you fell asleep with your face in the crook of my arm, and I lay awake a long time, conscious of your breathing, of the touch of your hair on my cheek, of the soft warm soles of your feet, of your slim waist and legs.

And in the morning, when the sunshine filled the room, I watched you while you slept — your slim body in repose, your face tranquil, your thin dark hands like sleeping butterflies; and then, when you woke, the beautiful untidiness of your hair and the drowsiness in your eyes. You lay folded up like a kitten, your limbs as untouched by self-consciousness as the limbs of a young and growing tree. And during the warmth of the day a bead of sweat rested on your brow like a small pearl.

I tried to remember what you looked like as a child. Even then, I had always been aware of your presence. You must have been nine or ten when I first saw you — thin, dark, plain-faced, always wearing the faded green skirt that was your school uniform. You went about barefoot. Once, when the monsoon arrived, you ran out into the rain with the other children, naked, exulting in the swish of the cool rain. I remembered your beautiful straight legs and thighs, your swift smile, your dark eyes. You say you do not remember playing naked in the rain; but that is because you did not see yourself.

I did not notice you growing. Your face did not change very much. You must have been thirteen when you gave up skirts and started wearing the *salwar-kameez*. You had few clothes; but the plainness of your dress only seemed to bring out your own radiance. And as you grew older, your eyes became more expressive, your hair longer and glossier, your gestures more graceful; and then, when you came to me in the hills, I found that you had been transformed into a fairy princess of devastating charm.

*

We were idling away the afternoon on our beds, and you were reclining in my arms, when Dinesh came in unexpectedly. He said nothing, merely passed through the room and entered his studio. Sunil got a fright, and you were momentarily confused. Then you said, 'He knows already,' and I said, 'Yes, he must know.'

Later I spoke to Dinesh. I told him that I wanted to marry ; that I knew I would have to wait until you were older and had finished school — probably two or three years — and that I was prepared to wait although I knew it would be a long and difficult business. I asked him to help me.

He was upset at first, probably because he felt I had been deceptive (which was true), and also because of his own responsibility in the matter. You were his niece, and I had made love to you while he had been preoccupied with other things. But after a little while, when he saw that I was sincere and rather confused, he relented.

'It has happened too soon,' he said. 'She is too young for all this. Have you told her that you love her?'

'Of course. Many times.'

'You're a fool, then. Have you told her that you want to marry her?'

'Yes.'

'Fool again. That's not the way it is done. Haven't you lived in India long enough to know that?'

'But I love her.'

'Does she love you?'

'I think so.'

'You think so. Desire isn't love, you must know that. Still, I suppose she does love you, otherwise she would not be holding hands with you all day. But you are quite mad, falling in love with a girl half your age.'

'Well, I'm not exactly an old man. I'm thirty.'

'And she's a schoolgirl.'

'She isn't a girl any more, she's too responsive.'

'Oh, you've found that out, have you?'

'Well . . .' I said, covered in confusion.

'Well, she has shown that she cares a little. You know that it's years since I took any interest in a girl. You called it unnatural on my part, remember? Well, they simply did not exist for me, that's true.'

'Delayed adolescence,' muttered Dinesh.

'But Sushila is different. She puts me at ease. She doesn't turn away from me. I love her and I want to look after her. I can only do that by marrying her.'

'All right, but take it easy. Don't get carried away. And don't, for God's sake, give her a baby. Not while she's still at school! I will do what I can to help you. But you will have to be patient. And no one else must know of this, or I will be blamed for everything. As it is, Sunil knows too much, and he's too small to know so much.'

'Oh, he won't tell anyone.'

'I wish you had fallen in love with her two years from now. You will have to wait that long, anyway. Getting married isn't simple matter. People will wonder why we are in such a hurry, marrying her off as soon as she leaves school. They'll think the worst!'

'Well, people do marry for love, you know, even in India. It's happening all the time.'

'But it doesn't happen in *our* family. You know how orthodox most of them are. They wouldn't appreciate your outlook. You may marry Sushila for love, but it will have to *look* like an arranged marriage!'

*

Little things went wrong that evening.

First, a youth on the road passed a remark which you resented; and you, most unlady-like, but most Punjabi-like, picked up a stone and threw it at him. It struck him on the leg. He was too surprised to say anything, and limped off. I remonstrated with you; told you that throwing stones at people often resulted in a fight; then realised that you had probably wanted to see me fighting on your behalf.

Later you were annoyed because I said you were a little absent-minded. Then Sunil sulked because I spoke roughly to him (I can't remember why), and refused to talk to me for three hours, which was a record. I kept apologising but neither of you would listen. It was all part of a game. When I gave up trying, and turned instead to my typewriter and my unfinished story, you came and sat beside me and started playing with my hair. You were jealous of my story, of the fact that it was possible for me to withdraw into my work. And I reflected that a woman had to be jealous of something. If there wasn't another woman, then it was a man's work, or his hobby, or his best friend, or his favourite sweater, or his pet mongoose, that made her resentful. There is a story in Kipling about a woman who grew insanely jealous of a horse's saddle, because her husband spent an hour every day polishing it with great care and loving kindness.

Would it be like that in marriage, I wondered — an eternal triangle: you, me and the typewriter?

But there were only a few days left before you returned to the plains, so I gladly pushed away the typewriter and took you in my arms instead. After all, once you had gone away, it would be a long long time before I could hold you in my arms again. I might visit you in Delhi, but we would not be able to enjoy the same freedom and intimacy. And while I savoured the salt kiss of your lips, I wondered how long I would have to wait until I could really call you my own.

Dinesh was at college, and Sunil had gone roller-skating, and we were alone all morning. At first you avoided me; so I picked up a book and pretended to read; and barely five minutes had passed before you stole up from behind and snapped the book shut.

'It is a warm day,' you said. 'Let us go down to the stream.'

Alone together for the first time, we took the steep path down to the stream, and there, hand in hand, scrambled over the rocks until we reached the pool and the waterfall.

'I will bathe today,' you said; and in a few moments you stood beside me, naked, caressed by sunlight and a soft breeze coming down the valley. I put my hand out to share in the sun's caress, but you darted away, laughing, and ran to the waterfall as though you would hide behind a curtain of gushing water. I was soon beside you. I took you in my arms, and kissed you, while the water crashed down upon our heads. Who yielded — you or I? All I remember is that you had entwined yourself about me like a clinging vine, and that a little later we lay together on the grass, on bruised and broken clover, while a whistling-thrush released its deep sweet secret on the trembling air.

Blackbird on the wing, bird of the forest shadows, black rose in the long ago of summer, this was your song: it isn't time that's passing by, it is you and I.

*

It was your last night under my roof. We were not alone; but when I woke in the middle of the night and stretched my hand out, across the space between our beds, you took my hand, for you were awake too. Then I pressed the ends of your fingers, one by one, as I had done so often before, and you dug your nails into my flesh. And as our hands made love, much as our bodies might have done. They clung together, warmed and caressed each other, each finger taking on an identity of its own and seeking its opposite. Sometimes the tips of out fingers merely brushed against each other, teasingly, and sometimes our palms met with a rush, would tremble and embrace, separate, and them passionately seek each other out. And when sleep finally overcame you, your hand fell listlessly between our beds, touching the ground; and I lifted it up, and after putting it once to my lips, returned it gently to your softly rising bosom.

And so you went away, all three of you, and I was left alone with the brooding mountains. If I could not pass a few weeks without you, how was I to pass a year, two years? This was the question I kept asking myself. Would I have to leave the hills and take a flat in Delhi? And what use would it be — looking at you and speaking to you but never able to touch you? Not to be able to touch that which I had already possessed would have been the subtlest form of

220

torture.

The house was empty but I kept finding little things to remind me that you had been there — a handkerchief, a bangle, a length of ribbon — and these remnants made me feel as though you had gone forever. No sound at night, except the rats scurrying about on the rafters.

The rain had brought out the ferns, which were springing up from tree and rock. The murmur of the stream had become an angry rumble. The honeysuckle creeper, winding over the front windows, was thick with scented blossom. I wish it had flowered a little earlier, before you left. Then you could have put the flowers in your hair.

At night I drank brandy, wrote listlessly, listened to the wind in the chimney, and read poetry in bed. There was no one to tell stories to; and no hand to hold.

I kept remembering little things — the soft hair hiding your ears, the movement of your hands, the cool touch of your feet, the tender look in your eyes and the sudden stab of mischief that sometimes replaced it.

Mrs. Kapoor remarked on the softness of your expression. I was glad that someone had noticed it. In my diary I wrote: 'I have looked at Sushila so often and so much that perhaps I have over -looked her most compelling qualities — her kindness (or is it just her easy-goingness?), her refusal to hurt anyone's feelings (or is it just her indifference to everything?), her wide tolerance (or is it just her laziness?) . . . Oh, how absoutely ignorant I am of women!'

*

Well, there was a letter from Dinesh, and it held out a lifeline, one that I knew I must seize without any hesitation. He said he might be joining an Art School in Delhi, and asked me if I would like to return to Delhi and share a flat with him. I had always dreaded the possibility of leaving the hills and living again in a city as depressing as Delhi; but love, I considered, ought to make any place habitable . . .

*

And then I was in a bus, on the road to Delhi.

The first monsoon showers had freshened the fields, and everything looked much greener than usual. The maize was just shooting up, and the mangoes were ripening fast. Near the larger villages, camels and bullock-carts cluttered up the road, and the driver cursed, banging his fist on the horn.

Passing through small towns, the bus-driver had to contend with cycle-*rickshaws*, *tonga*-ponies, trucks, pedestrians, and other buses. Coming down from the hills for the first time in over a year, I found the noise, chaos, dust and dirt a little unsettling.

As my taxi drew up at the gate of Dinesh's home, Sunil saw me and came running to open the car door. Other children were soon swarming around me. Then I saw you standing near the front door. You raised your hand to your forehead in a typical Muslim form of greeting: a gesture you had picked up, I suppose, from a film.

For two days Dinesh and I went house-hunting, for I had decided to take a flat if it was at all practicable. Either it was very hot, and we were sweating, or it was raining and we were drenched. (It is difficult to find a flat in Delhi,even if one is in a position to pay an exorbitant rent, which I was not. It is especially difficult for bachelors. No one trusts bachelors, especially if there are grown-up daughters in the house. Is this because bachelors are wolves, or because girls are so easily seduced these days?)

Finally, after several refusals, we were offered a flat in one of those new colonies that sprout like mushrooms around the capital. The rent was two hundred rupees a month, and although I knew I couldn't really afford so much, I was so sick of refusals, and already so disheartened and depressed, that I took the place, and made out a cheque to the landlord, an elderly gentlemen with his daughters all safely married in other parts of the country.

There was no furniture in the flat except for a couple of beds, but we decided we would fill the place up gradually. Everyone at Dinesh's home — brothers, sisters-in-law, aunts, nephews and nieces — helped us to move in. Sunil and his younger brother were the first arrivals; later the other children some ten of them, arrived and debouched all over the rooms. You, Sushila, came only in the afternoon, but I had gone out for something and only saw you when I returned at tea-time. You were sitting on the first-floor balcony, and smiled down at me as I walked up the road.

I think you were pleased with the flat; or at any rate, with my courage in taking one. I took you up to the roof, and there, in a corner under the stairs, kissed you very quickly. It had to be quick, because the other children were close on our heels. There wouldn't be much opportunity for kissing you again. The mountains were far, and in a place like Delhi, and with a family like yours, private moments would be few and far between.

Hours later, when I sat alone on one of the beds, Sunil came to me, looking rather upset. He must have had a quarrel with you.

'I want to tell you something,' he said.

'Is anything wrong?'

To my amazement he burst into tears.

'Now you must not love me any more,' he said.

'Why not?'

'Because you are going to marry Sushila, and if you love me too much it will not be good for you '

I could think of nothing to say. It was all too funny and all too sad.

But a little later he as in high spirits, having apparently forgotten the reasons for his earlier dejection. His need for a affection stemmed perhaps from his father's long and unnecessary absence from the country.

*

Dinesh and I had no sleep during out first night in the new flat. We were near the main road, and traffic roared past all night. I thought of the hills, so silent that the call of a nightjar startled one in the stillness of the night.

I was out most of the next day, and when I got back in the evening it was to find that Dinesh had had a rumpus with the landloard. Apparently the landlord had really *wanted* bachelors, and couldn't understand or appreciate a large number of children moving in and out of the house all day.

'I thought landlords preferred having families,' I said.

'He wants to know how a bachelor came to have such a large family!'

'Didn't you tell him that the children were only temporary, and wouldn't be living here?'

'I did, but he doesn't believe me.'

'Well, anyway, we're not going to stop the children from coming to see us,' I said indignantly.(No children,no Sushila!). 'If he doesn't see reason, he can have his flat back.'

'Did he cash my cheque?'

'No, he's given it back.'

'That means he really wants us out. To hell with his flat! It's too noisy here anyway. Let's go back to your place.'

We packed our bedding, trunks and kitchen-utensils once more; hired a bullock-cart; and arrived at Dinesh's home (three miles distant) late at night, hungry and upset.

Everything seemed to be going wrong.

*

Living in the same house as you, but unable to have any real contact with you (except for the odd, rare moment when we were left alone in the same room and were able to exchange a word or a glance) was an exquisite form of self-inflicted torture: self-inflicted, because no one was forcing me to stay in Delhi. Sometimes you had to avoid me, and I could not stand that. Only Dinesh (and of course Sunil and some of the children) knew anything about the affair — adults are much slower than children at sensing the truth — and it was still too soon to reveal the true state of affairs, and my own feelings, to anyone else in the family. If I came out with a declaration that I was in love with you, it would immediately become obvious that something had happened during your holiday in the hill-station. It would be said that I had taken advantage of the situation (which I had), and that I had seduced you — even though I was beginning to wonder if it was you who had seduced me! And if a marriage was suddenly arranged, people would say: 'Its been arranged so quickly. And she's so young. He must have got her into trouble.' Even though there were no signs of your having got into that sort of trouble.

And yet I could not help hoping that you would become my wife sooner that could be foreseen. I *wanted* to look after you. I did not want others to be doing if for me. Was that very selfish? Or was it a true state of being in love?

There were times — times when you kept at a distance and did not even look at me — when I grew desperate. I knew you could not show your familiarity with me in front of others; and yet, knowing this, I still tried to catch your eye, to sit near you, to touch you fleetingly. I could not hold myself back. I became morose, I wallowed in self-pity. And self-pity, I realised, is a sign of failure; especially of failure in love.

It was time to return to the hills.

*

Sushila, when I got up the morning to leave, you were still asleep and I did not wake you. I watched you stretched out on your bed, your dark face tranquil and untouched by care, your black hair spread over the white pillow, your long thin hands and feet in repose. You were so beautiful when you were asleep.

And as I watched, I felt a tightening around my heart, a sudden panic that I might somehow lose you.

The others were up, and there was no time to steal a kiss. A taxi was at the gate. A baby was bawling. Your grandmother was giving me advice. The taxi driver kept blowing his horn.

Goodbye, Sushila!

We were in a middle of the rains. There was a constant drip and drizzle and drumming on the corrugated tin roof. The walls were damp, and there was mildew on my books and even on the pickle that Dinesh had made.

Everything was green, the foliage almost tropical, especially near the stream. Great stagferns grew from the trunks of trees, fresh moss covered the rocks, and the maidenhair fern was at its loveliest. The water was a torrent, rushing through the ravine, and taking with it bushes and small trees. I could not remain out for long, for at any moment it might start raining. And there were also the leeches, who lost no time in fastening themselves on to my legs and fattening themselves on my blood.

Once, standing on some rocks, I saw a a slim brown snake swimming with the current. It looked beautiful and lonely.

I dreamt a dream, a very disturbing dream, which troubled me for days.

In the dream, Sunil suggested that we go down to the stream.

We put some bread and butter into an airbag, along with a long bread-knife, and set off down the hill. Sushila was barefooted, wearing the old cotton tunic which she had worn as a child. Sunil had on a bright yellow T-shirt and black jeans. He looked very dashing. As we took the forest path down to the stream, we saw two young men following us. One of them, a dark, slim youth, seemed familiar. I said, 'Isn't that Sushila's boy friend?' But they denied it. The other youth wasn't anyone I knew.

When we reached the stream, Sunil and I plunged into the pool, while Sushila sat on the rock just above us. We had been bathing for a few minutes when the two young men came down the slope, and began fondling Sushila. She did not resist; but Sunil climbed out of the pool and began scrambling up the slope. One of the youths, the less familiar one, had a long knife in his hand. Sunil picked up a stone and flung it at the youth, striking him on the shoulder. I rushed up and grabbed the hand that held the knife. The youth kicked me on the shins and thrust me away, and I fell beneath him. The arm with the knife was raised over me, but I still held the wrist. And then I saw Sushila behind him, her face framed by a passing cloud. She had the bread-knife in her hand, and her arm swung up and down, and the knife cut through my adversary's neck as though it were passing through a ripe melon.

I scrambled to my feet, to find Sushila gazing at the headless corpse with the detachment and mild curiosity of a child who has just removed the wings from a butterfly.

The other youth, who looked like Sushila's boy friend, began running away. He was chased by the three of us. When he slipped and fell, I found myelf beside him, the blade of the knife poised beneath his left shoulder-blade. I couldn't push the knife in. Then Sunil put his hand over mine, and the blade slipped smoothly into the flesh.

*

At all times of the day and night I could hear the murmur of the stream at the bottom of the hill. Even if I didn't listen, the sound was there. I had grown used to it. But whenever I went away, I was conscious of something missing, and I was lonely without the sound of running water.

I remained alone for two months, and then I had to see you again, Sushila. I could not bear the long-drawn-out uncertainty of the situation. I wanted to do something that would bring everything nearer to a conclusion. Merely to stand by and wait was intolerable. Nor could I bear the secrecy to which Dinesh had sworn me. Someone else would have to know about my intentions —someone would have to help. I needed another ally, to sustain my hopes; only then would I find the waiting easier.

You had not been keeping well, and looked thin; but you were as cheerful, as serene as ever.

When I took you to the pictures with Sunil, you wore a sleeveless *kameez* made of purple silk. It set off your dark beauty very well. Your face was soft and shy, and your smile hadn't changed. I could not keep my eyes off you.

Returning home in the taxi, I held your hand all the way.

Sunil (in Punjabi): 'Will you give your children English or Hindi names?'

Me: 'Hindustani names.'

Sunil (in Punjabi): 'Ah, that is the right answer, uncle!'

*

And first I went to your mother.

She was a tiny woman and looked very delicate. But she'd had six children — a seventh was on the way — and they had all come into the world without much difficulty and were the healthiest in the entire joint family.

She was on her way to see relatives in another part of the city, and I accompained her part of the way. As she was pregnant, she was offered a seat in the crowded bus. I managed to squeeze in beside her. She had always shown a liking for me and I did not find it difficult to come to the point.

'At what age would you like Sushila to get married?' I asked casually, with almost paternal interest.

'We'll worry about that when the time comes. She has still to finish school. And if she keeps failing her exams, she will never finish school.'

I took a deep breath and made the plunge.

'When the time comes,' I said. 'When the time comes, I would like to marry her.' And without waiting to see what her reaction would be, I continued: 'I know I must wait, a year or two, even longer. But I am telling you this, so that it will be in your mind. You are her mother, and so I want you to be the first to know.' (Liar that I was! She was about the fifth to know. But what I really wanted to say was, 'Please don't be looking for any other husband for her just yet.')

She didn't show much surprise. She was a placid woman. But she said, rather sadly, 'It's all right, but I don't have much say in the family. I do not have any money, you see. It depends on the others, especially her grandmother.'

'I'll speak to them when the time comes. Don't worry about that. And you don't have to worry about money or anything — what I mean is, I don't believe in dowries — I mean, you don't have to give me a Godrej cupboard and a sofa-set and that sort of thing. All I want is Sushila . . .'

'She is still very young.'

But she was pleased; pleased that her flesh and blood, her own daughter, could mean so much to a man.

'Don't tell anyone else just now,' I said.

'I won't tell anyone,' she said with a smile.

So now the secret — if it could be called that — was shared by at least five people.

The bus crawled on through the busy streets, and we sat in silence, surrounded by a press of people but isolated in the intimacy of our conversation.

I warmed towards her — towards that simple, straightforward, uneducated woman (she had never been to school, could not read or write), who might still have been young and pretty had her circumstances been different. I asked her when the baby was due.

'In two months,' she said. She laughed. Evidently she found it unusual and rather amusing for a young man to ask her such a question.

'I'm sure it will be a fine baby,' I said. And I thought: That makes six brothers-in-law!

*

I did not think I would get a chance to speak to your uncle Ravi (Dinesh's elder brother) before I left. But on my last evening in Delhi, I found myself alone with him on the Karol bagh road. At first we spoke of his own plans for marriage, and, to please him, I said the girl he'd chosen was both beautiful and intelligent.

He warmed towards me.

Clearing my throat, I went on. 'Ravi, you are five years younger than me, and you are about to get married.'

'Yes, and it's time you thought of doing the same thing.'

'Well, I've never thought seriously about it before — I'd always scorned the institution of marriage — but now I've changed my mind. Do you know who I'd like to marry?'

To my surprise Ravi unhesitatingly took the name of Asha, a distant cousin I'd met only once. She came from Ferozepur, and her hips were so large that from a distance she looked like an oversized pear.

'No, no,' I said. 'Asha is a lovely girl, but I wasn't thinking of her. I would like to marry a girl like Sushila. To be frank, Ravi, I would like to marry Sushila.'

There was a long silence, and I feared the worst. The noise of cars, scooters and buses seemed to recede into the distance, and Ravi and I were alone together in a vacuum of silence.

So that the awkwardness would not last too long, I stumbled on with what I had to say. 'I know she's young and that I will have to wait for some time.' (Familiar words!) 'But if you approve, and the family approves, and Sushila approves, well then, there's nothing I'd like better than to marry her.'

Ravi pondered, scratched himself, and then, to my delight, said: 'Why not? It's a fine idea.'

The traffic sounds returned to the street, and I felt as though I could set fire to a bus or do something equally in keeping with my high spirits.

'It would bring you even closer to us,' said Ravi. 'We would like to have you in our family. At least I would like it.'

'That makes all the difference,' I said. 'I will do my best for her, Ravi. I'll do everything to make her happy.'

'She is very simple and unspolit.'

'I know. That's why I care so much for her.'

'I will do what I can to help you. She should finish school by the time she is seventeen. It does not matter if you are older. Twelve years difference in age is not uncommon. So, don't worry. Be patient, and all will be arranged.'

And so I had three strong allies — Dinesh, Ravi, and your mother. Only your grandmother remained, and I dared not approach her on my own. She was the most difficult hurdle, because she was the head of the family and she was autocratic and often unpredictable. She was not on good terms with your mother, and for that very reason I feared that she might oppose my proposal. I had no idea how much she valued Ravi's and Dinesh's judgement. All I knew was that they bowed to all her decisions.

How impossible it was for you to shed the burden of your relatives! Individually, you got on quite well with all of them; but, because they could not live without bickering among themselves, you were just a pawn in the great Joint Family Game.

*

You put my hand to your cheek and to your breasts. I kissed your closed eyes, and took your face in my hands, and touched your lips with mine; a phantom kiss in the darkness of the verandah. And then, intoxicated, I stumbled into the road and walked the streets all night.

I was sitting on the rocks above the oak forest when I saw a young man walking towards me down the steep path. From his careful manner of walking, and light clothing, I could tell that he was a stranger, one who was not used to the hills. He was about my height, slim, rather long in the face; good-looking in a delicate sort of way. When he came nearer, I recognised him as the young man in the photograph, the youth of my dream — your late admirer! I wasn't too surprised to see him. Somehow, I had always felt that we would meet one day.

I remembered his name and said, 'How are you, Pramod?'

He became rather confused. His eyes were already clouded with doubt and unhappiness; but he did not appear to be an aggressive person.

'How did you know my name?' he asked.

'How did you know where to find me?' I countered.

'Your neighbours, the Kapoors, told me. I could not wait for you to return to the house; I have to go down again tonight.'

'Well then, would you like to walk home with me, or would you prefer to sit here and talk? I know who you are, but I've no idea why you've come to see me.'

'It's all right here,' he said, spreading his handkerchief on the grass before sitting down on it. 'How did you know my name?'

I stared at him for a few moments, and got the impression that he was a vulnerable person — perhaps more vulnerable than myself. My only advantage was that I was older and therefore better able to conceal my real feelings.

'Sushila told me,' I said.

'Oh. I did not think you would know.'

I was a little puzzled, but said, 'I knew about you, of course. And you must have known that, of course, or you would hardly have come here to see me.'

'You knew about Sushila and me?' he asked, looking even more confused.

'Well, I know that you are supposed to be in love with her.'

He smote himself on the forehead. 'My God! do the others know, too?'

'I don't think so.' I deliberately avoided mention of Sunil.

In his distraction he started plucking at tufts of grass 'Did *she* tell you?' he asked.

'Yes.'

'Girls can't keep secrets. But in a way I'm glad she told you. Now I don't have to explain everything. You see, I came here for your help. I know you are not her real uncle, but you are very close to her family. Last year in Delhi she often spoke about you. She said you were very kind.'

It then occurred to me that Pramod knew nothing about my relationship with you, other than that I was supposed to be the most benevolent of 'uncles.' He knew that your had spent your summer holidays with me — but so had Dinesh and Sunil. And now, aware that I was a close friend of the family, he had come to make an ally of me — in much the same way that I had gone about making allies!

'Have you seen Sushila recently?' I asked.

'Yes. Two days ago, in Delhi. But I had only a few minutes alone with her. We could not talk much. You see, Uncle — you will not mind if I also call you Uncle? I want to marry her, but there is no one who can speak to her people on my behalf. My own parents are not living. If I go straight to her family, most probably I will be thrown out of the house. So I want you to help me. I am not well off, but I will soon have a job and then I can support her.'

'Did you tell her all this?'

'Yes.'

'And what did she say?'

'She told me to speak to you about it.'

Clever Sushila! Diabolical Sushila!

'To me?' I repeated.

'Yes, she said it would be better than talking to her parents.'

I couldn't help laughing. And a long-railed blue magpie, disturbed by my laughter, set up a shrill creaking and chattering of its own.

'Don't laugh, I'm serious, Uncle,' said Pramod. He took me by the hand and looked at me appealingly.

'Well, it ought to be serious,' I said. I was just thinking of how clever Sushila is — or how simple! 'How old are you, Pramod?'

'Twenty-three.'

'Only seven years younger than me. So please don't call me Uncle. It makes me feel prehistoric. Use my first name, if you like. And when do you hope to marry Sushila?'

'As soon as possible. I know she is still very young for me.'

'Not at all,' I said. 'Young girls are marrying middle-aged men every day! And you're still quite young yourself. But she can't get married as yet, Pramod, I know that for a certainty.'

'That's what I feared. She will have to finish school, I suppose.'

'That's right. But tell me something. It's obvious that you are in love with her, and I don't blame you for it. Sushila is the kind of girl we all fall in love with! But do you know if she loves you? Did she say she would like to marry you?'

'She did not say — I do not know . . . There was a hunted, hurt look in his eyes, and my heart went out to him. 'But I love her — isn't that enough?'

'It *could* be enough — provided she didn't love someone else.'

'Does she, Uncle?'

'To be frank, I don't know.'

He brightened up at that. 'She likes me,' he said. 'I know that much.'

'Well, I like you too, but that doesn't mean I'd marry you.'

He was despondent again. 'I see what you mean . . . But what is love, how can I recognise it?'

And that was one question I couldn't answer. How do we recognise it?

*

I persuaded Pramod to stay the night. The sun had gone down and he was shivering. I made a fire, the first of the winter, using oak and thorn branches. Then I shared my brandy with him.

I did not feel any resentment against Pramod. Prior to meeting him, I had been jealous; and when I first saw him coming along the

232

path, I remembered my dream, and thought, 'Perhaps I am going to kill him, after all. Or perhaps he's going to kill me.' But it had turned out differently. If dreams have any meaning at all, the meaning doesn't come within our limited comprehension.

I had visualised Pramod as being rather crude, selfish and irresponsible, and unattractive college student, the type who has never known or understood girls very well and looks on them as strange exotic creatures who are to be seized and plundered at the first opportunity. Such men do exist; but Pramod was not one of them. He did not know much about women; neither did I. He was gentle, polite, unsure of himself I wondered if I should tell him about my own feelings for you.

After a while he began to talk about himself and about you. He told me how he fell in love with you. At first he had been friendly with another girl, a classfellow of yours but a year or two older. You had carried messages to him on the girl's behalf. Then the girl had rejected him. He was terribly depressed, and one evening he drank a lot of cheap liquor. Instead of falling dead, as he had been hoping, he lost his way and met you near your home. He was in need or sympathy, and you gave him that. You let him hold your hand. He told you how hopeless he felt, and you comforted him; and when he said the world was a cruel place, you consented. You *agreed* with him: what more can a man expect from a woman? Only fourteen at the time, you had no difficulty in comforting a man of twenty-two. No wonder he fell in love with you!

Afterwards you met occasionally on the road and spoke to each other. He visited the house once or twice, on some pretext or another. And when you came to the hills, he wrote to you.

That was all he had to tell me. That was all there was to tell. You had touched his heart once; and touching it, had no difficulty in capturing it.

Next morning I took Pramod down to the stream. I wanted to tell him everything, and somehow I could not do it in the house.

He was charmed by the place. The water flowed gently, its music subdued, soft chamber music after the monsoon orchestration. Cowbells tinkled on the hillside, and an eagle soared high above.

'I did not think water could be so clear,' said Pramod. 'It is not muddy like the streams and rivers of the plains.'

'In the summer you can bathe here,' I said. 'There is a pool further downstream.'

He nodded thoughtfully. 'Did she come here too?'

'Yes, Sushila and Sunil and I . . . We came here on two three occasions.' My voice trailed off and I glanced at Pramod standing at the edge of the water. He looked up at me and his eyes met mine.

'There is something I want to tell you,' I said.

He continued staring at me; and a shadow seemed to pass across his face — a shadow of doubt, fear, death, eternity, was it one or all of these, or just a play of light and shade? But I remembered my dream and stepped back from him. For a moment both of us looked at each other with distrust and, uncertainty; then the fear passed. Whatever had happened between us, dream or reality, had happened in some other existence. Now he took my hand and held it, held it tight, as though seeking assurance, as though identifying himself with me.

'Let us sit down,' I said. 'There is something I must tell you.'

We sat down on the grass, and when I looked up through the branches of the *banj*-oak, everything seemed to have been tilted and held at an angle, and the sky shocked me with its blueness, and the leaves were no longer green but purple in the shadows of the ravine. They were your colour, Sushila. I remembered you wearing purple — dark smiling Sushila, thinking your own thoughts and refusing to share them with anyone.

'I love Sushila too,' I said.

'I know,' he said naively. 'That is why I came to you for help.'

'No, you don't know,' I said. 'When I say I love Sushila, I mean just that. I mean caring for her in the same way that you care for her. I mean I want to marry her.'

'You, Uncle?'

'Yes. Does it shock you very much?'

'No, no.' He turned his face away and stared at the worn face of an old grey rock; and perhaps he drew some strength from its permanency. 'Why should you not love her? Perhaps, in my heart, I really knew it, but did not want to know — did not want to believe. Perhaps that is why I really came here — to find out. Something that Sunil said . . . But why didn't you tell me before?'

'Because you were telling me!'

'Yes, I was too full of my own love to think that any other's was possible. What do we do now? Do we both wait, and then let her make her choice?'

'If you wish.'

'You have the advantage, Uncle. You have more to offer.'

'Do you mean more security or more love? Some women place more value on the former.'

'Not Sushila.'

'Not Sushila.'

'I mean you can offer her a more interesting life. You are a writer. Who knows, you may be famous one day.'

'You have your youth to offer, Pramod. I have only a few years of youth left to me — and two or three of them will pass in waiting.'

'Oh, no,' he said. 'Yes will always be young. If you have Sushila, you will always be young.'

Once again I heard the whistling-thrush; its song was a crescendo of sweet notes and variations that rang clearly across the ravine. I could not see the bird; but its call emerged from the forest like some dark sweet secret, and again it was saying, 'It isn't time that's passing by, my friend. It is you and I.'

*

Listen. Sushila, the worst has happened. Ravi has written to say that a marriage will not be possible — not now, not next year; never. Of course he makes a lot of excuses — that you must receive a complete college education ('higher studies'), that the differences in our ages is too great, that you might change your mind after a year or two — but, reading between the lines, I can guess that the real reason is your grandmother. She does not want it. Her word is law; and no one, least of all Ravi, would dare oppose her.

But I do not mean to give in so easily. I will wait my chance. As long as I know that you are with me, I will wait my chance.

I wonder what the old lady objects to in me. Is it simply that she is conservative and tradition-bound? She has always shown a liking for me, and I don't see why her liking should change because I want to marry her grandniece. Your mother has no objection; perhaps that's why your grandmother objects.

Whatever the reason, I am coming down to Delhi to find out how things stand.

Of course the worst part is that Ravi has asked me — in the friendliest terms and in a most roundabout manner — not to come to the house for some time. He says this will give the affair a chance to cool off and die a natural (I would call it an unnatural) death. He assumes, of course, that I will accept the old lady's decision and simply forget all about you. Ravi has yet to fall in love.

*

Dinesh was in Lucknow. I could not visit the house. So I sat on a bench in the Talkatora Gardens and watched a group of children playing *gulli-danda*; then recalled that Sunil's school gave over at three o'clock and that if I hurried I should be able to meet him outside St. Columbas's gate.

I reached the school on time. Boys were streaming out of the compound, and as they were all wearing green uniforms — a young forest on the move — I gave up all hope of spotting Sunil. But he saw me first. He ran across the road, dodged a cyclist, evaded a bus, and seized me about the waist.

'I'm so happy to see you, Uncle!'

'As I am to see you, Sunil.'

'You want to see Sushila?'

'Yes, but you too. I can't come to the house, Sunil. You probably know that. When do you have to be home?'

'About four o'clock. If I'm late, I'll say the bus was too crowded and I couldn't get in.'

'That gives us an hour or two. Let's go to the exhibition ground. Would you like that?'

'All right, I haven't seen the exhibition yet.'

We took a scooter-*rickshaw* to the exhibition grounds on Mathura Road. It was an industrial exhibition, and there was little to interest either a schoolboy or a lovesick author. But a cafe was at hand, overlooking an artificial lake, and we sat in the sun consuming hot dogs and cold coffee.

'Sunil, will you help me?' I asked.

'Whatever you say, Uncle.'

'I don't suppose I can see Sushila this time. I don't want to hang about near the house or her school like a disreputable character. It's all right lurking outside a boy's school; but it wouldn't do to be hanging about the Kanyadevi Pathshala or whereever it is she's studying. It's possible the family will change their minds about us later. Anyway, what matters now is Sushila's attitude. Ask her this, Sunil. Ask her if she wants me to wait until she is eighteen. She will be free then to do what she wants, even to run away with me if necessary — that is, if she really wants to. I was ready to wait two years. I'm prepared to wait three. But it will help if I know she's waiting too. Will you ask her that, Sunil?'

'Yes, I'll ask her.'

'Ask her tonight. Then tomorrow we'll meet again outside your school.'

*

We met briefly next day. There wasn't much time. Sunil had to be home early, and I had to catch the night train out of Delhi. We stood in the generous shade of a *peepul* tree, and I asked, 'What did she say?'

'She said to keep waiting.'

'All right, I'll wait.'

'But when she is eighteen, what if she changes her mind? You know what girls are like.'

'You're a cynical chap, Sunil.'

'What does that mean?'

'It means you know too much about life. But tell me — what makes your think she might change her mind?'

'Her boy friend.'

'Pramod? She doesn't care for him, poor chap.'

'Not Pramod. Another one.'

'Another! You mean a new one?'

'New,' said Sunil. 'An officer in a bank. He's got a car.'

'Oh,' I said despondently. 'I can't compete with a car.'

'No,' said Sunil. 'Never mind, Uncle. You still have me for your friend. Have you forgotten that?'

I had almost forgotten; but it was good to be reminded.

'It is time to go,' he said. 'I must catch the bus today. When will you come to Delhi again?'

'Next month. Next year. Who knows? But I'll come. Look after yourself, my friend.'

He ran off and jumped on to the footboard of a moving bus. He waved to me until the bus went round the bend in the road.

It was lonely under the *peepul* tree. It is said that only ghosts live in *peepul* trees. I do not blame them: for *peepul* trees are cool and shady and full of loneliness.

I may stop loving you, Sushila; but I will never stop loving the days I loved you.

When You Can't Climb Trees Any More

He stood on the grass verge by the side of the road and looked over the garden wall at the old house. It hadn't changed much. There's little anyone can do to alter a house built with solid blocks of granite brought from the river-bed. But there was a new outhouse, and there were fewer trees. He was pleased to see that the jack-fruit tree still stood at the side of the building, casting its shade on the wall. He remembered his grandmother saying: 'A blessing rests on the house where falls the shadow of a tree.' And so the present owners must also be the recipients of the tree's blessings.

At the spot where he stood there had once been a turnstile, and as a boy he would swing on it, going round and round until he was quite dizzy. Now the turnstile had gone, the opening walled up. Tall hollyhocks grew on the other side of the wall.

'What are you looking at?'

It was a disembodied voice at first. Moments later a girl stood framed between dark red hollyhocks, staring at the man.

It was difficult to guess her age; she might have been twelve or she might have been sixteen: slim and dark, with lovely eyes and long black hair.

'I'm looking at the house,' he said.

'Why? Do you want to buy it?'

'Is it your house?'

'It's my father's.'

'And what does your father do?'

'He's only a colonel.'

'*Only* a colonel?'

'Well, he should have been a Brigadier by now.'

The man burst out laughing.

'It's not funny,' she said. 'Even mummy says he should have been a Brigadier.'

It was on the tip of his tongue to make a witty remark ('Perhaps that's why he's still a colonel'), but he did not want to give offence. They stood on either side of the wall, appraising each other.

'Well,' she said finally. 'If you don't want to buy the house, what are you looking at?'

'I used to live here once.'

'Oh.'

'Twenty-five years ago. When I was a boy. And then again, when I was a young man . . . until my grandmother died, and then we sold the house and went away.'

She was silent for a while, taking in this information. Then she said. 'And you'd like to buy it back now, but you don't have the money?' He did not look very prosperous.

'No, I wasn't thinking of buying it back. I wanted to see it again, that's all. How long have you lived here?'

'Only three years.' She smiled. She'd been eating a melon, and there was still juice at the corners of her mouth. 'Would you like to come in — and look — once more?'

'Wouldn't your parents mind?'

'They've gone to the Club. They won't mind. I'm allowed to bring my friends home.'

'Even adult friends?'

'How old are you?'

'Oh, just middle-aged, but feeling young today.' And to prove it he decided he'd climb over the wall instead of going round by the gate. He got up on the wall all right, but had to rest there, breathing heavily. 'Middle-aged man on the flying trapeze,' he muttered to himself.

'Let me help you,' she said, and gave him her hand.

He slithered down into a flower-bed, shattering the stem of a hollyhock.

As they walked across the grass he noticed a stone bench under a mango tree. It was the bench on which his grandmother used to sit, when she tired of pruning rose bushes and bougainvillaea.

'Let's sit here,' he said. 'I don't want to go inside.'

She sat beside him on the bench. It was March, and the mango tree was in bloom. **A sweet**, rather heavy fragrance drenched the garden.

They were silent for some time. The man closed his eyes and remembered other times — the music of a piano, the chiming of a grandfather clock, the constant twitter of budgerigars on the verandah, his grandfather cranking up the old car . . .

'I used to climb the jackfruit tree,' he said, opening his eyes. 'I didn't like the jackfruit, though. Do you?'

'It's all right in pickles.'

'I suppose so . . . The tree was easy to climb, I spent a lot of time in it.'

'Do you want to climb it again? My parents won't mind.'

'No, I don't think so. Not after climbing the wall! Let's just sit here for a few minutes and talk. I mention the jackfruit tree because it was my favourite place. Do you see that thick branch stretching out over the roof? Half-way along it there's a small hollow in which I used to keep some of my treasures.'

'What kind of treasures?'

'Oh, nothing very valuable. Marbles I'd won. A book I wasn't supposed to read. A few old coins I'd collected. Things came and went. There was my grandfather's exactly, because he was British and the Iron Cross was a German decoration, awarded for bravery during the War — that's the first World War — when Grandfather fought in France. He got it from a German soldier.'

'Dead or alive?'

'Pardon?' Oh, you mean the German. I never asked. Dead, I suppose. Or perhaps he was a prisoner. I never asked Grandfather. Isn't that strange?'

'And the Iron Cross? Do you still have it?'

'No,' he said, looking her in the eye. 'I left it in the jackfruit tree.'

'You left it in the tree!'

'Yes, I was so busy at the time — packing, and saying goodbye to friends, and thinking about the ship I was going to sail on — that I just forgot all about it.'

She was silent, considering, her finger on her lips, her gaze fixed on the jackfruit tree.

Then, quietly, she said, 'It may still be there. In the hollow of the branch.'

'Yes,' he said. 'After twenty-five years, it may still be there. Unless someone else found it.'

'Would you like to take a look?'

'I can't climb trees any more.'

'I can! I'll go and see. You just sit here and wait for me.'

She sprang up and ran across the grass, swift and sweet of limb. Soon she was in the jackfruit tree, crawling along the projecting branch. A warm wind brought little eddies of dust along the road. Summer was in the air. Ah, if only he could learn to climb trees again!

'I've found something!' she cried.

And now, barefoot, she runs breathlessly towards him, in her outstretched hand a rusty old medal.

He takes it from her and turns it over on his palm.

'Is it the Iron Cross?' she asks eagerly.

'Yes, this is it.'

'Now I know why you came. You wanted to see if it was still in the tree.'

'I don't know. I'm not really sure why I came. But you can keep the Cross. You found it, after all.'

'No, you keep it. It's yours.'

'But it might have remained in the tree for a hundred years if you hadn't gone to look for it.'

'Only because you came back —'

'On the right day, at the right time, and with the right person.' Getting up, he squeezed the hard rusty medal into her soft palm. 'No, it wasn't the Cross I came for. It was my lost youth.'

She understood this, even though her own youth still lay ahead of her, she understood it, not as an adult, but with the wisdom of the child that was still part of her. She walked with him to the gate and stood there gazing after him as he walked away. Where the road turned, he glanced back and waved to her. Then he quickened his step and moved briskly towards the bus stop. There was a spring in his step. Something cried aloud in his heart.

A Love of Long Ago

Last week, as the taxi took me to Delhi, I passed through the small town in the foothills where I had lived as a young man.

Well, it's the only road to Delhi and one must go that way, but I seldom travel beyond the foothills. As the years go by, my visits to the city — any city — are few and far between. But whenever I am on that road, I look out of the window of my bus or taxi, to catch a glimpse of the first-floor balcony where a row of potted plants lend colour to an old and decrepit building. Ferns, a palm, a few bright marigolds, zinnias and nasturtiums — they made that balcony stand out from others; it was impossible to miss it.

But last week, when I looked out of the taxi window, the balcony garden had gone. A few broken pots remained; but the ferns had crumpled into dust, the palm had turned brown and yellow, and of the flowers nothing remained.

All these years I had taken that balcony garden for granted, and now it had gone. It jerked me upright in my seat. I looked back at the building for signs of life, but saw none. The taxi sped on. On my way back, I decided, I would look again. But it was as though a part of my life had come to an abrupt end; a part that I had almost come to take for granted. The link between youth and middle-age, the bridge that spanned that gap, had suddenly been swept away.

And what had happened to Kamla, I wondered. Kamla, who had tended those plants all these years, knowing I would be looking out for them even though I might not see her, even though she might never see me.

Chance gives, and takes away, and gives again. But I would have to look elsewhere now, for the memories of my love, my young love, the girl who came into my life for a few blissful weeks and then went out of it for the remainder of our lives.

Was it almost thirty years ago that it all happened? How old was I then? Twenty-two at the most! And Kamla could not have been more than seventeen.

She had a laughing face, mischievous, always ready to break into smiles or peals of laughter. Sparkling brown eyes. How can I ever forget those eyes? Peeping at me from behind a window curtain, following me as I climbed the steps to my room — the room that was separated from her quarters by a narrow wooden landing that creaked loudly if I tried to move quietly across it. The trick was to *dash* across, as she did so neatly on her butterfly feet.

She was always on the move — flitting about on the verandah, running errands of no consequence, dancing on the steps, singing on the rooftop as she hung out the family washing. Only once was she still. That was when we met on the steps in the dark, and I stole a kiss, a sweet phantom kiss. She was very still then, very close, a butterfly drawing out nectar, and then she broke away from me and ran away laughing.

'What is your work?' she asked me one day.

'I write stories.'

'Will you write one about me?'

'Some day.'

I was living in a room above Moti-*Bibi's* grocery shop near the cinema. At night I could hear the sound-track from the film. The songs did not help me much with my writing, nor with my affair, for Kamla could not come out at night. We met in the afternoons when the whole town took a siesta and expected us to do the same. Kamla had a young brother who worked for Moti-*Bibi* (a widow who was also my landlady) and it was through the boy that I had first met Kamla.

Moti-*Bibi* always a sent me a glass of *Kanji* or sugar-cane juice or lime-juice (depending on the season) around noon. Usually the boy brought me the drink, but one day I looked up from my typewriter to see what at first I thought was an apparition hovering over me. She seemed to shimmer before me in the hot sunlight that came slashing through the open door. I looked up into her face and our eyes met over the rim of the glass. I forgot to take it from her.

What I liked about her was her smile. It dropped over her face slowly, like sunshine moving over brown hills. She seemed to give out some of the glow that was in her face. I felt it pour over me. And this golden feeling did not pass when she left the room. That was how I knew she was going to mean something special to me.

They were poor, but in time I was to realise that I was even poorer. When I discovered that plans were afoot to marry her to a widower of forty, I plucked up enough courage to declare that I would marry her myself. But my youth was no consideration. The widower had land and a generous gift of money for Kamla's parents. Not only was this offer attractive; it was customary. What had I to offer? A small rented room, a typewriter, and a precarious income of two to three hundred rupees a month from freelancing. I told the brother that I would be famous one day, that I would be rich, that I would be writing bestsellers! He did not believe me. And who can blame him? I never did write bestsellers or become rich. Nor did I have parents or relatives to speak on my behalf.

I thought of running away with Kamla. When I mentioned it to her, her eyes lit up. She thought it would be great fun. Women in love can be more reckless than men! But I had read too many stories about runaway marriages ending in disaster, and I lacked the courage to go through with such an adventure. I must have known instinctively that it would not work. Where would we go, and how would we live? There would be no home to crawl back to, for either of us.

Had I loved more passionately, more fiercely, I might have felt compelled to elope with Kamla, regardless of the consequences. But it never became an intense relationship. We had so few moments together. Always stolen moments — on the stairs, on the roof, in the deserted junk-yard behind the shops. She seemed to enjoy every moment of this secret affair. I fretted and longed for something more permanent. Her responses, so sweet and generous, only made my longing greater. But she seemed content with the immediate moment and what it offered.

And so the marriage took place, and she did not appear to be too dismayed about her future. But before she left for her husband's house, she asked me for some of the plants that I had owned and nourished on my small balcony.

'Take them all,' I said. 'I am leaving, anyway.'

'Where are you going?'

'To Delhi — to find work. But I shall come this way sometimes.'

'My husband's house is on the Delhi road. You will pass that way. I will keep these flowers where you can see them.'

We did not touch each other in parting. Her brother came and collected the plants. Only the cactii remained. Not a lover's plant, the cactus! I gave the cactii to my landlady and went to live in Delhi.

*

And whenever I passed through the old place, summer or winter, I looked out of the window of my bus or taxi and saw the garden flourishing on Kamla's balcony; leaf and fern abounded, and the flowers grew rampant on the sunny ledge.

Once I saw her, leaning over the balcony railing. I stopped the taxi and waved to her. She waved back, smiling like the sun breaking through clouds. She called to me to come up, but I said I would come another time. I never did visit her home, and I never saw her husband. Her parents had gone back to their village, her brother had vanished into the great grey spaces of India.

In recent years, after leaving Delhi and making my home in the hills, I have passed through the town less often; but the flowers have always been there, bright and glowing in their increasingly shabby surroundings. Except on this last journey of mine . . .

And on the return trip, only yesterday, I looked again, but the house was empty and desolate. I got out of the car and looked up at the balcony and called Kamla's name — called it after so many years — but there was no answer.

I asked questions in the locality. The old man had died, his wife had gone away, probably to her village. There had been no children. Would she return? No one could say. The house had been sold; it would be pulled down to make way for a block of flats.

I glanced once more at the deserted balcony, the withered, drooping plants. A butterfly flitted about the railing, looking in vain for a flower on which to alight. It settled briefly on my hand, before opening its wings and fluttering away into the blue.

MORE ABOUT PENGUINS

For further information about books available from Penguins in India write to Penguin Books (India) Ltd, B4/246, Safdarjung Enclave, New Delhi 110 029.

In the UK: For a complete list of books available from Penguins in the United Kingdom write to Dept. EP, Penguin Books Ltd, Harmondsworth, Middlesex UB7 0DA.

In the U.S.A.: For a complete list of books available from Penguins in the United States write to Dept. DG, Penguin Books, 299 Murray Hill Parkway, East Rutherford, New Jersey 07073.

In Canada: For a complete list of books available from Penguins in Canada write to Penguin Books Canada Ltd, 2801 John Street, Markham, Ontario L3R 1B4.

In Australia: For a complete list of books available from Penguins in Australia write to the Marketing Department, Penguin Books Australia Ltd, P.O. Box 257, Ringwood, Victoria 3134.

In New Zealand: For a complete list of books available from Penguins in New Zealand write to the Marketing Department, Penguin Books (N.Z.) Ltd, Private Bag, Takapuna, Auckland 9.

A WRITER'S NIGHTMARE
R.K. Narayan

R.K. Narayan, perhaps India's best-known living writer, is better known as a novelist but his essays are as delightful and enchanting as his stories and novels. *A Writer's Nightmare* includes essays on subjects as diverse as weddings, higher mathematics, South Indian coffee, umbrellas, monkeys, the caste system—all sorts of topics, simple and not so simple, which reveal the very essence of India.

'(A book) to be dipped into and savoured'— *Sunday*